D0897700

First Light

A JOHN BEKKER MYSTERY

First Light

Al Lamanda

FIVE STAR
A part of Gale, Cengage Learning

GALE
CENGAGE Learning®

Farmington Hills, Mich • San Francisco • New York • Waterville, Maine
Meriden, Conn • Mason, Ohio • Chicago

LIBRARY OF CONGRESS CATALOGING-IN-PUBLICATION DATA

Lamanda, Al.
First light : a John Bekker mystery / Al Lamanda.
pages cm
ISBN 978-1-4328-2865-3 (hardcover) — ISBN 1-4328-2865-7 (hardcover)
1. Bekker, John. 2. Private investigators—Fiction. 3. Adopted children—Fiction. 4. Missing persons—Investigation—Fiction. 5. Political corruption—Fiction. I. Title. II. Title: John Bekker mystery.
PS3612.A5433F57 2014
813'.6—dc23 2014006955

First Edition. First Printing: July 2014
Find us on Facebook– https://www.facebook.com/FiveStarCengage
Visit our website– http://www.gale.cengage.com/fivestar/
Contact Five Star™ Publishing at FiveStar@cengage.com

Printed in the United States of America
1 2 3 4 5 6 7 18 17 16 15 14

FIRST LIGHT

Chapter 1

It was a perfect early summer afternoon for trying on wedding dresses. I had a front-row seat to this extravaganza at the patio table in my bride-to-be's backyard. Armed with a mug of coffee and Molly, the stray cat I adopted a year ago, I watched the fashion show unfold before me with clockwork precision.

The wedding dress consultant marked the dress Janet wore with white chalk, then pinned and tugged. Janet is not your typical forty-seven-year-old bride, in that she's tall and extremely fit, so the consultant was having problems with the dress because it belonged to Janet's mother, who was neither.

Making matters worse, my nineteen-year-old daughter, Regan, was being a first-class pain, insisting in her limited way that her bridesmaid's dress match Janet's in style and color.

Molly went from my lap to the table for a better view of the show. I scratched her ears, which she appreciated highly, and watched along with her, although she was more interested in her ears than fashion.

Janet was close to tears. Regan was stomping her foot. The consultant was doing her best to calm the situation and restore order.

Molly purred.

I sipped coffee.

In desperation, Janet turned her eyes to me. "What do you think?" she said.

"I don't even have an opinion," I said. "I'm just here for the free coffee."

Janet looked at my daughter. "He's useless, Regan."

"Pretty much," I agreed. I scratched Molly's ears. "But the cat loves me."

I glanced at the sliding doors that led to Janet's kitchen and saw Mark, Janet's fourteen-year-old son from her first marriage, peeking out. He had the good sense to stay out of the line of fire.

As the groom, I had no choice but to jump into the frying pan.

An eternity ago, I was married to Janet's sister Carol. We had one child, Regan. I was a detective assigned to Special Crimes. When Regan was five years old, Carol was murdered in our home by a mobster's son. Regan was forced to watch from her hiding spot in a closet.

Regan spent the next twelve years in an institution for traumatized children and didn't speak a word until just six months ago, when I sobered up from a ten-year-long booze binge and began visiting her on a regular basis.

Once sober, I reestablished old ties with my former sister-in-law. She became Aunt Janet, then just Janet, and finally girlfriend and soon-to-be second wife. Along the way, I opened the door to my friend and ex-partner Walter Grimes and he stepped through it as if time stood still. I was too old and too long away from the job for reinstatement, so a private investigator's license seemed the way to go to supplement my meager pension.

After I'd solved a few high-profile cases and nearly gotten killed in the process, Janet agreed to marriage only if I found a new profession. I agreed and the funny thing is I don't even remember proposing.

It's a good match. Regan loves Janet as a mother and Janet loves Regan as a daughter; Mark calls my daughter his sister;

and Molly loves everybody who scratches her ears.

What isn't a good match is a middle-aged man in search of a new career when all he knows how to do is his old one. Too young to retire, too old to teach new tricks to, a third of my salary in pension benefits, and no other source of income—none of that is exactly the way I figured to walk down the aisle for the second time.

Still, I'm sober more than a year now, in reasonable good health, not as smart as I think I am, and not as dumb as I make out to be. It all kind of works for me in a strange, unexplainable way.

After another twenty minutes of chalk lines, pins, arguments, and sobs of stress, Janet and Regan were down to bare feet and white slips. At five foot nine or ten inches tall, Janet towered over Regan, but there was no mistaking that both were one hundred percent women—Janet in a mature way, Regan in a budding soon-to-be way.

That a woman like Janet loved and wanted to marry me made me feel decades younger than I had a right to feel, given my circumstances.

Seeing my daughter side-by-side with Janet and realizing that she was no longer a little girl made me feel like the ancient mariner I would soon become. Still, I felt pretty good about it. I missed so much of Regan's life while she was institutionalized and I was off trying to destroy my liver, and I can never get it back. But my daughter loves me and calls me Dad, and even though I didn't earn the title, I'll take it.

"Hey, tough guy," Janet said as the consultant was packing up. "We have to leave in twenty minutes."

"And why do you think I'm sweating inside this suit and tie?" I said.

"Give me ten and I'll be right out," Janet said, and dashed into the house.

Regan came over to the table. Molly dashed to her side.

"So what are you and Mark going to do while we're gone?" I said.

Regan looked at me for a moment. "Don't worry," she said. "We'll be fine."

"I know you will. I left money for two pizzas on the kitchen table. We should be home by eight or eight thirty."

Regan nodded, gave me a kiss on the cheek, and took Molly with her when she went inside.

Alone, I finished my coffee. When the cup was empty, Janet appeared wearing a light blue summer pantsuit with matching shoes.

"How'd you get ready so quick?" I said.

"A woman never reveals her secrets," Janet said.

I smirked. "Never?"

"Well, not all of them." Janet tossed me her car keys. "You drive."

I never argue with a woman, especially mine.

I drove.

CHAPTER 2

I drove Janet's two-year-old Ford from her home in the suburbs to the grand ballroom of the Bayside Hotel because she claims my ten-year-old Marquis smells like an ashtray.

I didn't argue the point. It does.

Janet is patient with my smoking. As a veteran of twenty-plus years nursing in major hospitals, she's seen it all and knows the value of a good vice when trying to kick another vice.

My body's been alcohol-free a year now and for that Janet and I are grateful to the powers that be, but a good cigarette with a mug of coffee is too much to sacrifice at the moment.

I'm weak.

Janet knows that.

We both deal with it, but there are rules I must follow. No smoking around Mark, and if I have to light up around Regan, I must be outside and downwind. Hey, life is compromise.

I smoke by the rules and I don't get nagged. It's a sweet deal.

We chatted on the drive.

"How does Regan like her room?" I said.

When first allowed to leave the institution under supervision, Regan would stay overnight. She slowly worked her way up to weekends until finally she was comfortable with large doses at a time. Janet reconverted her office back to a third bedroom, and now she and Regan live under the same roof as mother and daughter. Along with Mark, it's a really good fit. So good in fact that I often wonder what I'm needed for, since I'm not allowed to sleep over until the wedding.

Janet glanced over at me. "Jack, it's nothing to feel slighted over."

Most people call me John. Janet is one of the few who calls me Jack, unless she's pissed at me for something, then it's *John*!, said with a quiet tone that reeks of a *don't mess with me* smolder I can't help but find sexy.

"I don't feel slighted," I said. "Just not included."

"Explain to me the difference."

I thought about it and couldn't.

"If it makes you feel any better, I talked to Father Tomas about it," Janet said.

Father Tomas is the priest and psychiatrist in charge of the Catholic institution where Regan spent twelve years. Although she's been living with Janet for months now, Regan still sees Father Tomas once a week for counseling.

"And?" I said.

"Do you really want to hear this?"

"Yes."

"Regan is nineteen and even though she's made leaps and bounds the past year, maturity-wise she's right around Mark's age," Janet said.

"Fourteen?"

Janet nodded. "Right around the age when little girls grow noticeable breasts and curves, and start to hide things from Daddy for fear they will no longer be seen as Daddy's little girl," she said.

"I think I have to think about that one," I said.

"Two thinks in one sentence, you'll hurt yourself," Janet said.

I sighed.

"Don't sigh," Janet said.

I pouted.

"And don't pout."

"For Christ's sake, is there anything that I can do?" I said.

"Yes," Janet said. "You can marry me and allow Regan to grow to maturity at her own pace."

"I can do that," I said.

"And not be too upset that she has her first date this weekend," Janet said, so casually she might be ordering a hamburger from a menu.

"What?"

"Watch the road, Jack."

"I am watching the road."

"More importantly, stay on the road," Janet said.

I said, "When were you going to—"

"Today."

"And with who is—"

"My neighbor's nineteen-year-old son."

"What's his—"

"Justin Lester and he's a really nice kid, Jack."

"When do I—"

"Saturday afternoon if you'd like."

"No shit I'd like," I snapped.

"The road," Janet said.

"Where are they going on this date?"

"The movies."

"Have you told him I'd—"

"Yes, and he's okay with meeting you," Janet said.

"Why am I the last one to know?" I said.

"All dads are, silly," Janet said. "Now please watch the road. I'd like to get there in one piece."

"Yeah," I said.

"Don't pout," Janet said. "This is a big night for your closest friend."

"Should I sit up straight and eat all my peas?"

"That would be nice."

"I hate peas," I said.
"But you love your friend."

Chapter 3

It doesn't happen often that a police lieutenant is promoted to the rank of captain and precinct commander in the same breath. When it does occur, it's treated as a really big deal, which it is in police circles.

When it happens to your ex-partner and closest friend, it's more than a big deal; it's something very, very special.

Two hundred and fifty attended Walter Grimes's promotion dinner at the Grand Ballroom in the Bayside Hotel. Fellow cops, their spouses and children, friends and relatives, some media, the police commissioner, and the mayor composed the guest list.

Walt wore his dress blue uniform and did it proud, right down to the white gloves and polished buttons. At the podium, Walt accepted the promotion from the commissioner with a simple, humble thank you and reserved his speech for after dinner.

While waiters served the soup and salad, Walt made his way around the tables. Janet and I were seated in front, a few tables from the one reserved for Walt's family. He stopped by to see me first.

After a kiss on each of Janet's cheeks, Walt shook my hand. "Should have been you, Jack," he said to me. "We both know that."

I shook my head a bit. "The right man got the job," I said.

"Thanks, Jack," Walt said. "Well, my fan club waits."

Walt moved on.

I ate some salad, followed by some soup.

While the empty plates and bowls were being cleared to make room for the main course, Janet said, "Did the right man get the job, Jack?"

"Yeah," I said.

"You're sure?"

"Yeah."

Walt has something I lack. Call it inner strength. If it was Elizabeth, Walt's wife, who had been murdered and his two daughters went the way Regan did, he would not have spent a decade as a drunk mourning their loss. He would have acted like a husband, father, and cop, and dedicated himself to finding the guilty and punishing them.

Yeah, the right man got the job.

After a main course of baked chicken with dirty rice, Walt made a perfect, fifteen-minute speech, followed by dessert.

It was a grand occasion.

Janet and I stopped by Walt's table, where Janet and Elizabeth chatted weddings while Walt and I talked his new position.

"I don't know if I'm ready for command," Walt said.

"You're ready," I told him.

The evening ended on a high note when we posed with Walt for photographs.

Afterward, Janet and I drove home in silence. I was pouting and she let me.

Gotta love that woman.

Chapter 4

I was having morning coffee at the card table in front of my beachfront trailer. The tide was rolling in quickly and the waves rumbled like distant thunder when they crashed along the hard sand.

I've owned the trailer going on nine years. It's tiny and cramped, but while I was drinking, space didn't matter much. Neither did time, so it was a perfect place to drink my daily bottle in peace while the world passed by.

My only neighbor, a seventy-year-old black man named Oz, occupied a similar trailer a hundred yards to the right of mine. We drank away many a night watching baseball games on my old television. I'd bring it outside and we watched and sipped. Occasionally we would even eat something with our nightly bottle.

As Oz neared me, I could see two surf-casting poles in his right hand and a bag of donuts from Pat's Donut Shop in his left. It was only seven thirty in the morning. When did Oz find time to roll into town for donuts? He doesn't have a car and it's a half mile to town, another quarter mile to Pat's.

"When did you find the time to hit Pat's?" I said to Oz when he arrived.

"Yesterday," Oz said. "I stuck them in the fridge overnight and nuked them fifteen seconds this morning. What do you want to do first, eat donuts or dig for worms?"

"It's more pleasing to the senses to dig for worms with donut residue on your hands than vice versa," I said.

Oz set the poles down beside the card table and the bag on the table. "Got fresh coffee?" he said.

"Always."

We ate Boston creams, lemon creams, and crullers, drank coffee, and watched the tide raise the surf to the breaking point. Life is better when you wake up instead of come to after a night where you go to sleep instead of passing out.

Life is better when you can actually taste a donut.

We dug for sandworms and used them for bait to cast out the surf rods. I toted folding chairs and a thermos, and we sat and watched for bites with the sun on our faces.

"How goes the job hunt?" Oz remarked casually.

"Honestly, I'm finding I'm qualified for very little outside of police work," I said.

"Want I should call my brother at the DMV?" Oz said. "He might have something for you."

"God, no," I said.

"Honest work," Oz said.

"Honest and about as interesting as a Bruce Willis haircut. Thanks, but I'll keep looking on my own."

"Maybe you could keep working and not tell Janet about it?" Oz suggested.

"Secrets from my new bride," I said, "is no way to start a relationship."

"Neither is broke and unemployed," Oz said.

"It's not that bad. My pension is a third my old salary a year for life, plus a one-point-five-percent cost of living adjustment annually."

"So you're fine unless you want to take her to dinner, buy her something, have Christmas or take a vacation?" Oz said.

"I have—you're getting a bite—almost a hundred grand in the bank," I said. "Maybe I'll play the stock market?"

Oz stood up, grabbed his pole, and gave it a good tug. "Do that and you'll wind up with a hundred thousand pennies in the bank."

My pole jerked suddenly. I stood up and tugged, and the striper bass on the hook tugged back. Oz reeled his in and so did I. We landed two official keepers in the stripers department.

"Shall we catch some more?" Oz said.

"We shall," I said.

"This beats working, anyway," Oz said.

"It do," I said. "It certainly do."

"Do you really believe that?"

I looked at my friend. "No," I said. "But lying to myself is better than lying to Janet."

Chapter 5

Saturday began the way I usually start my days, with a workout on my hanging heavy bag, a slew of elevated push-ups, several hundred stomach crunches, and a three-mile run along the beach in ankle-deep water.

I followed up the workout with two cups of coffee and two cigarettes taken at the card table, where I listened to the battery-powered radio for company.

After that, a shave, and a shower, I was ready to go. I left the trailer and entered the Marquis wearing tan chinos and the nifty teal polo shirt Janet gave me because I needed to start dressing better. Black Reebok walking shoes completed the look.

Justin Lester was about my height, but a hundred pounds less than my weight. To say he was a gawky kid would be an understatement. His sandy hair was over his ears, his brown eyes stared at me softly, and his face was bumpy with pimples. My daughter gazed at him as if he were Tom Selleck circa 1980.

Janet and I were in the kitchen whipping up a late lunch. I glanced out the glass sliding door at the patio table where Regan and Justin sat with glasses of iced tea.

"She's not going to break, Jack," Janet said.

"For Christ's sake, he has pimples," I said.

"And you didn't when you were nineteen?"

"No, and I was never nineteen."

"Well, the good news is we're going with them," Janet said.

"What's the bad news?"

"We have to sit far enough in back of them we can't spy on their conversation."

"Whose idea was this?"

"Regan's," Janet said. "She told me she wasn't ready to be totally alone with a boy just yet."

"She tells you a lot of things," I said.

Janet cocked an eyebrow my way. "Are you jealous?"

"No," I said. "Maybe. Okay, but just a little."

Janet kissed the tip of my nose. "She's growing up, Jack," she said. "It's some kind of miracle she is where she's at, don't you think?"

"I do."

"Yet?"

"I've missed so much," I said.

"She's only nineteen, Jack," Janet said. "And she has a great deal of growing to do. After the wedding, when we're all under one roof, you'll see, it will be good."

"Speaking of under one roof, where's Mark?"

"At Clayton's for the night," Janet said. "So I wouldn't need a sitter."

"He's fourteen," I said.

"And capable of getting into all kinds of trouble left to his own devices."

"Let's have lunch," I suggested.

"Let's," Janet said.

I grabbed the plate loaded with smoked turkey sandwiches and was about to slide open the glass doors when Janet said, "Hold on a second, John."

"I'm in trouble," I said. "What did I do?"

"Nothing, why?"

"When Jack becomes John, I screwed something up. What?"

"You didn't, and shut up," Janet said.

"So what is it?" I said.

"I want you to do something for me," Janet said. "As a . . . favor."

"Sure. What?"

"Now listen, before you throw it back in my face. I know I said I didn't want you to do any more investigations, but this is an exception," Janet said. "Just this one last time."

"What is an exception?" I said.

"You're not angry?"

"No. Do you want me to be? I can fake it if you'd like."

"No, I do not and don't."

"Then maybe you'll tell me what you're talking about."

"After lunch."

"No fair," I said. "Tell me now or forever hold your peas."

"That's peace, idiot."

"I know, but I dislike peas. We established that, remember."

"I thought you didn't like broccoli."

"That, too, but nobody does and forever hold your broccoli doesn't cut it. So, what is the favor?"

"I need you to come to the hospital with me and talk to my boss."

"Who is?"

"Bob Gordon."

"Robert Gordon?" I said. "The chief of medicine at your hospital, that Robert Gordon? He's everybody's boss there, isn't he?"

"Yes."

"What does he want to talk to me about?"

"I'll leave that between you and him."

I looked into Janet's eyes. They told me *ask no more questions.* "Okay. When?"

"Tomorrow," Janet said. "I'm on four to midnight."

"Will there be payment?" I said in my wiseass tone.

"I'll stop by what you call a home around two tomorrow and advance you some premarital flesh," Janet said. "How's that?"

"I warn you, I do keep expense records," I said. "Detailed."

"Oh, shut up and serve lunch," Janet said.

I served lunch. Justin Lester, for all his slight build, ate like a starving plow horse. Conversation was at a minimum, mostly because Regan was too busy eyeing Justin with adoring glances and Justin was too busy stuffing his pimpled face.

After lunch, Janet and I sat fifteen rows behind Regan and Justin and watched Johnny Depp play pirates one more time on the silver screen. Or I should say, Janet watched Johnny Depp play pirates one more time and I watched Regan and Justin hold hands for the two-plus hours it took old Johnny to prance around on screen.

Janet took my hand and felt the tension in me. "Would you relax," she whispered. "It's better she grows up than stays a child for the rest of her life."

I thought about that for a moment. I relaxed a bit. "Must you always be smarter than me?" I whispered.

"I can't help it," Janet whispered. "Look who you're comparing me to."

Chapter 6

Robert Gordon had a large and cluttered office on the sixth floor of the hospital, the floor reserved for administration.

I wasn't sure if Gordon was late for our meeting so I would have time to browse his wall plaques, certificates, awards, and photos, or because something somewhere in the hospital required his attention.

It didn't really matter. I was alone in Gordon's office and perused the walls. A graduate of Harvard Medical School, Gordon served four years in the army overseas in a combat zone before returning home and assuming private practice. In conjunction with his practice, he joined the hospital as a surgeon on call and chief of medicine.

One certificate impressed me the most. Four years ago, the army medical staff in Iraq came across a three-year-old girl who needed immediate open heart surgery to repair two faulty valves. The girl was flown from Iraq to the hospital where Gordon performed the surgery and treated the girl afterward for two months until she was well enough to return home, and it was all done as a charity case, free of charge.

I would have read more, but the office door opened and Robert Gordon walked in with a container of Dunkin' Donuts coffee in his hand.

I'd met Gordon once before, at some hospital function Janet dragged me to about six or seven months ago. At that time, he stood about six-two or -three and went maybe two-twenty in weight, with thick snowy white hair. The Gordon who entered his office and looked at me through liquid brown eyes couldn't weigh more than one-forty and had hardly any hair at all.

Something was killing him, and quickly.

"John Bekker?" Gordon said softly.

"Yes."

He extended his right hand. We shook. The handshake should have been firm. It wasn't.

"Sit, please," Gordon said. "Would you like some coffee or tea?"

"I would," I said. "Coffee with milk, no sugar."

Gordon took a seat behind his desk, picked up the phone, and made a quick call. Within sixty seconds, a woman entered with a DD large and brought it to the desk.

"Hold all nonemergency calls for a bit," Gordon told the woman. "I'll let you know when."

She nodded at Gordon and left us alone.

I picked up the coffee and opened the tab. "Is there a DD in the hospital?"

"No." Gordon smiled. "However, I won't drink the swill they pass for coffee in the cafeteria, so I have a Box o' Joe delivered every morning with cups."

I sipped. It was good.

Gordon also sipped. I could tell he thought it was good, too.

"So, Mr. Gordon, what can I do for you?" I said.

"Janet tells me that you are very smart and very good at what you do," Gordon said.

"Maybe you can get her to tell me that," I said.

Gordon allowed a tiny smile to cross his lips. Then it faded. "I want you to find somebody for me, quickly and quietly. Can you do that?" he said.

"Missing person?"

"Sort of," Gordon said. "It's complicated."

"Mr. Gordon, I have a few rules when I work," I said. "I never break them, and if I see the work calls for breaking them, I won't take the job. First rule, no lying, no holding back. Second rule, if I don't like you or what you're hiring me to do, I won't take the job. Money won't make me break those rules. Simple rules, but I'm a simple guy. So, tell me what you think I can help you with."

"I'm sixty-two years old, Mr. Bekker," Gordon said. "Inoperable cancer in the lining of my lungs will soon take my life. Three months at best."

Gordon paused to sip some coffee.

My mind went backward in time to Eddie Crist, a mobster with months to live from the cancer that ate away at his flesh, who wanted to go out with a clear conscience.

"I won't help you clean your dirty underwear," I said. "I don't do that."

"I'm not asking you to," Gordon said when he was done sipping. "I haven't earned that right and I don't expect to."

"So back to the beginning, how can I help you?" I said.

"Forty years ago, I married my high school sweetheart," Gordon said. "We had an agreement. She would work full-time while I went to medical school. The best-laid plans of mice and men and all that."

"What happened?" I said.

"A baby happened two years into the marriage," Gordon said. "And as things turned out, my wife had a heart defect that took her life on the delivery table. The baby, a girl, lived."

I sipped some coffee.

Gordon sipped some coffee.

We looked at each other.

"I was twenty-four at the time, a full-time student and unemployed," Gordon said. "My father's brother, my uncle, is—or was—an attorney. I spoke to him about giving the baby up for adoption. He suggested a quicker, more profitable avenue to travel."

"You sold the baby on the black market," I said.

"My uncle did," Gordon said. "I allowed him to do it."

"I can't help you," I said and stood up.

"Wait," Gordon said. "Hear me out. Please?"

I sat back down. "Clock's ticking."

"I don't want you to find her so we may have a deathbed reunion," Gordon said. "I want you to find her and wait until after I'm gone, and then have my attorney Percy Meade contact her with my final will. She will be left all that I have minus some gifts to charity. I'm not looking to win a seat at the big table, Mr. Bekker, but maybe I can make her life a little bit better after I'm gone."

"Any clues as to her whereabouts?" I said.

"None."

"What about your uncle the lawyer?"

"Mr. Meade will answer all your questions, give you a contract and expenses, and work with you start to finish," Gordon said. "After today, we will probably never see each other again."

"Where do I find Mr. Meade?" I said.

Gordon slid open the top desk drawer and pulled out Meade's business card. "He's expecting your call," he said.

I looked at the card.

Chapter 7

"I didn't know," Janet said with a mixture of surprise and disgust in her voice. "If I had, I would have told him you were retired."

"Don't be so quick to judge," I said. "I'm guilty of practically the same thing."

"I'd hardly call a little girl witnessing her mother being murdered and you having a breakdown over it the same thing as selling your own flesh," Janet said.

I dumped some hot sauce on my scrambled eggs and stirred them around a bit.

"He sold a newborn instead of placing her for adoption," I said. "That means he sold her to a family with money and the ability to provide. Who knows where she would have wound up had she gone through regular channels?"

I ate some hot sauce–spiced eggs.

"Don't tell me you approve of what he did, Jack," Janet said. She pointed to my eggs. "And that's disgusting."

"I didn't say that," I said. "I don't. However, as I am as weak as the next guy, I can understand it a bit better."

"You're not weak, Jack," Janet insisted.

"No," I said. "I married your sister and at our reception I ogled you and a few decades later, we're getting married, what would you call it?"

"Stupid, but not weak," Janet said. "And nobody uses the word 'ogled' anymore."

"What do they use?"

"Leer. Smirk. Snicker. Sneer. Simper. Eye-bang and a host of others."

"Eye-bang?" I said.

Janet shrugged. "It's a new century."

I tossed on some more hot sauce and Janet rolled her eyes. We were in her backyard, having Sunday brunch. Regan and Mark were playing a video game in the living room and every once in a while I could hear Mark snap, "Quit cheating."

"But an old me," I said.

"Not so old yesterday afternoon," Janet said.

"I'm still recovering," I said. "I pulled a muscle."

"So you're going to do this?" Janet said.

"Somewhere out there is a woman, possibly a wife and mother, who would benefit greatly if I did," I said. "So yes, I'm going to do this."

"Can you do it by our wedding?" Janet said.

"Afraid I'll turn into a pumpkin?" I cracked.

"No," Janet said and turned her head away from me. "Just afraid that I'll lose you."

CHAPTER 8

Percy Meade's office was located a few miles from the hospital. He had a view of the ocean from his fourth-floor window. It was cluttered with law books, file cabinets, legal pads, and files.

He worked alone with just a plumpish, middle-aged paralegal who manned the outer office. When I arrived, she stood from her desk and ushered me into Meade's office, then politely closed the door behind her.

Meade was looking out his office window. "Come see this," he said.

I went to the window and stood beside him.

"The sailboat passing by," Meade said.

A forty-foot sailboat with bright blue sails cruised by at maybe fifteen knots.

"Ever see blue sails like that before?" Meade said.

"No."

He shook his head, turned to me and extended his right hand. "Percy Meade."

"John Bekker."

We shook, broke apart, and Meade went behind his desk. I took one of three leather-back chairs facing it.

"How about some coffee?" Meade suggested.

"Sure."

As if on cue, the door opened and the plumpish paralegal returned with a tray that held two mugs of coffee. She set the tray on the desk and silently retreated from the office a second time.

"I took the liberty of doing some background gathering on you after Mr. Gordon told me he wanted to hire you," Meade said.

"And what did you find out?" I said as I reached for a mug.

"Highly competent, used to be an excellent police detective, had a few bad breaks, rebounded nicely, and most of all you're honest," Meade said.

"You left out drunk," I said.

"Not for the last thirteen months," Meade said. "I hope," he added.

"No."

"So Mr. Gordon briefed you on what he wants of you?"

"Yes."

"I took the liberty of drawing up a contract for your approval," Meade said. He opened a desk drawer, removed a folded document, and slid it across the desk to me.

I picked it up and read the one-page agreement. It was the standard private investigator–attorney contract. Billable hours submitted to Meade, advance on expenses, keep and file all receipts before additional expense money is advanced. If the investigation exceeds ninety days, the hourly rate increases by fifteen percent to compensate for lost jobs from new clients.

I set the paper down on the desk. "What can you tell me about Mr. Gordon's request?"

"Nothing," Meade said. "I first became aware of it when he came to see me two weeks ago and told me he wanted to hire a private investigator."

I sipped coffee and nodded. "How much is Gordon worth? Ballpark figure."

"Five-point-seven million," Meade said. "That includes two luxury homes, insurance policies, investments, automobiles, furnishings, and cash."

"So it's a big league ballpark," I said.

"Bigger once the insurance policies kick in."

"The only starting point I have so far is Gordon's lawyer uncle," I said. "Know where I can find him?"

"Actually, I do," Meade said. "That would be Donald Gordon. He's eighty-seven and lives in a nursing home for Alzheimer's patients. The Hillcrest Estates, about an hour's drive north. I'll give you the phone number and address."

I nodded and took a pen from my suit jacket pocket to sign the work agreement. "Expenses?" I said.

Meade took the signed agreement and placed it in his desk. From the same drawer, he removed a white envelope and passed it to me. "Ten thousand," he said. "Please keep accurate records and receipts of all expenses and, of course, your time to the nearest hour."

I placed the envelope in my jacket pocket. "I'll keep you updated as things progress," I said.

"Mr. Bekker," Meade said. "I've known Bob Gordon three decades. This isn't his valediction, if that thought crossed your mind. The crime isn't that he gave his infant daughter away to a better life than he could have provided at the time. The crime is if he kept her and never became a doctor and saved thousands of lives in the process. Keep that in mind as things develop."

"Mr. Meade," I said. "If there's one thing I've learned about people, it's that nobody ever really knows anybody."

CHAPTER 9

When there is very little in the way of facts, information, clu
or leads to work with, go fishing.

Not the kind Oz and I did the other morning at the bea
but the kind done with a computer at the library. Since
trailer didn't have cable, the library was my source for all
computer needs.

Armed with a container of coffee, a legal pad, and pen, I
at one of eight terminals and did some fact-finding to fill in
blanks. Not that I held any illusions about finding any real c
to the whereabouts of Gordon's daughter. I just wanted s
background material on the principal players.

A search for Robert Gordon brought up thousands of lin
whittled it down to a manageable hundred and read the
that gave insight into the man's character. If you were str
with heart disease and required the best care and surgery,
don was your man on the East Coast. In addition to ru
the hospital, Gordon owned three private practice c
throughout the state. Known for charity work, his p
practices often treated patients with little money and no
ance *pro bono.* One report claimed that in his lifetime, G
had so far performed six million dollars' worth of charity
tions. He never remarried. His life was medicine.

Donald Gordon was a horse of an entirely different
For most of his legal career, Donald was a TV-adve
ambulance-chasing second-rater. His ads ran on late ni

angry guy saying if you'd been injured in an accident, you owed it to yourself to get what was coming to you. He made gobs of money, and from what I read of him, few friends. He outlived his wife by twenty years and had one daughter named Sylvia. I did a people search and located Sylvia, who lived in her father's home in the suburbs.

I printed some things I wanted to keep, made some notes on questions I wanted to ask, finished my coffee, and left the library.

On the drive back to my trailer, I made two quick stops. The first was at the Italian deli in town for two meatball subs and a large bottle of ginger ale. The second was at the potato chip factory store where they made a fresh batch of chips every fifteen minutes in a dozen different flavors. I picked up a pound bag each of barbeque chips and vinegar.

I park the Marquis in one of two places when I'm home. The first is at the municipal lot adjacent to the beach entrance. The second is in front of my trailer. Today I opted to drive the half mile across sand to my trailer since it was an overcast day and foot traffic was light.

I left the foil-wrapped subs on the kitchen counter and changed into gray sweats. I do my best thinking sometimes when trying not to think at all and working up a decent sweat.

Outside, I warmed up with some jump rope, then moved over to the heavy bag for twenty minutes of hard pounding. After that, I switched gears to push-ups and crunches, then took a three-mile run in ankle-deep water along the beach.

When I returned to my trailer, Oz was in his customary chair, waiting on me. He tossed me the towel on the card table as I flopped into my seat.

"I got subs," I said.

"Meatball from that Eye-talian place?"

"Of course."

"Chips?"

"A bag for each of us."

"What you waiting on?"

I went in, removed the foil from the subs, heated them for one minute in the microwave, and toted them out with the bags of chips, glasses, and ginger ale.

Oz dug right into his sub and didn't mind at all when sauce dribbled down his short, gray beard.

"Feel like working?" I said.

"I retired, in case you hadn't noticed," Oz said as he cracked open the vinegar chips. "Work and feel like are unrelated to each other."

"Twelve bucks an hour to keep records, answer the phone, and write reports," I said.

"Nobody gonna shoot me like last time?" Oz said as he licked sauce off his fingers. "I'm too old to be getting shot again."

"Missing persons case, and unless the missing person shows up with a gun and a grudge, I'd say the odds are pretty slim on that happening," I said.

"What about my expenses?"

"Expenses? All you have to do is walk from your trailer to mine."

"Wear and tear on the feet," Oz said.

"Twelve an hour plus one free bag of chips a week," I said.

"Two bags," Oz said. "Least you can do seeing as how I was almost killed for you twice for free."

"Deal," I said.

"When I start?"

"Right after you wipe the sauce from your beard."

"I get a gun?"

"No, but I'll toss in a third bag of chips."

"Deal," Oz said.

CHAPTER 10

Later in the afternoon, after Oz put together a logbook for calls, another for receipts and expenses, and a third for notes, I left him to finish his bag of chips, and probably mine along with it, and took a walk to town.

When I reached the pavement, I walked a few blocks to Main Street, turned left, and went a few more blocks to the *Ames Family Owned Jewelry Store since 1959,* and entered.

The grandson of Ames, the founder, stood behind a long glass counter and greeted me with a bright smile that reeked of *can't wait to take your money.* "Mr. Bekker, nice to see you again," he said.

I pulled the stub from my pocket and gave it to grandson Ames. "Is it back yet?" I said.

"Came in this morning," grandson Ames said. "I'll get it for you right away."

It was my mother's diamond wedding ring that I had reset into a modern setting in Janet's size. It set my father back a year's salary nearly six decades ago. Along with my mother's ring, I had my wife's diamond ring set into a pendant on a thin, eighteen-karat gold chain.

I'd left a deposit of half a few weeks ago. I paid for the balance in cash and then started back to the beach. Along the way, I stopped at Pat's Donut Shop and bought a half dozen mixed for tonight's ball game. Nothing says night baseball like a gut full of fried donut.

The beach was empty except for a few die-hard surfers catching the afternoon break and some gulls searching for snacks. The gulls must have caught wind of the bag of donuts in my hand, because suddenly I was extremely popular. I shooed them away and reached my trailer with me and the bag in one piece.

After tucking the Pat's bag in the fridge, I made some fresh coffee and took a mug and my cell phone outside to my rusty lawn chair. I rested the mug on the card table, lit a cigarette, and scanned my notes for Sylvia Gordon's phone number.

I punched in the number and listened to an electronic voicemail box tell me to press 1 to leave a message or press 2 to leave a callback number. I pressed 1 and left a message for Sylvia to return my call in regards to her father.

I drank my coffee and finished the cigarette. Three refills and four cigarettes later, my cell phone rang.

"John Bekker," I said.

"Mr. Bekker, Sylvia Gordon returning your call," Sylvia said. "Your message said you wanted to speak to me about my father."

"Yes," I said. "I'm a private investigator employed by a law firm to track down a missing person who may have had contact with your father when he was practicing law. I know it's a long time ago, but if you can spare some time I'd like to talk with you."

"Oooh, intriguing," Sylvia said. "Tell you what, Mr. Bekker. I've just walked in the door. I need a shower and a change, so why don't you meet me in, say, an hour. Know where I live?"

"I have the address," I said. "I'll find it."

"Don't be late," Sylvia said. "I have a dinner appointment at eight."

The phone went silent. I set it aside and lit a fresh cigarette. The donuts would have to wait until later.

CHAPTER 11

Sylvia Gordon's home wasn't in the mansion category, but definitely out of reach of the working middle class. My untrained eye put the home in the seven-hundred-thousand-dollar range.

I parked in the driveway beside a late-model Mercedes and walked past a manicured lawn to the front door. I rang the bell and waited. An intercom mounted beside the door crackled to life.

"Walk around back, Mr. Bekker," Sylvia Gordon said over the intercom speaker.

I did as instructed and followed a stone path that cut in half a lush green lawn with a dozen flowerbeds. I found Sylvia Gordon seated at a shaded patio table that overlooked a decent-size swimming pool. A wireless remote for the intercom rested on the table.

"John Bekker," I said.

Sylvia Gordon was about fifty years old, dressed in a lightweight silk pantsuit that shimmered teal when she stood up to greet me. Her eyes were green, her hair too black to be real, and her body as tight as a taut bow string.

"I just got home from Zumba and kettlebell class when I returned your call," Sylvia said as she shook my hand with a firm grip. "I'm having a screwdriver before I leave for dinner, care to join me?"

"No, thank you," I said. "Would you like to see my ID before we start?"

"I did an online search of you before I called," Sylvia said. "You're real or I would have deleted your number. Sit, please."

I sat. So did Sylvia.

"So how can I help you?" Sylvia said. "My father has been in a nursing home for Alzheimer's patients for a decade now."

"I think I know what kettlebell is, but I'm not so sure on the Zumba," I said.

"It's something that keeps my ass firm and tummy flat, and that's not easy to do at my age," Sylvia said.

"I think it isn't easy at any age," I said.

"I don't know, from what I see of you, you look pretty hard," Sylvia said.

"I do my best," I said. "So, how bad off is your father?"

"Good moments of clarity, bad moments of pure vegetable," Sylvia said. "No way of knowing when he'll have a good or bad moment, so it's a crap shoot he'll remember me, or anything for that matter."

I nodded. "Were you ever involved in his practice prior to his illness?"

"My father was an ambulance-chasing son of a bitch, but he knew how to make money," Sylvia said. "For his clients and for him. The only involvement I ever had was in spending what he earned. He provided me with a first-class education that I never had to use in the form of employment. He left me everything and I plan to spend every red cent before I check out because what else am I going to do with it?"

"Ever been married?" I said.

"Why, are you asking?"

"No," I said. "Just thinking a few questions ahead."

"Such as?"

"Any of your husbands close to your father?"

"Number one was fairly close. Worked for Dad for a while until they had a falling out," Sylvia said. "Two and three barely spoke to him."

"When was number one?"

"I was twenty-two," Sylvia said. "Almost twenty-nine years ago."

I nodded. "Is your father up for visitors?"

"Like I said, most of the time he doesn't know you're in the room."

"What's husband number one's name?" I said. "And what was the falling out about?"

"You like to jump all over the place, don't you?"

"It's an interviewing technique designed to keep the subject off guard and prevent prepared answers," I said.

"Am I your subject?" Sylvia said.

"No. Did your father keep any records in the house?"

"Not until he closed his offices about ten or eleven years ago," Sylvia said. "That's why my car is parked in the driveway. The garage is filled with his cartons."

"Three more quick questions and I'll be out of your hair," I said.

Sylvia took a sip of her drink. "You're not in my hair," she said. "In fact, if you'd like to stick around and get in my hair, I'll skip my dinner plans."

"Can't," I said. "What's your first husband's name and where can I find him, and can I have a look at the cartons in the garage?"

"Jonathan Levine and you can find him in the book," Sylvia said. "He still practices law. I don't know what the falling out was over. Ask him. As for the garage, you could do me a favor and clean it out for all I care."

I didn't clean out the garage. I did, however, find three cartons of files from twenty-nine years ago and loaded them into the back seat of the Marquis.

Sylvia watched from the edge of the driveway as I went

through rows and stacks of cartons before finding the three I thought useful. "I could use an escort for dinner," she said when the third was safely in the back seat.

"Tell you what," I said. "When I return these boxes, I'll spring for lunch. How's that?"

"Just lunch?"

"Three months I'm a married man," I said.

"A lot can happen in three months."

"And a lot can't," I said. "Do me a favor and check with the nursing home and find out if I can see your father."

"Better be some fucking lunch," Sylvia said.

I got behind the wheel of the Marquis and drove away as fast as my six-cylinder engine would allow me.

In the rearview mirror, I caught a glimpse of Sylvia giving me the finger. It was nice to know I made somebody's day.

CHAPTER 12

"I think this should count as overtime," Oz said.

"I'll owe you a donut and a half," I said.

"We been at this four hours," Oz said. "Is there some point I'm missing?"

"No."

Since eight p.m., Oz and I had sat at my tiny kitchen table and rifled through the three cartons of files I took from Sylvia's garage. Almost three-decade-old legal cases involving mostly auto accidents, hit-and-runs, pedestrians and buses, kids on bikes, pedestrians on wet pavements, and the usual fanfare one would expect to find in the files of a lawyer who sued and settled for a living.

Donald Gordon worked as most accident claim lawyers do, on contingency. They file a lawsuit and settle out of court because it's cheaper for the company being sued than the cost of a trial, and the companies just pass the costs on to clients anyway. For his time and trouble, Gordon took a third of all money paid to the victim.

Even back then, Gordon made a lot of money by today's inflated standards. His average settlement was nine thousand. In a good month, he settled thirty cases. He was making a million dollars a year before seven figures deflated to six figures in buying power.

"What are we looking for exactly?" Oz said.

"Good question," I said. "I don't know."

"But you'll know it when you see it," Oz said.

"Kind of like not knowing anything about art, but knowing a masterpiece when you see one," I said.

"We looking for paintings?" Oz said.

"No, clues."

Oz sighed and ate another donut.

Around one-thirty in the a.m., Oz knocked off and went home. We were done anyway and accomplished nothing of consequence in our research. All I wanted to see was how avid a player Jonathan Levine was when employed by his father-in-law. In seventeen months, Levine was involved in sixty-seven filed lawsuits against insurance companies, three against townships, and two filed under "Other."

Then he fell off the Donald Gordon grid.

The "falling out."

I took a can of ginger ale and my smokes outside and sat in my lawn chair. I sipped, smoked, and listened to waves crash against the dark beach. Off in the distance, a few lights from town glowed softly.

A falling out over what?

Perhaps Jonathan Levine grew tired of the ambulance-chasing business and wanted to practice real law?

Maybe he didn't like selling flesh?

The best way to get an answer was to ask the question.

Chapter 13

I called Janet early the next morning to set up a dinner date at her house for tonight. Then I ventured out in the Marquis to find the law office of Jonathan Levine.

Levine had moved his office about fifteen years ago to a squat, one-story building on Main Street two towns over. I parked at a meter, fed it enough quarters to last two hours, and paused on the street long enough to smoke a cigarette.

The street was quaint, lined with fenced-in trees and with parking at a forty-five-degree angle to allow more room for cars. More cars equated to more tourists during summer months, and nothing attracted tourists like a beach with an amusement park, which this town held bragging rights to.

I tossed the cigarette into the very clean street, then walked up and opened the door to Jonathan Levine's office. I stepped into a cluttered reception area that was presently unmanned. Directly behind the reception desk to the left was a closed door with Levine's name printed on it in bold, black lettering.

I went and listened at the door. A man I presumed to be Levine spoke in hushed tones on the phone. I waited until I heard him say goodbye, then I knocked once and opened the door before he could respond.

Jonathan Levine sat behind a desk so piled with folders and files, it was impossible to see where the desk began and the clutter ended. Startled, Levine looked at me with wide, owl-like eyes.

"I'm not here to rob the place if that's what you think," I said.

"Is Jennifer not at her desk?" Levine said.

A muffled sound of a toilet flushing came through the walls.

"No," I said. "Unless her desk is in the bathroom."

"Do you have an appointment?"

"No."

"Do you require the services of an attorney?"

"Let's talk about that," I said.

"I don't understand," Levine said. "Talk about what?"

I removed my license from the nifty plastic wallet I keep in my pocket and showed it to Levine. He scanned it quickly and I put it away. "I've been employed to find a missing person," I said.

"A missing . . . who?" Levine said.

"Why don't you send Jennifer for coffee?" I said.

Levine looked at me.

"I wasn't asking," I said.

Levine continued to look at me for a moment or two, and then he picked up his phone and hit the intercom button. "Jenny, would you be a dear and grab two large coffees for me and my guest." He looked up at me.

"Milk, no sugar," I said.

"Two with milk, one with sugar," Levine said and hung up the phone.

I took one of three hardback chairs in the room. "You were married to Sylvia Gordon and worked for her father in his practice," I said. "That's what we'll talk about."

"Are you asking?" Levine said.

"No."

"Yes to both questions," Levine said. "What does that have to do with your missing person?"

"I went through every case you filed for Gordon while you

were employed there," I said. "Looks like you averaged about eleven grand a month in income from settled lawsuits. What do you pull in now thirty years later, maybe sixty K after expenses and payroll?"

"I don't see how that's—" Levine said.

"You quit a lucrative gig to enter a meager private practice. Why?"

"Sylvia and I were having marital problems," Levine said. "It didn't sit right with me to keep working for her father. What does that have to do with—"

"What were the marital problems about?"

Levine glared at me. "I'm one step away from calling the police."

"Which puts you a half step away from a broken arm," I said.

"I have a gun in my desk," he said.

"Hey, go for it," I said. "You'll have a broken neck before it's halfway out. Now answer the question."

"We married too young," Levine said. "We argued a lot and fell out of love. Now answer mine. What does that have to do with your missing person case?"

"Bob Gordon had a little sideline that I think you found out about and disapproved of," I said.

"I don't know what—" Levine said.

"Gordon knew his way around the black market baby circuit," I said. "He sold newborns to couples with the means to pay what the market demanded. I know this as fact. What do you know?"

Levine thought about sighing and decided not to. "I found out about it when there was an appointment mix-up and a young couple came to my office by mistake. I confronted Donald about it and we had a falling out, which led to my resignation and divorce."

"Did you go to the police?"

"No."

"Why not?" I said. "Selling infant human beings is trafficking. Gordon would have gotten twenty-five to life."

"That first night I went home after finding out," Levine said, "I wanted to tell Sylvia, but I decided to wait until morning. Shortly after we went to bed, I heard a noise downstairs. I thought Sylvia's cat got into something in the kitchen. I turned on the light and three men in ski masks were sitting at the table. I knew I was in trouble right then and there."

"What happened?" I said.

"The spokesman of the group told me I should forget anything I knew or thought I knew about Donald Gordon," Levine said. "He said if I wanted to keep breathing, I should divorce Sylvia and move on and keep very quiet about their visit. Then to make their point, the spokesman stood up and put a pistol in my mouth. I did as I was told and have never been visited since."

"I can't say as I blame you," I said.

There was a soft knock on the door. It opened and a middle-aged woman I assumed to be Jennifer entered with two containers of coffee. She set them on the desk, gave me a quick glance, and said, "Will that be all, Jon?"

"Yes," Levine said. "See if you can finish that Werner contract agreement before you leave for the day."

Jennifer nodded and left us alone.

I picked up my coffee, lifted the tab, and took a small sip.

"I'm not a coward," Levine said. He picked up his coffee. "But you can't fight armed, masked men who appear unexpectedly in the night with principles and expect to win."

"No," I said.

Levine took a sip from his container. "I assume your missing person was a baby Gordon was involved with placing," he said.

"Selling, and yes," I said. "What did he charge for his services?"

"The one I knew about, the young couple was prepared to pay seventy-five thousand for a newborn."

I did a quick inflation adjustment in my head on seventy-five thousand in today's market. "A lot of money," I said.

Levine nodded. "Don was always good at making money. As you can see, I'm not."

"Did he keep records somewhere of the children he arranged sales for?"

"I assume so, but I can't say where," Levine said. "How long ago are we talking about?"

"Almost forty years," I said.

"I can't help you with that," Levine said.

"I know."

"Then why the visit?"

"Reinforce what I've been told," I said. "I used to be a police detective and I don't like unconfirmed details."

"We all used to be something," Levine said. "I used to be a real lawyer."

I left Levine with that and drove home.

CHAPTER 14

When a beaming Janet showed her diamond engagement ring to my daughter, Regan scolded me by explaining the ring and proposal are supposed to be done at the same time and from bended knee.

"Couldn't be helped," I said. "The diamond needed a new setting and my knees ain't what they used to be. Besides, I had to wait for this."

I produced the gift box and placed it in Regan's hands. "On the big day, when you walk beside Janet, I would like you to wear this. It belonged to your mother."

Regan opened the box and looked at the diamond necklace. She stared at it for many long seconds, gently closed the box, and started to cry silent tears. I wrapped my arms around her and kissed her forehead.

"I'm a lucky man to have two such beautiful women in my life," I said.

I heard a soft sob and looked over at Janet just as she wiped away a teardrop.

That moment, Mark poked his head into the living room where we had gathered. "What's all the weeping about?" he said. "I'm hungry."

"Never mind weeping," Janet said. "Go change that shirt to something clean."

Regan decided to change as well. Janet and I had a few moments alone and we took advantage of them by waiting in the cool breeze blowing in the backyard.

"It's beautiful, Jack," Janet said. "Thank you."

"You're welcome," I said.

"Also beautiful what you did for Regan," Janet said. "Sometimes I swear your insides are nothing but one big pile of mush."

"That's me, good old mushy," I said.

"Well what does old mushy want in the way of dinner?" Janet said. "We could break our reservation and go for something new."

"Let the young ones decide," I said.

"That could wind us up at Chuck E. Cheese."

"Maybe we better stick to our reservation, then?" I said.

"Yes, maybe. Oh, by the way," Janet said, "our guest list may be upped by one."

"Who?"

"Justin Lester."

"No," I snapped.

"Jack, he and—"

"Still no."

"Jack, shut up and listen to me," Janet said. "You want Regan to have a normal life and become a whole person like she was meant to be, or do you want her to stay as she is? Dating boys is part of her progress, Jack. If you really want her to continue to grow, you'll allow her to bring Justin as her date."

I sighed in defeat. "There you go being right again."

"I can't help it, it's a bad habit," Janet said.

"Does she know . . . I mean, what if he tries . . . I mean, she has been sheltered by nuns and priests all her life," I said.

Janet did her best not to laugh at me. She failed. "Oh, Jack," she giggled. "Sister Mary Martin gave her the birds and bees lecture years ago."

"A nun gave Regan the facts-of-life talk?"

"Nuns are people, too, Jack."

"Yeah, well, someone telling you what it's like to drive a Ferrari is not the same as driving one yourself," I said.

"Am I your Ferrari, Jack?" Janet giggled again. "Would you like to go for a ride?"

Before I could think of a quick-witted response, Mark and Regan came outside looking for us. "Quit giggling like kids, you two, and let's go eat," Mark said.

"To be continued," I told Janet.

"Oh, most definitely," Janet said and took my arm. "The engine is just warming up."

Chapter 15

I chatted briefly with Percy Meade early the next morning and gave him what little updates I had worth mentioning.

"I'll try to see Donald Gordon this afternoon," I said. "And hope he has a moment of clarity."

"You think he kept records?"

"I do."

"Robert announced his retirement to the hospital this morning," Meade said. "A party is planned for his last day the end of the week."

"He's getting close, isn't he?"

"Ten weeks, maybe," Meade said. "A bit more if his strength holds out."

"Do you think he's up for a road trip?" I said.

"To see his uncle? Possibly, but I was under the assumption Mr. Gordon didn't want to know any of the details," Meade said.

"The only true starting point in this is Donald Gordon," I said. "It may not be avoidable, but I promise to keep him out of it as much as possible."

"I'll speak to him this morning," Meade said.

"Call me back on my cell," I said.

I changed into shorts and a T-shirt and attached five-pound ankle weights to each ankle, opened the trailer door, and stepped out to greet Oz, who was in the process of sitting in his favorite chair.

I tossed him my cell phone. "You're on the clock."

"Any coffee inside?"

"Just made a pot," I said. "I'll be back in three miles."

"Who should be calling?"

"Lawyer named Meade," I said. "Take a message and I'll call him back."

I jogged down to the beach, turned right, and carved out a two-mile path in the hard sand. When I reversed direction, I skirted into ankle-deep surf. The canvas ankle weights took on water, so that by the time I returned to Oz, they'd increased in weight by several pounds.

I stripped off the weights and tossed them beside my chair to dry. "Anything?"

"Not yet," Oz said as he sipped from a mug.

"Feel like holding the mitts?" I said.

"Last time we did that, I couldn't hold a pen for a week," Oz said.

"Don't be an old woman."

"Is it okay for me to be an old man?"

I left Oz to his coffee, put on the gloves, and proceeded to beat the snot out of my heavy bag. After a while, I switched to push-ups and cranked out repetitions until my arms gave out, then switched over to sit-ups and did those until my stomach cramped.

Still no return call from Meade. I left Oz guardian of my phone and entered my trailer.

A shave, shower, and change of clothes later, I emerged from the trailer with a fresh mug of coffee to find Oz talking to Meade on my cell phone. "I'll tell him that, Mr. Meade," Oz said. "Just as soon as he returns. Thank you. Goodbye."

I flopped into my chair and lit a cigarette.

"You do all this shit running around exercising and then light a cigarette," Oz said. "Makes no sense."

"What did Meade have to say?" I ignored the critique of my bad habit.

"The man say to meet him at the hospital at four this afternoon," Oz said.

"That's it, nothing else?" I said.

"Just meet him at four is all," Oz said.

"At the hospital?"

"What he said."

I glanced at my watch. I had four hours to kill. "Feel like a walk to town for lunch?" I said.

"You buying?"

"I suppose I could cheat on my expense report," I said.

"In that case I suppose I could let you," Oz said as he stood up.

Chapter 16

Janet was sporting her new engagement ring on her finger when I paid her a surprise visit fifteen minutes before four o'clock. After taking some kind of final exam after months of studying, Janet now worked on the cardiac ICU ward where patients received one-on-one care immediately after open-heart surgery.

After scrubbing my hands with sanitizer the consistency of glue, I entered the ward and found Janet seated in a chair facing a small stand with a laptop on it. Directly in front of her was her patient, an unconscious man in a large motorized bed with a dozen or more wires and tubes inserted in him.

Janet turned her head when I approached her. "Jack, how did you get in here?"

"I have connections," I said.

"Did you scrub your hands on the way in?"

"I did. Can I kiss you?"

"Only if you want me to get fired."

"That won't happen," I said. "I have an in with the boss."

"Is that why you're here, to see Bob?"

"Yes."

"Why you're wearing a suit?"

"Yes."

"He announced his retirement this morning."

"I know."

A few cubicles down, alarms suddenly went off. Janet stood up. "I have to go," she said and dashed to the cubicle along with a dozen other nurses and doctors.

I watched for a few seconds as the crowd gathered inside the cubicle. A great deal was going on in there of which I knew nothing. If you ever want to feel small and insignificant, watch doctors and nurses rush to save somebody's life.

I left the floor, went outside, and smoked a cigarette across the street from the hospital while I waited for Percy Meade to arrive.

Around five past four, a large black Lincoln pulled up in front of the main hospital entrance doors. I crossed the street and got in. Meade and Gordon were already seated in back. I sat to Meade's right. Gordon sat to Meade's left beside the door.

"Driver," Meade said to the man behind the wheel. "The Hillcrest Estates."

CHAPTER 17

We reached the Hillcrest Estates about ninety minutes later. Conversation was held to the occasional word from Meade to the driver. At some point on the ride, Gordon fell asleep and didn't stir until Meade nudged him gently and told him we'd arrived.

The Hillcrest Estates was a long horseshoe-shaped building that consisted of 202 private rooms, all on one floor. Blue with white trim, lush flower beds and lawn, it more resembled a resort hotel in the mountains than a specialty nursing home.

Meade had phoned earlier in the day and made the appointment. A nurse in crisp whites escorted us to Donald Gordon's private room, situated in the center of the building with a nice view of the backyard gardens. Robert Gordon walked under his own steam behind the nurse. I stayed close by, as did Meade, just in case.

"Mr. Gordon, you have visitors," the nurse said when we arrived at Donald Gordon's room.

Donald Gordon was seated in a leather chair facing a tall open window. He was staring at the gardens, or off into space, anybody's guess. He didn't move.

"Can he hear us?" Robert said.

The nurse went to Donald and placed a hand on his shoulder. "Visitors, Donald," she said.

Donald slowly turned to look up at her.

"Your nephew and some friends," the nurse said.

Slowly, Donald Gordon stood up and turned around. He may have been an old man, but he still had his strength and walked effortlessly toward us. "Do I know you?" he said in a slightly booming voice.

"I'll leave you alone for a while," the nurse said. "If you want to sit outside, there's an exit two doors to the left."

"Uncle Don, it's Robert, your nephew," Robert said.

Donald stared at Robert for a moment. "My nephew?"

"Yes, Uncle," Robert said.

"Who are they?" Donald said.

"Friends," Robert said.

"What do you want?" Donald said.

"To talk to you," Robert said. "Why don't we sit outside? It's a beautiful afternoon."

"Can I have tea?" Donald said. "I always have tea when I sit outside."

"Sure," Robert said. "We'll all have tea. That would be nice."

Ten minutes later we sat at a shaded table in the garden and drank tea from actual tea cups with handles so small my fingers wouldn't fit into the loop.

"How are you, Uncle Donald?" Robert said.

"Who are you again?" Donald said.

"Your nephew. Robert."

"Robert, yes," Donald said. "And them?"

"Friends," Robert said.

"My friends? I don't recognize them. What do they want?"

"Just to keep me company, Uncle Donald," Robert said. "I need to ask you some questions about long ago."

"Questions?" Donald said.

"About long ago," Robert said.

"Questions about what?" Donald said.

"When you practiced law," Robert said.

"I was a lawyer?" Donald said. "When?"

"Your whole life," Robert said.

I sipped tea and listened to Robert and Donald exchange useless dialogue. Finally, I set the cup on the table and looked at Donald. "My name is John," I said. "It's nice to meet you, Donald."

Donald turned his head slightly and looked at me through a haze of confusion. "John?" he said. "Are we friends?"

"Yes," I said. "I admire the way you helped so many people start families."

"I used to do that?"

"Yes," I said. "I remember how you helped Robert with his problem."

Donald turned to Robert. "What problem?"

"When his wife died in childbirth and you helped find a home for the baby, remember?" I said.

A little of the haze in Donald's eyes cleared up. "I . . . remember," he said softly.

"You found the baby a home," I said. "Do you remember the name of the family?"

Donald looked directly at me. His eyes were clearer, but not all the way there. He shook his head no.

"What about records, Donald?" I said. "You must have kept track of all the children you helped?"

"I think . . . maybe," Donald said. "Have you checked my safe deposit box?"

"No," I said. "What box, where?"

"At my bank," Donald said.

"What bank?" I said. "What's the name of the bank?"

Donald's eyes hazed over again and he picked up his teacup. "Why don't we all have some tea?" he said. "It's a lovely afternoon."

"We're losing him," Robert said.

"Donald?" I said.

"I do enjoy my afternoon tea," Donald said.

"He's gone," Robert said.

"It was nice talking to you, Donald," I said.

Donald looked at me. "Who are you?"

"Nobody," I said. "Just somebody having tea in the afternoon."

Chapter 18

I grilled some steaks and watched a ball game with Oz that ended in the eleventh inning when the relief pitcher walked in the winning run after three consecutive singles. Not a good way to end a game, but the thing about baseball is, tomorrow is always a brand-new game and a chance at redemption.

I went to bed early and awoke when the gulls made a racket on the beach as they did battle for scraps of food.

I wore a lightweight summer suit and blasted the AC in the Marquis to keep from sweating through my shirt on the drive to Sylvia Gordon's home. The second I left the car and felt the near-ninety-degree heat, my back was beaded with droplets of sweat.

Sylvia had no such problem. She was swimming laps in the pool when I went around the house to the backyard. She saw me and waved in mid-stroke.

"Only thirteen laps to go," Sylvia said. "Fix a cold drink and go sit in the shade."

I crossed the tiled walkway to the outdoor bar, filled a tall glass with ice cubes and ginger ale, and took a chair under a wide umbrella. I lit a smoke, sipped ginger ale, and watched Sylvia swim laps. She was a powerful swimmer with a stroke that sliced through the water with barely a ripple. When she finally emerged from the pool, I saw she was wearing a blue racing suit as tight as skin. Oddly enough, she was pale as a ghost, probably from wearing strong sunblock.

"You owe me lunch," Sylvia said as she took the chair to my left.

"I'm here on business," I said.

"Not mine," Sylvia said as she wrung out her hair.

"I spoke to your dad yesterday," I said.

Sylvia quit wringing her hair and looked at me. "Oh? Was he lucid or did he sit around and ask for tea?"

"He was plenty lucid," I said. "We had a nice chat."

"About your missing person?"

"Yes. There might be a clue in his safe deposit box," I said. "Do you know where the key is and what bank?"

Sylvia looked at me as if I'd suddenly walked over her grave.

"You do, don't you?" I said.

"I don't see what that has to do—"

"How much cash did you find in the box, Sylvia?" I said.

"I don't have to tell you anything," Sylvia said.

"No, you don't," I said. "But you would have to tell the IRS if they found out about it."

Sylvia gave me a hard look.

"We don't have to fight about it," I said. "Just tell me what I want to know and your secret is forgotten."

"What do you want to know?"

"Besides the unclaimed cash, what else was in the box?" I said.

"A solid gold Rolex, a small pouch of cut diamonds, a brick of solid gold, and some papers and an old notebook," Sylvia said.

"A gold brick?" I said.

Sylvia shrugged. "I sold the Rolex, had the diamonds made into a necklace, and I keep the brick in the wall safe in my bedroom."

"The papers and notebook?"

"The garage," Sylvia said. "The box marked 'miscellaneous.' "

"I didn't see it last time."

"It's under the workbench against the wall."

"Let me in," I said.

I followed Sylvia into the house, where she opened a connecting door that led to the garage. She pointed to the workbench. "There."

Past the rows and rows of file boxes, against the far wall, sat an unused workbench cluttered with old coffee cans and tools. Under the bench sat a cardboard shoebox with a lid.

I lifted the box onto the bench and removed the lid. Sylvia came and stood beside me. "Is that what you're looking for?" she said.

"I don't know," I said.

"Take it and then get the fuck out," Sylvia said. "If you come back again, you'll have to deal with my lawyer."

"What, no lunch?" I said.

"Fuck you. Get out."

Not one to miss a hint, I took the box and left. This time I didn't bother to check for Sylvia's middle finger in the rearview mirror, but I knew it was there.

Chapter 19

The papers were mostly useless. Old insurance policies, leases on Gordon's office, an application for a concealed-carry gun permit, none of them remotely current. The notebook was the kind a kid uses in school to make notes in and was at least forty years old.

I filled a mug with fresh coffee, sat in my rusty chair, lit a cigarette, and opened the notebook. Donald Gordon wrote in pencil. On the first page was a name, a date, and a cash amount of fifty thousand dollars. Below the name was a second date about a year later with the cash amount of twenty-five thousand. Below that, dated two years later, fifteen thousand.

More of the same on the second and third pages. Gordon used a separate page for each name, each baby sold. Each baby bought. He'd made a small fortune selling infants on the black market.

I skipped to the last page. It was dated twenty years ago. Something or someone had made Donald Gordon quit the baby-selling business.

I skipped backward. There on page seventeen was the name Robert Gordon. The cash amount was sixty thousand paid by Mr. and Mrs. David Gertz of Queens, New York. Wife's name, Michele. No other dates or cash amounts were recorded.

I thought about that for a while.

Donald Gordon sold babies on the black market, then followed up with blackmail to the parents and buyers. The buyers didn't want to give up the baby and the seller didn't want the baby back. Gordon worked a double-edged sword and profited highly from it. His records showed he gave his nephew a break.

What a sweetheart.

If Donald Gordon had half a bag of marbles left, I'd be showing the notebook to the FBI. I still might, but for the moment my interest was in the Gertz family of Queens, New York.

Chapter 20

The librarian on duty at the public library came by the computer I was using to tell me closing time was in thirty minutes.

I thanked her and told her I was done anyway.

I gathered up the documents I'd printed and said goodnight to the librarian on the way out. It was just past seven in the evening and still very warm. I removed my jacket and slung it over my shoulder, then walked two blocks to a coffee shop near the beach.

I took a booth and ordered coffee.

My records search had produced very little in the way of pertinent information. David and Michele Gertz owned a home in Kew Gardens, Queens, for thirty years. They owned a men's clothing store on Queens Boulevard in the neighborhood of Forest Hills. They were members of local business owners' organizations, sat on the Rotary Club, and were leaders in local charity groups. One daughter, Sarah. Went to Kew Gardens Middle School and graduated from Forest Hills High School twenty-two years ago. She attended NYU and studied political science after high school, and then the information train came to an abrupt stop.

A people search showed the house still listed under the Gertz name, but without a current phone number. Michele Gertz's age was listed as seventy-four. Neither David nor Sarah was listed beside Michele as active contacts.

Something happened around twelve years ago that changed the Gertz family, and not for the better. To speculate on what that something was would be a waste of my time. Two things every good detective learns from experience: not to speculate when you lack facts and never waste time when you could be doing something productive.

I left a five-dollar bill for my buck-fifty coffee and walked home.

CHAPTER 21

"Maybe they retired and moved to Florida?" Janet said.

"Maybe."

"Or he could have died?" Janet said.

"That, too," I said. "People have been known to do that after eighty or so years."

"It's possible they just like to mind their own business and all this is perfectly innocent?" Janet said.

"Also that," I said.

"But you don't think so?"

"No."

We were in Janet's backyard, having a midnight snack and enjoying the cooler air that had settled in from the northwest.

"I'm sorry I involved you in this," Janet said. "Had I known what Bob truly wanted, I would have told him you retired."

"I could have turned him down," I said.

"Why didn't you?"

"A woman with possibly a family benefits greatly if I find her," I said. "And doesn't if I don't. The dos outweigh the don'ts."

"And if you don't, who benefits then?"

"Besides the IRS," I said. "Some very needy and worthy charities."

"And you?"

"I'll submit a bill for services, but I would hardly call it a benefit."

"I don't mean money," Janet said. "I'm talking about that void in your chest that neither I nor Regan can fill. That need you have to solve the problems of the world. I'm afraid you'll get that taste again in your mouth and I'll lose you."

"I'm not saying I'll do any more work after this, but say that I did," I said. "Why would that cause you to lose me?"

"Because I won't compete for your love," Janet said. "I waited a long time for us and I won't share. I'm at the age where a woman becomes greedy, and I'll end us and send you packing, ring and all."

"Just like that?"

"I'll cry and I'll mourn you as if you had died for a long time, but I won't be married to a man who needs his work more than he needs me. Don't put me to the test."

"I was just saying," I said.

"Don't."

"What if I found a cushy corporate security job where the most danger I'd be in was from paper cuts?" I said.

"That would be lovely," Janet said. "I'm a nurse. I know how to fix paper cuts."

"Not as lovely as you," I said.

"No you don't, buster," Janet said. "You don't get rid of my mad that easy."

"Would some frisky advances from an attractive older man do the trick?" I said.

"Sure," Janet said. "Send him over."

"Ouch."

"I have to go to work," Janet said. "Just because school is out doesn't mean Mark gets to play video games all night and eat pizza."

"No problem," I said. "I am a strict disciplinarian."

"Right. Walk me to my car."

I escorted Janet to where she kissed me before getting into

her car and driving to work. I glanced at my watch. It was a few minutes past eleven. I walked back around and entered the house through the kitchen. Mark and Regan were on the sofa, watching a rerun of a seventies sitcom.

"Mom left for work," I said.

"I thought she'd never leave," Mark said.

Regan grabbed the video baseball game from under the sofa.

"Shall we order pizza first?" I said.

"With sausage," Mark said.

"And broccoli," Regan said.

"That's gross," Mark said.

"I'll get one of each," I said.

"And garlic rolls," Mark said. "Don't forget them."

"Yes," Regan said.

"I'll phone it in," I said.

I used the phone in the kitchen to call in the order. No sooner did I hang up than the phone rang.

"So tell me how long it took to order pizza and break out the video games?" Janet said before I even said hello.

"Are you calling on a cell phone while driving?" I said. "That's dangerous."

"Hands-free and answer the question."

"More than one and less than ten seconds," I said.

"Oh, Jack," Janet sighed. "Just make sure they clean up afterward."

"Sure."

"And no pizza for Molly," Janet said. "Last time you gave her pizza, she spent a week in the litter box."

"No problem."

After hanging up a second time, I returned to the living room where Mark and Regan were in the first inning of video baseball.

"Mom said no pizza for Molly, right?" Mark said.

"Yeah."

"She's so predictable," Mark said as his video game batter hit a home run.

Chapter 22

I called Walt early the next morning and asked him to meet me for coffee at my trailer around nine thirty. Janet arrived home from work around eight forty-five and by then the breakfast dishes were done and Regan and Mark were in the backyard with Molly.

There was just time to share a kiss and a cup of coffee with Janet, then I was out the door and on my way.

Walt was fifteen minutes late. He had a good excuse. He'd stopped for a bag of nine from Pat's Donut Shop on the way over. "Receipt's in the bag," he said as he took a seat. "I figured you'd expense report it."

"That's cheating, isn't it?" I said.

"So is my being paid by the taxpayers to sit and eat donuts with you," Walt said.

"Not if you're working," I said.

Walt cocked an eyebrow in my direction. "Oh?"

"Eat a donut while I request the assistance of the state's newest police captain, and a damn fine one I might add," I said.

Walt grabbed a double chocolate donut from the bag and took a bite. "Kiss me first before you bend me over," he said.

"Nothing heavy," I said. "Just some background checks. Minor stuff."

"I thought you told Janet you were done with PI work," Walt said.

"I did," I said. "This was her idea."

"Really?"

"Yes, really."

Walt looked past me and said, "How does he smell donuts from a hundred yards?"

I turned and looked at Oz, who was crossing the sand toward us. "He's reporting for work."

"You?"

"I needed someone to help with paperwork."

"No you didn't," Walt said. "So, all right, what do you want now, you friggin' albatross?"

"A rundown on this family," I said, and gave Walt the prepared envelope I had on the card table.

"For?"

"Anything."

"Should I ask what you've been hired to do?" Walt said.

"And spoil your fun," I said.

Oz arrived, sniffed, and said, "I smell donuts."

"Can you do that with drugs?" Walt said. " 'Cause if you can, we could use you."

"What?" Oz said.

"Nothing," I said. "Walt was just leaving. Weren't you, Captain?"

"I'll call you later if I find anything out," Walt said.

After Walt was safely in his car, Oz grabbed a lemon cream from the bag. "Man seems uptight since his promotion," he said.

"Some people just can't handle their donuts," I said as I reached into the bag for a chocolate sprinkle.

CHAPTER 23

"Sarah Gertz is the daughter of Bob Gordon?" Meade said after I filled him in on the latest information.

"Apparently."

"And she's missing?"

"I didn't say that," I said. "People get old, families drift apart. Parents die, children lose touch, life goes on, and all that other stuff."

From behind his desk, Meade nodded. "So what now?"

I shrugged. "Wait. See what information Walt comes up with. Make a decision on my next move after that."

"And Robert?"

"He doesn't want to know details anyway," I said. "And right now I don't have any even if he wanted them."

"Captain Grimes is a good man," Meade said. "From his reputation, he's a great police officer."

"The best."

"You were partners once."

"Back in the day," I said. "Before I tried to drink every bottle of Scotch and bourbon within three states."

"I can't say I would have done any different had I been in similar circumstances," Meade said.

"Walt wouldn't have," I said. "That's why he is where he is and I'm where I am."

Meade nodded. "You'll let me know what you're going to do, then."

"As soon as I figure it out," I said. "You'll be the second to know."

CHAPTER 24

From my perch on the lawn chair in front of my trailer, I watched Walt walk toward me on the beach. The sun had already set and the sky over the ocean was filled with that strange afterlight glow that lasts for about fifteen minutes before actual darkness sets in.

I got up and went inside for a fresh mug of coffee, returned and sat, and lit a fresh cigarette. Walt was about a hundred feet closer now, in no hurry, but not moving slowly, either.

To my right, a light came on inside Oz's trailer.

Walt finally arrived by the time the cigarette was nothing but a filter between my fingers.

"You have a client?" Walt said as he flopped into Oz's chair.

"I do."

"The usual 'client can't talk about the case' bullshit in effect?"

"It is."

"Break it."

"Why?"

"Because life is hard enough," Walt said. "Being stupid only makes it harder."

"That's not an answer."

"How about because I said so?" Walt said.

"What, you're going to tell me I have to eat my peas next?" I said.

"No, but I sure as hell will withhold any information I have from you," he said. "Besides that, we're friends and ex-partners."

"That's all you had to say, Walt."

"I know, but I do so enjoy the joust of busting your balls."

"I have Janet for that," I said.

"Speak," Walt demanded.

I gave Walt the short version, leaving out any references to Donald Gordon's notebook. He listened, didn't move or nod his head, which I knew was his way of absorbing information and committing it to memory.

"Robert Gordon, the director of the hospital?" Walt said when I concluded.

"Not as of yesterday," I said.

"He resigned?"

"He's dying," I said. "Quickly."

Walt took in a huge breath of salt sea air and exhaled slowly. "No point arresting Gordon for trafficking in babies," he said.

"None."

"And what aren't you telling me?"

"Stuff I can't prove that has nothing to do with Gordon's daughter," I said. "When I can prove it, it's yours. Your turn."

"The Gertz family owned a clothing store for thirty years in Queens," Walt said. "Paid their taxes, took part in the community, not so much as a parking ticket. One daughter named Sarah, with an H like in the Bible. Graduated college with a degree in political science, whatever that is. Took a job in DC with a think tank. A dozen years ago, she vanished without a trace. A missing-persons report and investigation by DC Metro and the FBI came up empty. Back in Queens, her father committed suicide. Mom is in a nursing home in Jamaica Estates. The family home hasn't been sold, but as far as I can determine isn't lived in. Some cousins and a sister live nearby and that's about it."

"What's a think tank?" I said.

"You know, a political group that follows certain agendas and blogs about them," Walt said. "In her case, it was the environment. Even met with Congress a few times."

I nodded.

"Don't give me that bullshit head-nod crap, John," Walt said. "I see the gears in that little brain of yours spinning."

"I have tiny little gears, Walt," I said.

"Don't give me that crap, either," Walt said. "I know you too well."

"Look, the job is find the girl and wait until after Gordon is gone to tell her she inherits his millions," I said. "That's it."

"Except that the girl is missing and there's nobody on the food chain left to claim the inheritance," Walt said.

I lit a fresh cigarette off the old one and puffed away while I sorted things out in my mind. "How extensive an investigation was held for the missing girl?" I said.

"Metro did their best, the FBI spent some time on it only because she worked for some federal groups in DC," Walt said. "When nothing turned up inside of a few weeks, well, you know how that goes."

"Yeah."

"Yeah, what?"

"I don't know."

"Bullshit," Walt said. "You know."

"I don't, but I'll keep plugging away and see what develops, and I'll keep you in the loop if you're interested," I said.

"That would be nice," Walt said. " 'Cause I sure have nothing else to do these days except fuck around with your dumb shit."

"How are Elizabeth and the kids?" I said.

"Fuck you."

I grinned.

"Asshole," Walt added.

"Still want me and Janet to come over for a home-cooked meal?" I said.

"That depends on who's home and who does the cooking," Walt said. "If you mean mine and Elizabeth, I don't inflict that kind of pain on friends."

"How about we do Janet's?" I said.

"Excellent. When?"

"As soon as I get permission."

"God, you're whipped."

"You don't know the half of it," I said.

"She's a good woman, Jack," Walt said. "Whatever you do, don't fuck that up."

"Yeah," I said.

Chapter 25

Janet wasn't exactly what I would describe as angry when I told her I'd be out of town for a few days, but she wasn't thrilled either. The words *cold shoulder* described her mood best.

I told her not to worry and that I would call her later on tonight. Then I drove an hour to the airport and got on a business flight to New York City that touched down at Kennedy Airport in the borough of Queens. I booked a room at a hotel just off the airport grounds via a courtesy phone, then rented a mid-sized car and drove it to the hotel. After I checked in and dropped off my one bag, I returned to the rental and got on the expressway.

I'm no expert on New York, but I know enough to navigate around and the dashboard GPS did the rest. I took the exit for Queens Boulevard, drove through Forest Hills to Kew Gardens, and found the Gertz home on a picturesque side street that was lined with trees and manicured front lawns.

I parked in the Gertz driveway.

It was a nice Tudor-style home with freshly cut lawn and a bed of flowers out front. A large For Sale sign with the agency listing was posted on the lawn. The agency claimed to be "#1 in New York."

Doubting that claim, I punched the address into the GPS and followed the directions a mile south on Queens Boulevard to a neighborhood called Rego Park where the real estate agency was run out of what was once a private home.

I parked on the street, fed the meter quarters, and entered. Immediately, a blast of cold air hit me in the face. Six agents at desks looked up. They had that dollar-sign look in their eyes.

I cut them off at the pass. "Who has the Gertz home on their board?" I said.

A dark-haired woman of about thirty stood up. She wore a business suit of the mini-skirt type with black pumps. "I do," she said excitedly.

"Feel like showing it?" I said.

The woman grinned broadly. I could see her calculating her commission in the back of my mind. "Delighted to," she said.

We stood in the living room of the Gertz home. Her nametag read *Valerie.* I said, "I'll be honest with you, Valerie, I have no interest in buying this home or any other home."

The cheery smile on Valerie's face fell like a sack of potatoes. "I don't understand," she said. "Why did . . . ?"

I dug out my identification and held it up to her. "I've been hired to find a missing person. Sarah Gertz. She grew up in this home. I'd like two things from you. First is to look around for photos of Sarah Gertz, and second are the name and number of who put the home on the market."

"Isn't this, like, illegal?" Valerie said. "False pretense and all that?"

"No, it isn't," I said. "I could have let you show me around and checked out photos without you knowing it, and I can find the Gertz relatives easily enough on my own. It's hot and I'd like to save a few steps."

Valerie looked at me.

"Besides," I said and removed a white envelope from my jacket pocket. "I'll pay you five hundred dollars for your time."

Valerie took the envelope and peeked at the five one-hundred-dollar bills inside. "Where would you like to start?" she said.

Sarah Gertz had been a lovely young woman, with thick black hair, piercing dark eyes, and a wonderful smile. After examining household photos hung around various rooms that took Sarah from about a few months old to around the time she disappeared, it was easy to conclude she was fun-loving and full of life.

I drove back to my hotel a bit saddened that something had befallen so young a woman who was filled with such promise. In my room, I cranked the AC and stripped down to my shorts. I had requested a smoking room, and I lit up at the desk as I reached for the phone.

Ann Marie Hoffman answered on the third ring. She politely said, "Hello?"

I wasn't sure if Ann Marie was one word or hyphenated, so I introduced myself first. "This is John Bekker calling," I said. "I'm a private investigator looking for a missing person by the name of Sarah Gertz. Are you a relative by any chance?"

If a pin dropped at that moment, I would have heard it.

Finally, Ann Marie spoke. "Is this some kind of sick joke?"

"I assure you that it's not," I said. "I'm a licensed, bonded private investigator and this is a real missing persons case."

"I . . . don't understand," Ann Marie said. "Why now after all these years?"

"My client is her biological father," I said. "He's dying and wants to make her the beneficiary of his estate. It's considerable."

There was a short pause before Ann Marie said, "This is one of those Ponzi scams, isn't it. Well, I have very little in—"

"Call Police Captain Walter Grimes at this number," I said, and gave her the number. "Speak with him and then call me back at my hotel." I gave her the number for that, too. "If after that you still have doubts, you don't have to see me."

I hung up, grabbed a Coke from the small fridge beside the TV, pulled the tab, and settled in to wait on the bed. I finished the Coke and another cigarette before the phone rang.

I stood and grabbed the phone off the desk. "John Bekker."

"This is Ann Marie, Mr. Bekker," she said. "Captain Grimes said you're highly trustworthy and an excellent investigator. He also said you have a weakness for donuts."

"Any particular kind?" I said.

"What? Oh, the donuts. He said you'd bite fingers off for the last Boston cream."

"Not true," I said. "Double chocolate with sprinkles gets me every time."

"Well, now that I know you're who you say you are and we've established your fondness for donuts, what now?" Ann Marie said.

"You have a beautiful home, Mrs. Hoffman," I said.

"Call me Ann Marie," she replied. "And thank you."

We were in the backyard of Ann Marie's home just across the Queens border in the town of Valley Stream on Long Island. The three-hundred-foot-square area was filled with rows and circular plots of flowers and orchards in which a small aquatic plant pond sat centered. The floral aroma drifting my way was like sweet perfume.

Ann Marie served strong tea with milk and homemade scones just out of the oven. Above our heads, a retractable awning gave us welcome shade from the sun and the temperature was a good twenty degrees cooler.

"My husband, Daniel, was an excellent provider," Ann Marie said. "He was a self-employed CPA with a very long client list on the Island and in the City. He left the business to our son when he passed away three years ago."

I guessed her age at about seventy-five, a year or two younger than her sister Michele. "Children?" I said.

"That was my job," Ann Marie said. "My oldest son just turned fifty. He's a CPA like his father. My youngest daughter is forty-two. I have two more wedged in between."

I took a nibble on the scone. It was tasty and still warm. I added a sip of tea and swallowed. "I have a daughter myself. She's nineteen."

"Divorced?" Ann Marie said.

"Widower."

"I am sorry," Ann Marie said. "You're so young to be a widower."

"It was a long time ago and I'm not that young anymore, I'm afraid."

Ann Marie smiled. "So after you comment on my gardens, we can get down to what you came here for," she said.

I smiled. "You have a beautiful garden and the scents are just lovely."

"Thank you," Ann Marie said. "So ask your questions."

"You knew that Sarah was adopted?" I said.

"Of course," Ann Marie said. "My sister was twenty-two when she married David. They tried for ten years to conceive a child before finally adopting. Low sperm count, the doctors said. Anyway, the answer is yes, the entire family knew."

"What can you tell me about Sarah?" I said.

Ann Marie took a sip of tea. "Well, she was a very happy child," she said. "Smart and funny, bright as can be. She was very popular in school, had many friends and boyfriends, though none serious. When she moved to Washington to work for those environmental groups, she didn't have a steady boyfriend at the time. I can't speak to that once she left."

"Did she know she was adopted?"

"Yes, and she didn't care," Ann Marie said. "She knew David and my sister as her parents and loved them as much as they did her."

"What happened to your sister?" I said.

Ann Marie lowered her eyes for a moment as most people do when recalling a painful memory. "After Sarah . . . disappeared, David took his own life," she said. "Michele suffered a nervous breakdown from which she's never recovered. She's been in a hospital for mental patients on Long Island for ten years now. That's why I put the house on the market. Her savings and investments are gone, and Social Security doesn't make a dent in the monthly bills."

"Did you ever talk to the DC police or the FBI?"

"Yes," Ann Marie said. "Two men flew in a few days after Sarah went missing. They were interested in her boyfriends, jealous lovers, and possible enemies. I'm afraid I was able to provide them with very little information other than what I just told you."

"Did they ever get back to you later on?"

"A few times, but it was always to ask some question they forgot or to tell me they were still actively investigating her disappearance," Ann Marie said. "Then after about six months they stopped calling. I phoned once and they told me they weren't closing the case, but they moved it to inactive."

I nodded. "That happens a lot with missing persons."

Ann Marie sighed. "I suppose."

"The house, I visited it this morning," I said. "I noticed a lot of photos still on the walls and furniture."

Ann Marie nodded. "I didn't have the heart to take them down," she said. "I suppose I'll have to at some point. I did remove Sarah's letters she wrote from Washington. I brought them to my sister. She keeps them in a chest beside her bed. I think it gives her some comfort to read Sarah's thoughts once in a while."

"I understand," I said.

"How about you, Mr. Bekker, will you give up, too?" Ann Marie said.

"Not for a while," I said.

"But eventually?"

"I never get ahead of myself," I said.

"You will keep me advised?" Ann Marie said.

"That I can do," I said and took another sip of tea.

Chapter 26

"Where are you that the reception is so bad?" I said to Janet from the phone in my hotel room.

"The mall with Regan," Janet said. "Indoors."

"What are you doing there?"

"What does a woman usually do at a mall, Jack?"

"Buy shoes."

"I resent that," Janet said. "Women do other things in a mall besides buy shoes."

"How many pairs so far?"

"Eight between us."

"Between you there's only four feet," I said.

"It's a woman's rite-of-passage thing," Janet said. "I'm passing the baton."

"Men don't have one of those," I said.

"Oh, yes you do," Janet said. "Only it usually takes place alone in the shower at about the age of thirteen with a wet bar of soap."

"Give me a minute to think of a snappy comeback," I said.

"No time. Shoes awaiting. Call us later tonight," Janet said and hung up.

I lit a cigarette and stared out my window for a while. There was really nothing worthwhile to see down below, but sometimes staring out into space is the way to go when all else fails.

I turned away from the window when I grew tired of planes landing and taking off in the background and picked up the phone. I called the desk and asked for a long distance line, then placed a call to FBI headquarters in Washington and asked for Paul Lawrence.

After press 1 for this and press 2 for that, I was forwarded to Paul's voicemail box and left him a message to call me back at the hotel number. Then I did something productive and took a nap.

Three hours later, the ringing phone in my ear woke me with a jumpstart. I grabbed it and barked out, "John Bekker."

"Jack, it's Paul Lawrence," Lawrence said. "I wake you?"

"I fell asleep waiting for your call," I said as I sat up and grabbed my pack of smokes off the nightstand.

Paul Lawrence and I go back to my rookie days on the force. He was a top-notch forensics specialist for the county before the FBI stole him away to Washington.

"So what federal law do you want me to bend this time?" Lawrence said.

"I can't just be calling to say hi?" I said.

"You could, but you're not."

I set fire to a cigarette and blew smoke. "Old missing persons case, goes back a dozen years," I said. "The FBI investigated along with Metro PD. Can you dig around and let me know what you find out?"

"Why did the Bureau investigate a local Metro case?" Lawrence said.

I gave him the background along with Sarah Gertz's name. "She worked on the Hill and knew a lot of the right people, so I guess it caused a fuss with the feds."

"And you are involved in this how?"

I gave him the background on that, too, stretching the truth a bit by stating Sarah was adopted, and added, "My client doesn't have long to go, so time is a factor. He just wants to leave her something in his will."

"You coming to DC?"

"Tomorrow morning."

"That donut shop in—"

"Say no more," I said. "See you around noon."

"Assorted," Lawrence said.

"Do they come any other way?" I said.

As soon as I hung up with Lawrence, I called information for my area code and got the number for Pat's Donut Shop. I asked Pat to airmail express a dozen assorted donuts to Paul Lawrence at his office in the Federal Building. After that, I called the airlines and booked a ticket to Washington on a business-class flight that got me there around eleven in the morning. Hopefully, the donuts would arrive before I did.

There was little else to do the rest of the afternoon and evening except jot notes and think. I decided I did my best thinking on a full stomach and took the notebook with me to the restaurant on the sixth floor of the hotel.

I ordered a steak. They charged hotel restaurant prices.

Since it was Gordon's dime, I asked for extra steak fries and had double layer cake for dessert, and didn't feel the least bit bad about it. When I returned to my room, the red light on the phone was blinking.

I checked the incoming number and then dialed Janet's home number. Mark answered on the third ring.

"Hello," Mark said above the loud sounds of video baseball.

"Mark, it's me," I said. "Is your—"

"Mark, quit cheating," Regan yelled in the background.

"Hold on, Uncle—I'm not cheating—Jack," Mark said.

"Let me speak to—" I said.

"You can't score on the third out, Mark," Regan said in the background.

"Mark, put your mom on the phone," I said.

"Uncle Jack, tell Regan you can score on the third out if it's a strikeout and the catcher drops the ball," Mark said.

"Mark, put your mother on the phone."

"Mom had to go to work," Mark said. "She called you before she left."

"Are you alone with Regan?" I said.

"Don't worry, Uncle Jack, she's watching me," Mark said.

I thought, *yeah, but who's watching her?* I said, "Let me talk to Regan."

"Sure," Mark said and passed the phone to Regan.

"Hi, Dad," Regan said. "Don't worry. We're fine."

"I can call someone to come over," I said.

"Dad, Aunt Janet trusts me," Regan said. "Can you?"

"I can and I do," I said. "I'll be home tomorrow night. Tell Janet for me and do your best not to let Mark change the rules too much."

"I will, Dad," Regan said. "And thanks."

CHAPTER 27

From my spot on a bench in the Mall, I watched Paul Lawrence make his way through thousands of tourists. He was close to my age now, but still looked thirty except for the slightly receding hairline.

I had a bag with two containers of coffee in it next to me on the bench. Lawrence held a bag that I hoped contained a few of Pat's best donuts. Behind him, the White House loomed large in the distance.

When he neared, I stood and extended my right hand. Lawrence did the same.

"Coffee?" Lawrence said.

"Donuts?" I said.

"Arrived this morning fresh as a daisy."

I exchanged a coffee for two double chocolates.

I bit. Lawrence sipped.

"And?" I said.

"Sarah Michele Gertz disappeared without a trace twelve years ago," Lawrence said. "She was twenty-six at the time. She moved to DC from Queens three years prior to take a job with a political group that lobbied for the EPA on the Hill. They called themselves Citizens for Saving the Planet. She wrote text and speeches, took notes at hearings in Congress, stuff like that. She was recruited by the EPA lobbyist group for the UN and spoke at sessions in New York a few times, but mostly here in Washington. Just when she was making a name for herself, she vanished. Metro put a six-man team on it and we got involved when the EPA and her group made some noise. I read every report last night and this morning, Jack. They did all they could and came up empty. Not a clue, a witness, a motive, nothing."

"Random?" I said.

"Random happens a lot, Jack," Lawrence said. "You know that."

"I also know that men who commit random acts of rape and murder don't stop at just one," I said.

"We looked for patterns and found a few possibles, but it didn't pan out," Lawrence said. "The EPA and her employer put pressure on us for months, but an investigation is only as good as the facts, and those we didn't have. You also know that facts make a case."

"I also know young women just don't up and vanish like a fart in the wind, Paul," I said. "And so do you."

"If you're thinking we missed something, we didn't," Lawrence said. "Her one-bedroom apartment was swept by our own people. Every person she knew and came in contact with, including members of the Senate and Congress, was interviewed. We used receipts for clothing and food purchases to interview stores where she shopped. We traced every phone call she made from work, home, and by cell phone. We read her letters home and return letters, appointment books, even notes on her refrigerator. And then we did it again."

"Was she a jogger?" I said.

"No."

"Belong to a gym?"

"No."

"Like to visit dance clubs?"

"No," Lawrence said. "What she liked to do was work and apparently did so round the clock."

"Evidence?"

"Locked away in storage," Lawrence said. "Her office belongings and work-related stuff from home. Her personal belongings tagged non-evidence were shipped to her home in Queens."

"What am I allowed to see?" I said.

Lawrence reached into his suit jacket pocket for the visitor's badge and handed it to me. "I knew you'd be a pain in the ass about this," he said.

"Whose ass?" I said. "Mine or yours?"

CHAPTER 28

After five hours at a table in what Paul Lawrence called the Bureau reading room, my back felt like peanut brittle.

Lawrence stayed with me most of the time, reading old reports, watching as I jotted a note or two, taking calls on his cell phone.

I read every report written by the Metro police and detectives. The same for the Bureau agents assigned to investigate Sarah's disappearance. I read interviews from senators and congressmen and women who knew and dealt with Sarah in the course of her activities as a lobbyist. The same for her coworkers and members of the UN who knew and worked with her.

What it came down to was this. On a Friday afternoon twelve years ago in May, Sarah and several members of the UN Environmental Group met with the environmental watchdog committee that consisted of six sitting senators and chaired by Senator Oliver Koch of Maine. The meeting lasted two hours. Sarah left for home and when she didn't return calls or report for work on Monday, a colleague stopped by her apartment to check on her. When the colleague didn't get a response to knocking or a call on her cell phone, she called the police.

A hotline set up by the Bureau and Metro produced not a single useable lead or clue. Even her expense report book was scrutinized to establish driving habits and pinpoint meeting times, dates, and places.

Nothing.

Not a single shred of evidence worth pursuing.

It was as if twenty-six-year-old Sarah Gertz up and fell right off the Earth.

"You want to keep going?" Lawrence said.

"Do you have someplace to be?" I said.

"I enjoy going home at least once a day if possible," Lawrence said.

"Feel like a steak dinner at the best place in town?"

"Sure, as long as I don't have to pay for it."

"Give me an hour," I said.

"I have to hit my office and check messages," Lawrence said. "I'll be back in one hour to pack all this shit up."

I nodded, sat alone after Lawrence left, and thought a bit.

Then I thought some more.

I shifted reports to look at Sarah Gertz's final day at work. She kept meticulous expense records. From her apartment just across the line in Virginia to Capitol Hill was a distance of twenty-seven miles. She made an entry in her log book that the police found in the glove box of her car, which was parked in its reserved spot at her building. *TO CONGRESS,* the entry read.

I flipped pages and found a dozen or more entries for Congress with the exact mileage listed. There was nothing listed for the return trip home for that day. I flipped back again and found entries listed for return trips made to Congress when she didn't go to her office that day, a common practice for those lucky enough to be reimbursed for mileage.

Maybe she forgot to make the entry?

Maybe she would do it at another time along with other entries?

Maybe she never got the chance?

I shuffled some papers and found the forensics report on her car. Sarah's prints were lifted off the glove box, rearview mirror, and radio knobs.

But not the outside door handle or steering wheel.

Otherwise the car was clean, close to immaculate.

I read the forensics report for Sarah's apartment. The only prints found anywhere in the apartment belonged to her. The same for hair and DNA samples from her toothbrush.

Lawrence returned.

"Ready?" he said.

"Yeah."

"Help me pack this stuff up and I'll drive us over to the Capitol Steakhouse," Lawrence said. "We may even see a senator."

"I'll do my best not to faint in the presence of such royalty," I said.

I waited until dessert and coffee to talk shop. While we ate our steaks, we chatted about Regan, my pending marriage to Janet, and other such lighthearted subjects.

As we sliced into giant hunks of strawberry cheesecake, I said, "Sarah Gertz's car was tagged as evidence—is it still in storage?"

"I don't know," Lawrence said. "Why?"

"Forensics reports no fingerprints on the driver's side door handle or steering wheel," I said. "And her last entry for mileage is missing in her expense report book."

Lawrence stared at me for a moment. "I skimmed right over that," he said. "Are you sure?"

"Yup. Rearview mirror and glove box, but nothing on the door handle or steering wheel."

"Maybe she wore gloves?"

"In mid-May and then took them off to adjust the mirror, open the glove box, turn on the radio, and then put them back on to drive?" I said.

Lawrence stared at me some more.

"Who does that in May in Virginia?" I said.

Lawrence quit staring at me and ate a piece of his cheesecake. "I'll find out if her car is still in evidence," he said.

"Something else," I said. "I read detective's reports on her apartment. Said she was very neat but highly cluttered. Boxes of EPA stuff everywhere, books, notebooks, stacks of reports and papers in every room. Even the bathroom. They determined nothing had been gone through or disturbed. Same reports called the interior condition of her car close to immaculate. Generally a person's car reflects their home. Clutter in the house—"

"Clutter in the car," Lawrence said.

"Except it was neat as a pin," I said. "She just came from a meeting and no briefcase on the seat, no notes or notebook, nothing. Not in her apartment, either. They said they could find nothing to indicate she was ever at the meeting, even though other attendees confirmed she was, so I'm thinking her briefcase with her notes in it never turned up."

"Or they missed it?" Lawrence added.

"They didn't miss it," I said. "They did what we would have done; follow the evidence to where it takes you. In this case, it took them to a dead end. We can speculate on missing notebooks and lack of fingerprints all we want, but it doesn't move things closer to a suspect. Only evidence does and there just doesn't seem to be any."

"I've known you a long time, Jack," Lawrence said. "We worked together a lot back home in the day. I've seen you turn lack of details into a lead that closed a murder case. I think I know how your mind works a bit, so you tell me what you think and I'll tell you if I can help you."

I ate a hunk of cheesecake and washed it down with coffee. "I think somebody killed her and disposed of the body, drove her car to her apartment, wiped down the steering wheel and door handle, and took her briefcase with them," I said. "And so do you and so did the Metro detectives and FBI who worked the case twelve years ago."

Lawrence nodded. "I'll check and see if the car is still in evidence in the morning."

I ate another piece of cheesecake. "I'll hold my room over tonight."

"Meet for breakfast, you buy?" Lawrence said.

"My client will buy and let's make it nine at that coffee shop on the Hill where all the powerful people get their morning cup of joe," I said. "Maybe I could get some autographs."

Chapter 29

I sat in the chair opposite the bed in my hotel room and sipped room service coffee to accompany the cigarette I just lit.

Both tasted really good.

Most things that do are really bad for you.

I think it's a rule. Bad things taste good. Good things taste like spinach. Things with no taste don't matter.

By all accounts Sarah Gertz had been an ideal daughter and student, and grew up to be a fine young woman. She loved her parents and country and worked to make the world a better place through her environmental work in Washington.

I read the pages of notes Lawrence allowed me to make and keep.

I saw the frustration in the reports written by Metro and FBI agents when I read their later accounts of the investigation. It stalled and they knew it. They had nothing and they knew it. Whoever made Sarah Gertz disappear got away with it and they knew it.

And they didn't like it.

Neither did I.

I poured a second cup of coffee from the carafe sent up by room service and accompanied it with another smoke.

A random act perpetrated upon Sarah Gertz was how all accounts, reports, and conclusions read between the lines.

Random.

An accidental occurrence.

You're walking down the street and a safe falls on your head. That's an accidental occurrence.

What do you call it when you leave your house to drive to a meeting and your car is found parked in front of your apartment and you're never seen or heard from again despite the efforts of the police and FBI?

I don't know.

I flipped back in my notes. The meeting with the committee started at two and ended at four. It was Friday. Sarah probably drove straight home afterward and arrived around five in the afternoon.

Was someone waiting for her outside her apartment building?

Did she drive off with that someone in their car?

What if it wasn't random?

What if Sarah Gertz had secrets the way all of us do? The human heart is a deep ocean of secrets, most of which we never want exposed.

What if her secret caught up to her?

What if she died because that secret was about to come to light?

And that secret would have damaged somebody beyond repair?

Problem is that Washington is full of powerful somebodies past and present with secrets that would damage them beyond repair.

I lost count of disgraced senators and congressmen caught in sex, drug, and tax scandals. Most of them just go away. A few reemerge with that *I'm cured from rehab* speech and actually win new elections. Others get talk shows on television and radio.

Few ever commit murder.

I was spinning my wheels on ice and I knew it.

As far as anybody knew, Sarah Gertz didn't even have a boyfriend at the time of her disappearance, in Washington or back home.

Maybe Sarah Gertz wasn't interested in men?

Maybe Sarah Gertz leaned the other way and had a girlfriend?

Maybe that girlfriend was a woman of power in DC circles and had a great deal to lose if their illicit affair came to light?

Enough to warrant having Sarah Gertz killed and disposed of?

Stranger things have happened. Just watch the nightly news and see.

Secrets.

It always came down to secrets.

We all have them. Most are innocent and have meaning to no one except ourselves.

Some will ruin your life. A very few will get you killed.

Or drive you to murder.

What secrets did Sarah Gertz have locked away inside of her?

I stood up to stretch my back. I took my coffee to the window. Night had settled in and the airport lights dominated the night sky. DC was lost in the brightness of the airport, as was any chance at seeing stars.

Technically, my job was done. I'd located Gordon's biological daughter. That she was missing for twelve years and presumed dead wasn't part of our agreement. On the other hand, my contract was to find Gordon's daughter and I hadn't actually done that yet. She could be locked in a safe at the bottom of the Potomac River for all I knew.

I returned to the chair, sat, and refilled the coffee cup.

What bugged me most was the cleanliness of her disappearance. Sanitized, almost. It bothered the Metro detectives and Bureau agents as well. I could feel their frustration in their reports.

Criminals, especially those inclined to murder, are like slugs. They leave a slimy trail in their wake, and even those adept at disguising their trail leave something behind a trained eye can follow.

Somebody really good made Sarah Gertz disappear.

Or somebody powerful.

I lit a cigarette and continued to think about it.

Good and powerful. Probably both.

Not a good combination when murder is involved.

Chapter 30

I met Paul Lawrence at the coffee shop on the Hill where DC power brokers hang out to be seen and make deals with others doing the like. We both ordered pancakes with scrambled eggs, a side order of bacon, juice, and coffee.

"Her car's in Virginia in the evidence garage," Lawrence said. "As long as the case stays inactive the car will sit in storage as evidence. Some cars are there as long as twenty or more years pending closure."

I knew the routine. Once a case is closed, a car, truck, or boat is sold at auction. Money raised goes to the victim's family, or if none, to a charitable fund of some sort. Sometimes, if a car or boat is perfect for undercover work, it is kept for that purpose.

I didn't see Sarah Gertz's twenty-year-old Honda hatchback as worthy of undercover work. It would sit in the lot awaiting closure and then be sold for scrap or donated to charity if still in working order.

The evidence lot was thirty miles south in Virginia. Lawrence gave me a visitor's badge and an attendant on duty led us to Sarah Gertz's Honda, one of almost two thousand cars being held in evidence.

At the time she disappeared, the Honda was eight years old. Burnt orange in color, it was exactly the kind of car a single woman might own to tool around DC in on a daily basis. Small enough to dodge heavy traffic, good gas mileage, some pep in the engine for highway driving if you didn't run the AC on high.

I walked the exterior of the Honda and looked for dents, scrapes, and scratches. There were a few shopping cart dings, but nothing to indicate the car had ever been in an accident.

"Got any rubber gloves?" I asked Lawrence.

He produced two pairs of disposable rubber gloves and gave me a pair. We slipped them on and I opened the driver's side door. The ignition key was taped to the sun visor.

I sat behind the wheel.

Lawrence opened the front passenger door and got in beside me.

"Was the car driven or towed here, do you know?" I said.

"Towed, according to Metro reports," Lawrence said.

I waved to the attendant standing close by. He came over.

"Are the cars ever driven or started?" I said.

"Not this one," he said. "We get orders from time to time to move a car for a trial or drain the gas, things like that, but usually hot cars the department wants to keep. Most sit here like this one and rot from the inside out."

I nodded. The attendant moved back away to answer his cell phone.

"How tall are you, Paul?" I said.

"Five-eleven," Lawrence said.

"I'm three inches taller," I said.

"I could wear lifts when we're together," Lawrence said.

"How is your seat?" I said. It was adjusted all the way front for a much shorter person.

"My knees are in my mouth," Lawrence said.

"Look at mine," I said.

The driver's seat was as far back on the track as it would go. "All the missing-persons reports I read on Sarah Gertz listed her height at five foot five inches tall," I said. "If she drove with the seat like this, she'd need wood blocks on the gas and brake."

I looked at the rearview. "The angle of the mirror is set for a much taller person," I said. "Same with the side mirror. If Sarah Gertz drove with the mirrors set like this she wouldn't be able to see a thing in them."

Lawrence looked at me.

"So either someone messed around with the car during its time here in the lot," I said. "Or the last person to drive it was around my height and wore gloves."

Lawrence looked at me some more.

"Any of the investigating detectives or Bureau agents who investigated still around?" I said.

"I knew you were going to ask that," Lawrence said. "I checked. They were all senior men close to pension. All but two are retired and those two have passed away."

"I'm booked on the five-o'clock business flight home," I said. "Maybe we can go over those reports one more time in case we missed something."

"Like what?"

"Like any reference to the seat or mirrors being moved," I said. "Minor details that at the time seemed noteworthy but meant nothing in the way of evidence."

"When you get home, I expect another care package from Pat's," Lawrence said.

I opened the car door. "That could be classified a bribe," I said.

"Not once I eat the evidence," Lawrence said.

Chapter 31

I occupied my time on the flight home by thinking about Sarah Gertz's final day on Earth. All accounts by witnesses who attended the meeting at Congress said she was present and an active participant. The meeting lasted two hours. In attendance were the six members of the Senate, four members from the UN, and Sarah Gertz and her three-man team.

After the meeting, according to those in attendance, Sarah said goodbye and left quickly, even though several members were going for drinks afterward.

So where did she rush off to?

Meet a boyfriend?

Meet a girlfriend?

An appointment of some sort?

Business?

Or personal?

There wasn't a scrap of evidence left behind to say which, or if that was even the case. For all anybody knew, Sarah Gertz rushed home to catch her favorite TV show on that night, wash her hair, or curl up with a good book she was reading.

It could have been bill-paying night. Detectives and agents ran a check on her finances. She lived well within her means, paid her bills on time, and had a small nest egg set aside for emergency use.

What made tracking her final day or locating her so frustrating was a total lack of evidence or clues left behind. Her disappearance predated the possibility of gleaning information from posts on Facebook or tweets on Twitter. There had been no calls on her cell phone or land line, no blood to analyze, no hair fibers or DNA, no emails or texts. Investigators rely on these and a host of other links to give them something to go on when something doesn't exist.

When there's nothing, as was the case with Sarah Gertz, sleeves are rolled up and shoes hit the pavement. With enough shoes running around, somebody usually says the right thing and points a finger to a clue or lead. Sometimes reward money is offered to activate the snitches and bring them forward.

When everything fails, a case is shifted to the open/unsolved file where it sits forgotten until a tip or lead comes in or it's finally closed.

A lifetime ago, when Walt and I were partners in Homicide and we drew a case similar to Sarah Gertz, we moved on to other cases and said we were waiting for the victim to speak to us from the grave.

In her case, did Sarah Gertz speak?

Did anybody listen?

Was her voice from beyond ignored?

I didn't know and I had no idea how to find out.

I had three choices. Make a final report to Meade, submit a bill, and close the book on Sarah Gertz. Continue on with nothing to guide me except my wits, a prayer, and luck. Or go backward and start at the beginning.

Shake some trees and see what fell out.

Maybe I'd get lucky and something would fall on my head.

Chapter 32

It was one of those perfect afternoons on the beach. The temperature hovered around eighty degrees. A cloudless sky seemed bluer than usual. High tide brought swells and body surfers to ride them. Gulls squawked and begged for scraps of food.

Janet and I occupied beach chairs a safe distance from incoming waves. Regan sprawled on a towel to cook under the sun beside her beau, Justin. I made her drench her skin in number thirty sunblock and I was about to do her back when she handed the bottle to Justin. Before I could grab the bottle from Kid Pimple, Janet placed her hand on my arm and gave me her no-no look, one that I was quickly becoming all too familiar with.

Mark rode the waves a safe distance from shore where we could keep an eye on him. In a bathing suit, he was still scrawny, but at least a good ten pounds heavier than a year ago.

Between us was a white cooler filled with soda and juice. I opened the lid, removed two sodas, and gave one to Janet. She wore a straw hat and sunglasses and a one-piece suit, and if I stared at her for too long I was sure I would go blind.

So I didn't stare.

I drank my soda and tried not to think about Sarah Gertz. Regan and Justin got up and walked down to the water to ride the waves with Mark.

I tried to think about the beautiful day, the fine-looking

woman by my side, how well my daughter was progressing, and the brats I would grill up later on in the afternoon.

Except that Sarah Gertz was a dark cloud hovering over my head. Her voice from the grave was crying to be heard and I couldn't hear it. Speculation about car seats and mirrors, her sexuality and personal life, added up to nothing more than guesswork and straw-grasping.

"Jack?" Janet said softly.

"Yeah?"

"Where are you right now, because you certainly aren't here with me."

"Sorry," I said. "Just hacking something out."

Janet sat up in her chair, turned, and looked at me. "I'm sorry I got you involved in Bob Gordon's personal business," she said. "Look at you, a fine-looking MILF by your side, your daughter has come a decade in a year, you're bone dry and healthy as an ox and all you can do is sit and mope."

"I'm not moping," I said. "And MILF?"

"It means—"

"I know what it means," I said. "Look, somebody made a twenty-six-year-old woman disappear for no apparent reason. If it were Mark, would you want me to quit on him because it's too much trouble to find out what happened?"

Janet stared at me for a moment. Then she lifted the shades and her tongue ran over her lips. She stood up and looked down to the water. "Mark, Regan, we're going to start the grill!" she shouted. "One hour and be careful."

Mark and Regan waved to us.

"Start the grill?" I said.

"Yes," Janet said. "Right after I start you."

I stood up and took Janet's hand. "I hope you're not planning on pouring starter fluid on me," I said.

"No, but I might just strike a match," Janet said.

CHAPTER 33

I was doing one-armed pushups on the hard sand in front of my trailer when Walt stopped by to drop off some wisdom.

As Walt flopped into Oz's chair, I switched from the left hand to right and cranked out ten reps.

"That looks painful," Walt commented as he lifted the coffee pot from the card table and filled an empty mug.

"Was a time," I gasped between reps, "we used to do these together."

Walt took a sip of coffee. "Was a time I was twenty-one and stupid, too."

I switched back to my left hand and pushed out ten more reps, then stopped, sat up, and looked at Walt. "Educate me," I said as I stood up.

"You tell Lawrence about the girl being sold?" Walt said.

"Not yet."

"So he's under the assumption she's adopted?"

"Yes."

"Has it occurred to you an old enemy of what's-his-name, Donald Gordon, is behind it?" Walt said.

"It has, but I don't see how killing Sarah Gertz hurts Robert Gordon when he has no knowledge that Sarah is his daughter," I said. "And I'll give Paul the full story if and when, and he can do with it as he pleases."

"If and when what?"

"If I can't find who killed her, or when I give up," I said.

"Either way."

I filled a mug with coffee, sat, and grabbed my smokes.

"When you give up?" Walt said. "We both know when that will be."

I lit my cigarette, blew smoke, and sipped coffee.

"How the hell can you go from push-ups to smoking?" Walt said.

"They're unrelated activities," I said.

"Did you make your usual thousand pages of notes?" Walt said.

"Yes."

"I got one hour."

Walt and I read my notes together at the card table. He pulled a yellow highlighter from his suit jacket pocket and every once in a while scrawled through a note or word.

"You're right," Walt said when he turned the last page.

"About?" I said.

"Somebody needs to speak for this girl," Walt said.

"Can you be more specific about the *about*?"

"She didn't drive her car home," Walt said. "Whoever did drive her car took her briefcase and notes, but overlooked her mileage book in the glove box. He wiped down the wheel and door and took all incriminating evidence with him."

"What would you do if this was your case?" I said.

"Same as you, go back to the beginning."

"Because I missed something?"

"Because they missed something. Because the Metro Police and FBI have a thousand other crimes to work on at the same time and you don't," Walt said.

I nodded.

"Because the bastard got away with murder and maybe more than one," Walt said. "And maybe just because."

"I think I'll ask her aunt if I can read her letters home from

Washington," I said. "I'm sure the FBI read them, but it's possible they . . ." I paused.

"What?" Walt said.

"Flip back there and read the list of personal items the police released to her family."

Walt flipped through my notes and scanned the page. "Letters, clothing, cookware from the kitchen, photographs, snow globes collection, and her personal finances."

I drew in smoke from the cigarette and exhaled slowly through my nose.

"What?" Walt said.

"It strikes me as odd how sanitized her apartment was," I said. "Not one mention of a birthday gift or card from a coworker or friend, a dinner date written on the refrigerator, something or anything to say she was a young woman with a life. Even a casual note from a movie and dinner date."

"Someone cleaned her apartment before the police got there," Walt said.

"The same someone who drove her car," I said.

"Because the son of a bitch had the key," Walt said.

"And all weekend to tidy up sight unseen," I said.

"Mother fucker," Walt said.

"Maybe I'll go read some letters and talk to the mother," I said.

Walt scanned my notes and stopped a few pages deep. "These committee members in Congress and the UN, any of them still around?"

"A few," I said. "Metro and the FBI conducted interviews and cleared them all."

"So go talk to Mom and read some letters," Walt said. "Maybe you can shake a few apples from the tree."

I tossed my spent cigarette to the sand and lit another. "Janet wants me to find a job," I said. "A job-type job and quit doing this."

"And you're okay with that?"

"I am," I said. "Just as soon as I figure out what I'm qualified to do."

"There's always some nice cushy security job with a major corporation," Walt suggested. "Want I should ask around?"

"Yeah."

"Don't sound so excited about the prospect, you might give yourself a heart attack."

"Yeah."

"Look, asshole, we both know it should be you wearing the captain's badge," Walt said. "I concede that. Point is, it ain't you and now you have a second chance to make a real life with Janet and the kids, so don't fuck it up, you asshole."

I stood up. "Feel like taking a jog on the beach?"

"I'm wearing a suit, moron," Walt said.

"Afraid you can't keep up?" I said.

"Afraid of you, ha," Walt said as he stood up. "Gimme a second to roll up my pants and take off my shoes."

"I'll give you a head start," I said.

"How about I just kick your ass," Walt snapped as he yanked off a shoe.

"Gotta catch me first," I said and took off running.

I made it to the water, turned left, and jogged about a hundred feet before Walt caught up with me. "Is this all you got?" Walt said.

"Something was missed," I said. "In her letters or the evidence."

"Then find it," Walt said.

We ran a quarter of a mile and then Walt started to lose steam. I pushed him a bit harder and he opened it up to keep pace with me.

We stayed in stride for another quarter mile until Walt started to gasp and wheeze, and I slowed the pace to a medium jog. A quarter mile after that, Walt stopped and placed his hands on his knees. "I think I'm gonna puke."

"Breathe in through your nose and out your mouth," I said.

"Fuck you," Walt said. "What kills me is you'll go back to your shithole trailer, sit in your rotten chair, and light a fucking cigarette."

"We all need a hobby," I said.

Walt stood up as his breathing slowly returned to normal. "Try collecting stamps."

We walked back to my trailer.

"Stamps," I said.

"What?"

"When I ask to read her letters home, it will be interesting to see if any are postmarked from other parts of the country," I said.

Walt looked at me with that frozen expression he generally reserved for something he hadn't thought of before.

"Yeah, it would, wouldn't it!" he said.

CHAPTER 34

"We can't go to New York, Jack," Janet said. "It's just not a good time."

"Why not?" I said.

We were at the dinner table in Janet's kitchen. I looked at Regan as she paused in mid-chew to look at me.

"Because it's not," Janet said.

Mark was sneaking something to Molly under the table and looked at Janet. " 'Because' is not an answer, Mom," he said. "Isn't that what you always tell me when I say 'because'?"

"You shut up," Janet said as she wagged a finger at Mark. "Or I'll give you a first-class because."

Mark grinned his wise-guy grin at me as if to say, *see what you're in for?*

"I'm going anyway, and you have the weekend off," I said. "And isn't this Mark's weekend with his father?"

"Do I have to see Dad this weekend?" Mark said.

"Yes, and quit feeding Molly under the table," Janet said.

I looked at Regan, who was laser-light focused on Janet. "Regan's never been to a city," I said. "She might as well start with the biggest. We'll stay at the Charter Arms on Central Park. I'll be back in time on Saturday for us to take in a Broadway show and dinner on the Way."

Janet looked at Regan. "Can you handle a plane ride and a hotel?"

Regan nodded gently. "Yes, I can," she said softly.

"And all those people in the streets?" Janet said.

Regan nodded a second time. Her eyes were as wide as dinner plates. "You'll be with me," she said.

"Tomorrow we'll go shopping for the appropriate clothes and shoes," Janet said. "A young woman should look the part in a major city."

Regan stared at Janet for a moment while it sunk in. Then she stood up and gave Janet a kiss and tight hug.

That was the moment when I realized I'd lost my daughter's need for approval to Janet. No matter how tight a father-daughter relationship is, a daughter's need for a mother's approval is the relationship that lasts forever.

Mark looked at me and rolled his eyes. "Jeeze," he said.

I rolled my eyes back at him.

"Women," Mark said.

That pretty much summed it up.

While Regan and Mark rinsed and stacked dishes in the dishwasher, Janet and I took coffee in the backyard at the patio table. Molly followed us out and jumped on Janet's lap where she seemed content to lie.

"You'll have to make it up to Mark," Janet said.

"I know."

"You haven't lost Regan, Jack," Janet said. "If that's what you're thinking."

"I'm not."

"She's just gained a mother, that's all."

"I know and I'm glad it's you."

Janet nodded.

We sipped coffee.

Molly purred.

"Didn't you just go shopping, by the way?" I said.

"Not for New York," Janet said. "Regan will need to look the part of a blossoming young woman if we're to stay on Fifth Avenue and take in the theatre."

"Regan and not you?" I said.

"This trip is your idea," Janet said.

"Yeah," I said. "You think maybe I should go buy a new pair of shoes?"

"Oh, shut up," Janet said.

I did and we listened to Molly purr. I reached over to scratch her ears and Janet took my hand.

"A new pairs of shoes wouldn't hurt you though, Jack," she said.

Chapter 35

I forked over the extra money for three seats in first class to try and minimize Regan's initial fear of being on a plane for the first time. I asked for an aisle seat for her, but she insisted on the window once we boarded, so I traded with her.

Turned out Regan was fascinated by the takeoff, excited by being above the clouds, and even more excited at the landing.

Go figure.

We landed at four in the afternoon at Kennedy Airport. Tens of thousands filled the massive terminals and baggage claim areas. Regan didn't exactly freak at being in such a crowd, but she gripped Janet's arm and didn't let go until I removed our bags from the carousel.

We went outside and stood in a very long line for a taxi.

"We're in the borough of Queens," I said to Regan. "We'll be taking a cab into Manhattan to the hotel."

Clutching Janet's arm, Regan nodded.

The seven-mile ride into the city took almost an hour. It was rush hour, which meant traffic crawled at a snail's pace, and sometimes not at all.

I'm not sure what Regan saw or didn't see as we crossed the bridge into Manhattan, as she said not a word. She just watched with wide-eyed wonder as the largest city in the country rolled by outside her window.

On Fifth Avenue, Regan stood on the sidewalk and looked up at the towering structure of the Charter Arms Hotel.

"We're on the fortieth floor," I said. "With a view of the park."

A doorman held the doors for us as we entered the lavish, very spacious lobby. A bellman took our bags and waited with us as I checked in at the desk. Our room was a suite, actually. Two bedrooms and a living room, and it didn't come cheap. However, a third of the bill and my plane fare would go on my expense report, so that helped a bit.

After I tipped the bellman, we explored the bedrooms. Janet and Regan took the larger room; I settled for the smaller, which was about the size of my entire trailer on the beach. The living room was double the size of the one in Janet's home and had every comfort. The view from the bay window, as I promised, was spectacular.

"That's Central Park," I said to Regan. "Maybe while I'm off working tomorrow, Janet can take you for a carriage ride?"

Regan looked at me. Her eyes misted up and she turned away, then scooted off to her bedroom.

I looked at Janet. "What?"

"Be right back," Janet said and followed off after Regan.

The bedroom door closed. I went to the desk and called down to reserve a car for the morning. Then I called room service for a pot of coffee. By the time it arrived and I was happily sipping my first cup, Janet emerged from the bedroom.

"And that was about?" I said.

Janet filled a cup with coffee and took a sip. "It appears that for the first time since she was five years old Regan feels like part of a real family," she said. "Oh, and she wants room service for dinner. Something expensive."

I nodded and looked away when a mist filled my eyes.

Janet sighed. "Why does every woman want a sensitive man until they have one?"

CHAPTER 36

Ann Marie Hoffman served tea in her backyard.

"I must admit I was surprised when you called back so soon after your last visit," she said.

"Like I said on the phone, it could be nothing at all," I said.

"If you thought that, you wouldn't be here right now," Ann Marie said.

"I'm very thorough," I said. "Even if a detail has no meaning, I like to know its origin."

"Because its origin may mean something," Ann Marie said.

"Possibly."

"Let's finish our tea and then take a drive to see my sister," Ann Marie said.

The drive east from Valley Stream to East Islip took about an hour because Long Island is just that, a very long island. One hundred and eighteen miles long, in fact, and home to some of the wealthiest people in the country.

I took the scenic route, avoiding the highway. Not because I was interested in sightseeing, but because Ann Marie only knew one way to the live-in hospital where her sister resided.

It also gave us some extra time to chat a bit more. Ann Marie gave me some insight as to what kind of a child Sarah was growing up in Queens. An excellent student all the way through college, she was also very popular with boys as well as girls.

"She had an army of friends and boyfriends, but none serious," Ann Marie said. "And even when she moved to Washington, she came home at every holiday and wrote twice a month like clockwork."

"Did she phone much, do you know?" I said.

"Every weekend," Ann Marie said. "But she always wrote as well. My sister taught her the value of writing a letter. With a letter, you can read it again and again, but with a phone call, what have you got?"

"She sounds like a wise woman, your sister," I said.

"Reserve judgment on that," Ann Marie said. "Until after you meet her."

The Islip medical facility and nursing home was a blue and white U-shaped building that consisted of two hundred private rooms, a lush courtyard garden, a large entertainment center, dining hall, library, and medical facility. It was filled to capacity, and all of the patients in residence were there because they were deemed mentally unfit to live at home for various reasons—severe depression being the most common. Care for the patients was excellent and easy. Most rarely left their rooms except to eat in the dining hall, sit in the gardens, or play bingo in the rec room.

Michele Gertz had never recovered from her breakdown brought on by Sarah's disappearance and her husband's suicide. She was tiny bit of a thing, overdressed for a hot day but seemingly unaware of the heat. She was in a chair in her large bedroom, knitting. She didn't look up when a nurse ushered us into her room.

"Michele, honey, it's Ann," Ann Marie said.

Michele kept right on knitting as if we weren't there.

Ann Marie sat on the bed and touched Michele's bony arm. "It's not polite to ignore company, Michele," she said.

The knitting continued.

I looked around the spacious bedroom. A large dresser against the wall had the snow globes collection found in Sarah's Virginia apartment. I counted forty of them. Most depicted winter scenes from various states. The Empire State Building, the Statue of Liberty, the Boston Common, the Washington Monument, Niagara Falls, and so on.

I picked up a globe depicting a sleigh ride down a hill and shook it. Snow fell gently around the horses and sleigh. It was heavy, around two pounds. I flipped it over and read the tiny metal plate.

To Sarah, Love Dad.

"One of her very first," Michele said in a soft voice.

I set the globe down and looked at her. She hadn't stopped knitting or looked up at me or Ann Marie. "They're beautiful," I said.

"I'm holding them for her," Michele said. "Until she asks for them back."

"Is it all right if I look at them?" I said.

Michele finally paused from her knitting long enough to look at me. "Don't break any," she said. "Sarah will be terribly upset if you broke any."

"I won't," I said.

I picked up a few of the globes, checked the engraving, looking for what I didn't know. Metro and the FBI had scrutinized every item in Sarah's apartment before releasing it to her family.

One globe caught my attention mostly because I didn't recognize the internal setting. I picked it up and looked closer at the all-white lighthouse by an ocean. I shook it and snow gently fell around the lighthouse.

I flipped the globe over. The engraving read, *With Love, Okay.*

I set the globe down and turned to Michele. "Mrs. Gertz, may I ask you a question?"

Michele looked up at me.

"Does Sarah write you much?" I said.

"All the time," Michele said. "She loves to write letters, my Sarah."

"Can I see them, the letters?" I said.

"Why?" Michele said.

"We're old friends," I said. "I promise not to damage any of them."

Michele turned to Ann Marie. "The closet," she said. "The shoebox."

Ann Marie stood up, went to the closet, and opened the door. From the top shelf she removed a covered shoebox and brought it to me. I set the box on the bed and laid the lid aside. Inside were about two hundred letters. About eighty were held together in a bunch by a large rubber band.

I removed the eighty. There were letters from Sarah to her parents that were sent from Washington. More than likely it was the FBI that separated them inside the shoebox.

I removed the rubber band and rifled through the envelopes to check postmarks. All but one had a Virginia or DC postmark. The seventy-seventh envelope had a different postmark, one that I didn't recognize.

I held the envelope to the light, but the ink was so faded I couldn't read the state seal or origin mark, just the zip coding for where it was mailed.

04107.

Where the hell was that?

I removed the letter and read it. Sarah wrote about her latest meeting with Congress and the progress they were making in getting new EPA legislation voted on. She wrote that she would like to take a vacation soon and come home to Queens for a week. Nothing about boyfriends, dating, or social activities.

I replaced the letter and looked at Michele. "Your daughter loves you very much," I said.

"Yes, she does," Michele said. "I'm making her this sweater."

She held up the knitting. "It gets cold in Washington in winter," she said.

"Yes, it does," I said.

Michele returned to her knitting as if Ann Marie and I were no longer there.

In her mind we probably weren't.

On the drive back, Ann Marie said, "And that's my sister."

"It's really unfortunate," I said. "But maybe it's best she doesn't remember."

"Or chooses not to remember," Ann Marie said.

"Either way it's less painful for her," I said.

"I suppose," Ann Marie said. "Well, now that you've met my sister, are you giving up or will you ponder on?"

"Ponder," I said. "Which brings me to a question. The snow globes. The lighthouse, do you know where that one is from?"

"Why, no, I don't," Ann Marie said. "I don't remember it in the box the FBI sent from Sarah's apartment."

"They sent the box to you?"

"Yes. My sister was in no condition to receive anything then," Ann Marie said. "Or now," she added.

"Maybe that globe was already in your sister's house?" I said.

"That's . . . no, she brought it with her," Ann Marie said. "I remember now."

"Sarah?"

"About a month before she . . . disappeared, Sarah came home for a few days after a conference at the UN," Ann Marie said. "She showed us that globe and left it behind. I think she forgot it and I must have added it in when I brought them to my sister."

"Do you know where that lighthouse is from?" I said.

"No, I don't. Do you?"

I shook my head. "Odd it's not marked with the name."

"On the bottom?"

"A metal tag with the engraving, *With Love, Okay.*"

"That's probably where the ID or brand was."

"What's that mean, 'okay'?" I said.

"I don't know," Ann Marie said. "But it sounds as if someone is asking for permission to love her."

"It does, doesn't it," I agreed.

CHAPTER 37

Before returning to the hotel, I dropped off the rental, then forked over one thousand dollars for three tickets to *Spider-Man the Musical* at the same-day-tickets booth in Times Square.

With my wallet considerably lighter, I walked north on Broadway, then east to the hotel. It wasn't rush hour, but that didn't matter. This was New York, a twenty-four-hour sandbox for adults. The sidewalks were clogged and the streets were jammed.

When I entered the suite, the master bedroom door was closed. I entered mine, removed jacket and tie, and flopped on the bed. It was early afternoon and I wasn't hungry. I thought about taking a nap, and while I was thinking about it, I fell asleep.

Tapping on the door woke me up about an hour later. "Jack, are you in there?" Janet said from the other side.

"Yeah," I said and sat up in bed.

Janet opened the door and came in wrapped in a white hotel robe. "I thought you were off working?" she said.

"I am," I said. "I was until a bit ago."

"Looks suspiciously like napping to me."

"Toss me a bag of donuts and it's like being back on the job," I said.

"Funny," Janet said. "So, where are we going for dinner and what are we going to see?"

"A surprise and a surprise," I said.

Janet sat on the bed. Her muscular legs peeked out at me. I did my best to glimpse without getting caught. "You don't suppose we could . . . ?" I said.

"No, and no," Janet said. "I need to shave my legs and take a shower. I suggest you do the same."

"Shave my legs?"

Janet grinned and shook her head. "Wait until you see your daughter."

The key word was *wait.*

I shaved, but just my face. I showered, then dressed in the suit I'd packed just for the occasion, ordered room service coffee, went downstairs to the street for a smoke, and still had to wait forty-five minutes on the sofa before the master bedroom door finally opened.

Janet came out first. She wore a short-sleeved, black dress with matching shoes and shoulder wrap. Her hair was swirled in an evening-out bun. Her makeup was flawless. Not that I'm an expert on women's makeup, but I know enough so that when you can't tell a woman is wearing any, she's done a pretty good job of applying it.

I was about to stand when Janet hushed me with a finger to her lips, then motioned for me to stay seated.

I looked past Janet at the open bedroom door.

Janet turned around. "Come on, Regan," she said. "We don't want to be late."

Shy as a tiny bird, my daughter wobbled out of the bedroom wearing a sleeveless black dress with matching wrap. Her feet were unsteady in three-inch black pumps and it struck me that this was probably the first time in her life she'd worn shoes with heels.

Regan's hair was in a complicated braid that must have taken Janet an hour to accomplish. What really threw me for a loop was how much older and more mature Regan's makeup made her appear.

Gone was the gawky teenage girl who played with coloring books to whittle away the painful years after her mother's death. In her place was a beautiful young woman full of hope and promise for a brighter, happier future.

"Well?" Janet said.

Regan looked at me for approval. I could see fear and worry on her face.

I stood up from the sofa.

"Wow," I said, and Regan's face glowed with a sudden, very bright smile.

With a beautiful woman on each arm, I was the envy of every man in the theatre lobby. Heads turned as we strolled in and took our place in line for the opening of the interior doors, and they weren't turning for me.

Regan still wobbled a bit in her heels, but she was getting the hang of it. Then the doors opened and I could feel the excitement in her body as she clutched my left arm on the way to our seats.

I didn't quite get the plot, but the sets were spectacular, the music fun, and people got to fly around on wires. Regan sat riveted the entire two hours as her eyes and ears and senses took it all in.

Afterward, we rode in a cab to Little Italy where we walked the crowded, narrow streets and mingled with a thousand tourists before settling on a restaurant for dinner. For dessert we traveled the streets in search of an outdoor café and settled on one with checkered tablecloths and lit candles.

At every table, men snuck glances at the two goddesses I was lucky enough to be blessed with. We ordered six different pastries and ate them all while sipping espresso.

I didn't think about Sarah Gertz once.

For the first time in a decade, I had faith that my daughter would have a life of her own and it would be a good one.

Me, too.

Chapter 38

I sat with Oz and drank coffee and listened to high tide roll in down at the beach. I lit a cigarette to accompany my coffee, and for twenty minutes or so, we were content to listen to the waves without exchanging words.

A bit earlier, I'd brought Oz up to speed and he made notes in his book as he listened. When I was an active detective on the job, I sometimes used a small recorder to talk out my notes, usually when I was stumped and had nowhere to go. I would play the tape back, listen to my own notes, and hope it sparked something in the way of a clue or missed detail.

Today Oz was my tape recorder.

I played him back. "Anything strike you or jump out at you?" I said.

"Yeah, somebody got away with murder," Oz said.

"Anything else?"

"The lighthouse, postmark thing is interesting," Oz said. "You think it means anything?"

"When clueless, everything means anything," I said.

"You clueless a lot, huh?" Oz said.

"Only about life, love, and women," I said.

Oz sipped coffee. "Ah, wisdom," he said.

"Feel like taking a walk?" I said.

"How far and where?"

"Town and the library."

"What about lunch?"

"What about it?"

"You buying, right?"

I didn't have a photogenic memory, but an experienced detective will tell you a memory for details is the key to being successful at solving puzzles. And most crimes are just that, puzzles.

Puzzles that don't end well.

And when the pieces all fit together, a pretty picture isn't made and somebody usually goes to prison.

"Why don't you spring for a laptop?" Oz said when we settled in before a computer at the library.

"Then I'd have no excuse to buy you breakfast in town," I said.

"My friendship, companionship, and insight ain't enough?"

"You need a hobby."

"I got a hobby."

"Drinking ain't a hobby," I said. "Although I tried to make it mine."

"So what are we looking for?" Oz said.

"Famous photos of lighthouses," I said.

"Because they'd use a famous photo for the snow globe?" Oz said.

"That must be some of that insight you mentioned," I said.

"I try to use it twice a day," Oz said. "More than that and I hurt myself."

I Googled famous lighthouses and got thousands of links.

"Aw, man," Oz said.

I limited the links to North America. Still thousands of links.

"Forget lunch and go for dinner," Oz said.

"How about we forget both and go for broke," I said.

"What?"

I did a search for lighthouses in the 04107 zip code.

And there it was.

The Portland Head Light.

Portland, Maine.

Where Sarah Gertz mailed the only letter home outside of the Washington area.

"That's it?" Oz said.

"That's it," I said.

I printed a few photographs and some history on the lighthouse.

"Now what?" Oz said.

"We go to lunch," I said. "And think about it."

CHAPTER 39

"What's it mean?" Oz said as he bit into a juicy burger from the coffee shop a block from the library.

I had a juicy burger of my own. "I don't know," I said as I took a bite.

Oz wiped his bearded chin with a napkin. "Well, it means something."

"Yes, it does."

I ate a few French fries and mulled things over. There was no mention of a trip to Maine in Sarah's letters home. She came for a visit and had the snow globe in her possession. If she'd mentioned a trip to the Lobster State at a family gathering, Ann Marie would have remembered and mentioned it to me.

From Portland, Maine, to Kennedy is about ninety minutes or less in the air. She could have met somebody in Maine and then zipped to Queens for a quick family visit. The snow globe could have been a gift or souvenir from the Maine trip, left behind when she went back to Washington.

The trip to Maine could have been for business reasons. Maine is a state very dependent upon the environment for its livelihood. The globe could have been a gift from whatever group she had met with, but if that was the case, would they inscribe it *With Love, Okay*?

And what the hell did *Okay* mean?

If Sarah purchased the globe for her collection, the engraving made even less sense, unless it was some kind of inside joke, which I doubted.

"Want dessert?" Oz said, snapping my thought process.

"Sure."

We ordered double-double chocolate cake and coffee, because there's no such thing as too much chocolate.

"Know what's bothering me?" Oz said when the cake and coffee arrived.

"What?"

"The word *antiseptic* comes to mind," Oz said. "How neat and clean everything is. Her car, the apartment, lack of evidence or anything."

"They had from Friday night to Monday morning to sterilize things," I said.

"Makes it premeditated, don't it?" Oz said.

"Not necessarily," I said. "It could have been a spur of the moment, crime of passion thing, and afterward when things cooled down, the murderer was left with a dead body to dispose of and clean up."

"So where's the girl's body?"

Good question.

No answer.

"Probably in the same place as the real evidence is," I said.

"Yeah, where's that?" Oz said.

Good question.

No answer.

We finished our cake and coffee and took a leisurely stroll back to my trailer.

Once safely in the confines of our lawn chairs, I called Paul Lawrence on my cell phone and left a message for him to call me back.

"What now?" Oz said.

"We wait."

Chapter 40

After three hours of waiting, Oz returned to his trailer for a nap. Another hour passed and I did the same. An hour or so into my snooze, my cell phone on the nightstand jangled me awake.

I scooped it up and checked the incoming number. It was Paul Lawrence.

"Hey, Paul, thanks for calling me back," I said.

"I was out of town when you called," Lawrence said. "Or I would have called sooner. So what do you got?"

"Questions," I said.

"Sorry, Jack, I really don't know the true meaning of life," Lawrence said. "I'm not sure about aliens and little green men, either."

"Ah, but can you get me a list of all committee members in Congress, the UN, and Sarah Gertz's think tank that are still around I can get in touch with?" I said.

"Well, now, this doesn't sound like the usual grasping-at-straws request," Lawrence said. "What have you been up to that the Bureau should know about?"

"Three weeks before she disappeared, Sarah Gertz took a trip to Maine," I said.

"There's nothing in the evidence that says that," Lawrence said.

"She brought a snow globe of the Portland Head Light home to Queens three weeks before she vanished," I said. "And she mailed a letter from Portland, Maine, right around the same time. An 04106 zip code. Maybe she did some work for an environmental group in the Lobster State or something along those lines."

There was a long pause on the phone.

"What's going through that mind of yours, Jack?" Lawrence said.

"Just following the evidence where it takes me," I said.

"Will you be around tomorrow?" Lawrence said.

"I will."

"I haven't been home in a while," Lawrence said. "I could use a little R&R, what do you think?"

"I think a nice trip east might be just what you need," I said. "Want a ride from the airport?"

"Hey, man, I'm the F . . . B . . . I . . . we don't stoop to begging for rides," Lawrence said.

"What time?"

"Around five."

"See you then," I said.

I hit the *end* button and lit a cigarette.

Follow the evidence and see where it takes me.

Maybe somewhere.

Probably nowhere.

Paul Lawrence was a top-shelf forensics expert all the way. A giant in his field. Maybe he thought I knew something I didn't?

Maybe he just missed the donuts?

CHAPTER 41

Walt put his feet up on his new captain's desk, sipped coffee from a mug decorated with a gold captain's badge and the words *World's Greatest Dad,* looked at me, and sighed openly.

I was seated in one of three guest chairs. "So this is how the other half lives," I said.

"What other half?" Walt said.

"The upper crust."

"Only crust around here is from my wife's stale sandwiches."

"Want to have dinner with me and Paul?" I said.

"Janet's?"

I shook my head. "Some prime steaks on the grill."

"At the beach?"

"Around seven," I said. "I have to pick up Paul in about an hour."

"I take it this isn't a social visit from Paul?" Walt said.

"He misses the donuts," I said.

"Let me call Elizabeth," Walt said. "If she's not too pissed at me, I'll stop by."

"See ya later," I said and stood up.

"Hey, Jack?" Walt said.

I looked at him.

"You found something, didn't you?"

"Just following the evidence," I said.

"I like my evidence medium," Walt said. "With a nice baked potato," he added.

Lawrence took a commercial flight in from Washington to stay under the radar. It wasn't an official Bureau investigation as yet, even though the book on Sarah Gertz had never been closed.

I parked in short term and met Lawrence at his gate. His plane was only ten minutes late, but he had a small carry-on bag so we skipped baggage claim and went right to my car. He was dressed casually in chinos and a teal pullover shirt that had a tiny alligator on the right side.

On the way to see Walt, I'd stopped by the meat market in town and selected three cuts of steak and on the way home; I stopped by to pick them up along with a fresh bag of charcoal and wood chips.

"I asked Walt to join us," I told Lawrence as we returned to my car from the market.

"How is Walt?" Lawrence said. "I haven't seen him since my last trip home."

"Captain Walt now," I said.

"I always knew he'd make captain," Lawrence said. "After you."

"Yeah."

We didn't talk shop. That was reserved for later. I drove the Marquis to my trailer and parked on the sand. Oz wouldn't stop by. Lawrence was federal and our conversation might be restricted. Oz understood. He knew I'd discuss what I could with him tomorrow.

I brewed a fresh pot of coffee, then filled the grill with new coals and started them going. While Paul sat in Oz's chair, I wrapped six large potatoes in foil and set them on the grill. Beside the card table was a bucket of water where six ears of corn had been soaking since early this afternoon. I pulled them from the bucket and set them on the grill with husks still in place.

Then I grabbed a mug of coffee, took my chair, and lit a cigarette.

Lawrence had been gazing at the waves crashing on the beach. "Two more years and I pull the pin," he said.

"Kind of young to go fishing," I said.

"Thirty years of looking at the worst possible crimes, I've had enough," Lawrence said. "I was thinking of moving back here and resting on my laurels."

"Resting on laurels is highly overrated," I said. "You can get bedsores from that."

Down at the beach, I saw Walt's sedan skirt around the parking lot and enter from the beach opening. Nearby gulls screeched and flew away in packs, only to resettle the moment the sedan was past.

I got up to turn the potatoes and corn. By the time I sat down again, Walt was stepping out of his car.

"Paul, what's it been, a year?" Walt said.

Lawrence stood up to shake Walt's hand. "At least," he said.

"Want some coffee?" I asked Walt.

"Only if it comes with a steak," Walt said and took the third chair.

I fetched Walt a mug, sat, and lit a smoke.

Walt sipped from the mug. "I feel compelled to say 'Meeting called to order,' but I'll refrain," he said.

"This is a rerun for Paul," I said and filled Walt in on my findings. I paused once to turn the potatoes and corn again, and then continued after refilling coffee mugs and lighting up a fresh smoke.

"Is there a chance she ordered the globe thing in the mail and was bringing it home?" Walt said.

"I thought of that, but her collection was in her Virginia

apartment," I said. "I think she bought the globe or was given it as a gift when she mailed the letter from the 04106 zip code."

"Portland, Maine," Walt said.

"Yeah."

"That *With Love, Okay,* what the hell does that mean?" Walt said.

I looked at Lawrence. "You got that list?"

Lawrence dug a folded sheet of paper from his shirt pocket. "DC is a transient town," he said. "People come and they go like you change your underwear."

"Once a week?" Walt cracked.

I got up to flip potatoes and corn and to make room for the steaks.

"Twelve years is a long time," Lawrence said. "That's a century in Washington. Anyway, every person on the UN committee she worked with is gone and out of the country. Her office has an almost entirely new staff top to bottom. Even the Senate Oversight Committee on environmental issues has five new members of the six. Only senator left is the chairman, Oliver Koch."

"That guy from Maine?" Walt said with a raised eyebrow.

I tossed the three steaks on the grill and they immediately made that satisfying sizzle of flesh hitting heated steel. "Something I didn't mention before," I said.

"Because?" Lawrence said.

"I want your gut reaction," I said.

"This can't wait until my gut is full?" Walt said.

I flipped the steaks to char the other side, then took my seat and lit another smoke. "The snow globe of the lighthouse, it was engraved, *With Love, Okay.*"

Walt looked at me.

Paul Lawrence looked at me.

I got up, looked at the steaks, and flipped them again.

"Okay, what?" Walt said.

"Shit," Lawrence said.

"What?" Walt said.

"Okay said another way is *O* followed by *K,*" Lawrence said. "*OK*. The initials for Senator Oliver Koch."

"Motherfucker," Walt said.

"Yeah," Lawrence added.

"Koch is some kind of big shot, isn't he?" Walt said.

"Twenty-four years in the Senate, two in the House," Lawrence said. "Sits on the Finance Oversight Committee, the Military Advisory Committee, Housing, and several others. He's the only registered Independent in the Senate. He's considered the most powerful senator because his vote could sway either party. The word in Washington is he'll seek a fifth term and bow out in two years to seek the VP nod. He's nobody to fuck with. For sure."

"Is he accessible?" I said.

"To what?" Lawrence said.

"Being interviewed," I said.

"By cable news when he's looking for a free plug, by the *Times* for some free publicity. By you, no," Lawrence said.

"You?" I said.

"I have no reason to," Lawrence said.

"Do you think it's a coincidence Sarah Gertz has a snow globe from Maine with *Okay* engraved on it and mailed a letter from Portland?" I said. "And that twelve years ago he chaired a committee she worked on in Washington?"

"None of that is a reason for me to interview Koch on a twelve-year-old missing-persons," Lawrence said. "The Bureau would have a first-class fit if I tried."

"What if I tried?" I said.

"He'd chew you up and spit you out for lunch," Lawrence said.

"Dammit, Paul, listen to me," I said. "There's something else. Sarah Gertz was a black market baby. Her father sold her for sixty grand after his wife died. How many times can one girl be fucked over in her life and not have anyone speak for her?"

"And you want to be that voice?" Lawrence said.

"No, I don't, but I'm stuck with it," I said.

Lawrence looked at Walt. "What do you say, Captain?"

"When Jack decides to do something, I'd hate to be the one to get in his way," Walt said. "Say no and he'll just do it anyway."

"The steaks done?" Lawrence said.

"Five minutes," I said.

I took my seat and lit another smoke.

"Koch is one powerful motherfucker," Lawrence said.

"Too powerful to even talk to?" I said. "Even God can be talked to."

"What if I called his office and requested a meeting?" Walt said. "I could tell him I'm opening up an old missing-persons case from DC that has ties to here. If he agrees, we might learn something. If he says no, well, we learn something from that, too. If he does agree and we pick up on something, well, the case was never closed by the Bureau, was it?"

"No," Lawrence said.

"Worth a shot," Walt said.

Lawrence nodded to me. "How do you explain Jack?"

"Tell him Jack's the private investigator who made the connection from missing persons to Sarah Gertz," Walt said. "He'll be a ride-along. A quiet ride-along, right, Jack?"

"A sphinx," I said.

"It will take some dancing," Lawrence said.

"I do a mean two-step," Walt said.

"What about Mr. Two Left Feet here?" Lawrence said.

"Jack will stay in the background and behave himself," Walt said. "Right, Jack?"

"I don't two-step," I said. "But I can foxtrot."

"Give me forty-eight hours to clear it with the Bureau bigwigs," Lawrence said. "They might want a seat at the table."

"I'm cool with that," Walt said.

Lawrence looked at me. "Jack?"

"Yes."

"Then let's eat some steak and watch the sunset," Lawrence said.

Chapter 42

Close to shore, high tide and a near full moon brought in some tall waves that broke with the sound of low rumbling thunder. Moonlight shimmered off the ocean in the distance.

I removed my shoes and left them at my chair. Walt and Lawrence did the same. We stood there and watched the waves, three barefoot guys with a long history of friendship and professional respect.

I lit a cigarette.

Walt took it away from me, put it in his mouth, and said, "These are bad for you."

I watched him puff on my cigarette. "But not for you?"

"I didn't say that," Walt said.

I lit another.

"The Bureau doesn't like egg on its face," Lawrence said.

"Who does?" Walt said in between puffs. "It's sticky and messy and can make you sick."

"A man like Oliver Koch can make a lot of trouble if he feels he's being picked on or wrongfully singled out," Lawrence said.

"Talking isn't picking," Walt said.

"These guys live in their own universe," Lawrence said. "Pampered rich men who do and say what they want when they want to. Some of them honestly believe the rules don't apply to them."

"They do," Walt said. "All of 'em, same as the rest of us."

"You don't get to Washington much, do you, Walt?" Lawrence said.

"Never is too often for me," Walt said.

"There's this thing called inside the Beltway rules," Lawrence said. "You won't read about them in a newspaper or hear about it on cable news, but they're real and everybody knows not to speak about them at parties."

"If you say, 'You need me on that wall,' I'm gonna puke," Walt said.

I saw Lawrence grin in the moonlight. "The rules say 'don't hold me accountable for my actions' and 'do as I say, not as I do,' " he said. "They say 'I get a free pass on what you'd be arrested for because I'm better than you because you chose me to represent you.' Violate the rules and they're like spiders, they eat their own."

"Like tweeting your private parts," Walt said. "Or throwing hooker parties on the taxpayer's dime in Vegas."

"Oh, hell, they all do and survive that," Lawrence said. "Only if they fuck with the media do they pay the price at the media's hands."

"So what rule are you talking about?" Walt said.

"He means murder, Walt," I said. "Isn't that right, Paul?"

"Hey, in that town you could dry-hump a goat on Election Day as long as you apologize to your wife and shed a misty tear for your hurt family and the people you let down back home," Lawrence said. "It's the old two-step; don't get caught with an underage girl or a dead boy, otherwise anything goes."

I looked at Lawrence. "What about a dead young woman?"

"That's grandfathered in," Lawrence said.

"Fuck their rules," Walt said. He looked at Lawrence. "Talk to whoever you got to back in DC, but I'm going to talk with Koch regardless of if your bigwigs approve or not. Fuck them, too."

"It's not your jurisdiction, Walt," Lawrence said.

"Hell it ain't," Walt said. "New evidence says the biological father lives here and has knowledge of a black market baby ring. That says it's mine."

"Forty-eight hours, Walt," Lawrence said. "That's all I'm asking for."

"You got it," Walt said.

"What about you, Jack?" Lawrence said.

"I don't have a jurisdiction," I said. "Remember?"

Chapter 43

Lawrence stayed at a small motel in town for the night. I met him for breakfast and then drove him to the airport. On the way home, I stopped by the library to do a computer search on Senator Oliver Koch.

His name brought up several thousand links.

I spent several hours reading and printing many of them.

Around noon, I gathered up the sixty or so sheets of paper I'd printed and walked a few blocks to the Italian deli. Armed with a bag full of meatball subs, chips, and ginger ale, I returned to my car and drove home to my trailer.

"The man's a real bigwig," Oz said as he bit into his meatball sub. "A player."

"Yes, he is," I agreed. "You got sauce in your beard."

"I'll wipe when I'm done," Oz said.

Oliver Koch was a silver-spoon baby from a wealthy Boston family that relocated to Falmouth, Maine, when he was five years old. Oliver's father, Olin, was an investment banker who specialized in increasing his own wealth by risking the wealth of others. The move to Maine came in '52 when cheap housing dotted the Portland landscape and Olin invested heavily in buying and developing property for the baby-boomer communities springing up all over in the postwar boom.

Young Oliver went to private schools in Portland, played varsity football and basketball, and graduated an A-plus student.

He attended Harvard and graduated there with a degree in political science and a minor in business. He was a member of the rowing team and selected as an alternate for the US Olympic Team in the 1976 games.

Back home in Maine, young Koch was elected to the state senate for two terms before running for Congress. He did one term in the House and then switched to the Senate, where he'd been for twenty-four years and counting.

Koch knew the game well and played it better than most. As an Independent he was wined and dined by both sides of the aisle and his vote was a giant stick he carried around DC like a war club. Many a bill was passed or lost on his tiebreaking vote. He was now seeking a fifth term, and it was rumored he had his eye on the VP slot next presidential election.

Married thirty-four years to Melissa Carey of Falmouth, he had sired three daughters and one son. All worked for him in one capacity or another, although none presently resided in Maine. The son, thirty-one-year-old Oliver Jr., recently started a PAC for the senator.

Known as a champion for human rights, the environment, and a strong military, Koch also appealed to the other side by supporting many social programs. Sixty on his last birthday, it was prime time for him to move into the VP seat at the White House.

I searched for dirt on Koch and came up empty. Not even a tiny nugget for the gossip tabloids. People in power who are that squeaky clean are usually so for two reasons. They are so feared that the print and television media are afraid to run anything negative, or enough money buys silence.

I wondered which applied to Oliver Koch.

"You sure you want to open this can of worms?" Oz said.

"First rule of investigation is to follow the evidence," I said.

"This evidence could take a big bite out of your ass and ruin two close friends," Oz pointed out. "Or worse."

"It could," I said.

Oz finished the last bite of his sub and finally wiped the sauce from his beard. "Maybe you should pay me in advance?" he said.

CHAPTER 44

Waiting is a tough game, not for the faint of heart or restless.

Time slows to a crawl unless thoughts are occupied with something to do. In my case, I brought Regan and Mark to the beach where we played a game of touch football, rode the waves, and barbequed burgers and dogs late in the day.

Once our bellies were full, I tossed a baseball with Mark while Regan read a book. Oz strolled by in time for coffee, cake, and a red ball sunset over the ocean.

I kept Regan and Mark until eleven, and then drove them home to Janet's. I stuck around until she came home from work at twelve-thirty.

We took coffee in the backyard, where a slight breeze made it more pleasant to sit outside than in.

"So we're full steam ahead on the missing girl?" Janet said.

"Things are sort of on hold for the moment," I said.

"Because of?"

"I don't think you want to know," I said.

Janet sipped some coffee. "If you don't reach a satisfactory conclusion by our wedding, what then?"

"I put things on hold until we return," I said. "After that, we'll see. Walt is keeping an eye open for me on a corporate job, so I'll have to make a decision on something sooner or later."

"Make it sooner, Jack," Janet said. "Before people start shooting at you again and we have to go into hiding like last time."

"This is different," I said. "No crazy killers or mobsters

involved here. Just a missing girl from twelve years ago."

Janet omitted a soft sigh I almost didn't catch.

"What?" I said.

"Nothing," Janet said. "Let's just enjoy the quiet for a bit."

Code words for *I don't want to talk about it.* Women have a lot of code words. The secret to happiness from a man's point of view is to learn the meaning of as many of those code words as possible. *I'm fine* means nothing of the sort, and *I don't want to talk about it* means you better start talking about it if you know what's good for you. I kept my mouth shut, sipped coffee, and listened to the soft breeze as it gently blew across the backyard.

"I'm sorry if I'm acting like a selfish teenage girl," Janet said.

"Don't be because you're not," I said.

"I don't mean that," Janet said. "I've been giving a lot of thought to what I've demanded of you and it doesn't seem quite fair. By all accounts, even Walt admits you're the best investigator around and I'm asking you to give that up because I want you home with me. You're not asking me to quit being a nurse, so my demands seem a bit selfish. That said, I can't find it in me to change my mind and I won't apologize for how I feel."

"You can't have everything," I said. "If you could, where would you put it?"

Janet looked at me and despite her best efforts to keep a straight face, cracked a smile. "Be right back," she said, as she got up and then walked into the house through the kitchen door.

I finished my coffee and thought about going for a refill, but Janet came back out with a blanket in her arms. She walked to the table but didn't sit.

"Kiddies are in bed," she said. "I'm taking this blanket to the end of the yard, to spread it on the grass under the tree and take my clothes off. You're invited to watch and participate in the festivities if you're not feeling too old."

Janet turned and walked toward the tree.

I jumped up. "Hey, not feeling too old is my middle name," I said.

And that's another way to occupy your time, maybe the best way of all.

Chapter 45

The call from Paul Lawrence came a few moments after I completed a three-mile run along the beach. I flopped into my chair to towel off and my cell phone rang. I checked the number and scooped it up off the card table.

"Jack, hold on a moment," Lawrence said. "I'm conferencing Walt."

I carried the phone inside my trailer, filled a mug with hour-old coffee, returned to my chair, and lit a smoke before Lawrence came back on the line.

"Walt, Jack, can you both hear me?" Lawrence said.

"Yes," I said.

"Same here," Walt said.

"I'm your silent partner for the moment," Lawrence said. "My bosses have agreed to let me reactivate the Gertz file if you bring something convincing enough if and when you get a meeting with Koch."

"That's it?" Walt said.

"Do you know the shit storm that will blow through DC if you fuck this up?" Lawrence said. "From the president on down the line, my bosses will be called on the carpet and they'll feed me to the hungry mouths to quiet things down."

"What constitutes fucking up?" Walt said.

"A pissed-off powerhouse of a senator who wants to be VP screaming at the Bureau because some cop made accusations he can't prove," Lawrence said. "Like that."

"Senators are above questioning now?" Walt said.

"No, but Koch's fucking DC royalty, so it's kid gloves or nothing," Lawrence said. "If you're worth shit as a cop, and I know that you are, you'll come away from a nice friendly chat with Koch knowing if we should proceed or stop. Agreed?"

"Agreed," Walt said.

"Jack?" Lawrence said.

"I'm just a ride-along," I said.

"Bullshit," Lawrence said. "You wanted me in, I'm in, but my rules apply."

"I never expected otherwise," I said.

"First things first," Lawrence said. "Get the appointment with Koch."

"I'll get it," Walt said.

"Second thing, you call me immediately with the date and time," Lawrence said.

"No problem," Walt said.

"Third thing, I can be there in ninety minutes if need be," Lawrence said.

"Faster if donuts are involved," Walt said.

Lawrence cracked up, which relieved the tension among us. "If Koch is guilty, I want his dick in my trophy case as much as you do," he said. "Just remember that pesky little thing we call the Constitution also applies to senators."

"You have a trophy case full of dicks?" Walt said.

"Why not, I live in a city full of them," Lawrence said. "Call me ASAP when you got the meeting."

We said our goodbyes and I set the phone down. It immediately rang back.

"I'll be right over," Walt said.

I was beating up the heavy bag when Walt's sedan entered the beach. I gave it a few more whacks before I went in for two mugs of coffee. By the time I came out, Walt was closing his car door.

I gave Walt a mug and we both sat in lawn chairs.

"Paul is right," Walt said. "I was just jazzing him."

"I know. So does he."

"Congress is out for a month. I checked," Walt said. "Means we'll have to go to Maine. What do you know about Maine?"

"I can find it on a map," I said.

Walt took a sip of coffee. "That's more than I know," he said.

"So when will you make the call?"

"This afternoon."

"So you stopped by for my delicious coffee?"

"Unicorp International," Walt said.

"What is it and why do I want to know about it?" I said.

"The third largest private health insurance company in the country," Walt said. "That's what they are. Why you want to know is, they are relocating their home office in our beautiful state due to large tax breaks. Their security director refuses to leave his present home in Miami, so they're on the lookout for a new one. I can get you an interview if you want it."

"How?"

"These companies usually try to hire ex-cops for the security slots," Walt said. "Their recruitment people call local captains to see who might be available. I told them I knew just the guy. They're waiting for my call back."

I grabbed my smokes and lit one.

"I realize how hard it must be to give all this up," Walt said and waved his hand at my trailer. "But this kind of opportunity doesn't knock very often."

I blew smoke and nodded. "Call them," I said.

"Right after I call Senator Fuck You and set up an appointment," Walt said.

"I better get myself a new suit, then," I said.

"Take my advice and let Janet pick it out," Walt said. "And maybe get a new pair of shoes as well."

"Go make your phone call," I said. "And I'll worry about my clothes."

Chapter 46

A look of frustration on the tailor's face was cause enough for Janet to stand up from her chair and walk to the mirrors where I was fidgeting uncomfortably inside a new suit jacket.

"Problem?" Janet said.

"No," I said.

"Yes," the tailor said. "Most men who wear a fifty-two jacket have considerable girth in the waist. Look how badly this jacket hangs on him."

Janet looked.

I looked.

The tailor sighed.

"Can you take the waist in a bit?" Janet said.

"A bit?" the tailor said.

"Why don't you take measurements while I pick out some shirts and ties," Janet said.

The tailor sighed again. "Let me get some chalk."

About an hour later, Janet and I walked down Main Street, me carrying a shopping bag full of new shirts and ties. A stub for my new suit was safely tucked away in my wallet, which was growing thinner by the moment, but just heavy enough for the new shoes I was about to buy. That took forty-five minutes as Janet drove the clerk and me crazy trying to find the right shoes for my new suit.

With yet another bag inside the shopping bag, we held hands and continued our walk. We stopped at an outdoor ice cream shop where we ordered two dishes. Janet went with maple walnut. I had vanilla, because I'm that kind of guy.

"What would a manager of security do for an insurance company?" Janet said. She ate ice cream by licking both sides of her spoon.

"I think it's called director of security, and I have no idea," I said. "I imagine since they deal with insurance, it has to do with insurance fraud."

"I imagine so," Janet said. "Healthcare and fraud seem to go hand in hand. You wouldn't believe what goes on at the hospital."

I ate some vanilla ice cream. It was speckled with tiny black vanilla bean dots.

"When is your interview?" Janet said.

"As soon as Walt gets back to me."

"And the thing you're doing for Bob Gordon?"

"Even if they hire me on the spot, it will be a month or more before they've relocated," I said. "I can do both."

"Meaning you're in it to the end," Janet said.

"Don't say it like that," I said.

"How should I say it?"

"How about, 'I have every confidence in you to solve the missing-persons case before you start your new job, which I'm sure you will excel at as well'?" I said.

"And if you don't solve it by our wedding?"

I looked at Janet over my dish of ice cream.

"I sound like a real bitch, don't I?" Janet said.

"No, but just enough to drive a man to drink," I said.

Janet's usually wide friendly eyes hardened to slits. "Don't ever say that again, Jack," she said. "Not even as a joke. Tell me to shut up, mind my own business, or quit being a bitch, but never say that to me again."

I ate some ice cream while I mulled that over. "You're not being a bitch and telling a woman to shut up is like asking cows to fly," I said. "All I want you to understand is I'd like to finish what I started."

"I guess that since you wouldn't be involved in this unless I asked you to be, that sounds like a reasonable request," Janet said.

I ate some more ice cream. "How do you like my new suit?"

Janet smirked. "It will be a miracle if he gets it to fit you properly."

"Hey, I'm a big believer in miracles," I said. "It's a miracle a beautiful, intelligent woman like you is interested in a mutt like me."

Janet stared at me for a moment.

"What?" I said.

"I have a shift in four hours," Janet said. "That gives us enough time to return to your love nest on the beach where I will rip your clothes off and ravish you."

So every once in a while I say the right thing. I started to get up from the chair.

"Finish your ice cream," Janet said. "You'll need the calories."

I was sipping coffee in my chair while Janet saved some time by taking a shower in my trailer. I lit a smoke and watched the sedan cruise slowly toward me. I recognized it immediately.

By the time my cigarette was spent, Walt emerged from his sedan. I lit a fresh smoke as he walked toward me.

"Pack an overnight bag," Walt said. "We leave for Maine tomorrow morning."

I drew in on my cigarette and then blew a picture-perfect smoke ring.

Chapter 47

We took Walt's sedan for the drive to Maine. He was on official business. The sedan was an official-looking car. Of course, Walt being Walt, I couldn't smoke in it and had to wait for a rest stop.

The drive was long, boring, and uneventful. Most long drives are, even the scenic routes, which this one wasn't.

Walt had spoken to Chad Handler, Senator Koch's personal assistant, who arranged for the meeting to take place aboard Koch's sailboat in the town of Boothbay Harbor.

With Congress out for a month or more, Koch was back at home and working from his office in Portland. He took a few weeks' vacation with his wife, Melissa, according to Chad, and would be sailing up the coast tomorrow. Hence the meeting scheduled for four o'clock today.

"I've always wanted to see the rocky coast of Maine," Walt said.

"I'm more interested in lighthouses," I said.

I talked Walt into a quick stop at the Portland Head Light on the way north. We were about an hour from the border of Maine when we stopped for gas and a quick coffee. I had a state map, which I spread out on the hood, and traced a path on it with a yellow highlighter. Even with the stop at the lighthouse, we would arrive in Boothbay an hour or more early.

Walt came out of the rest stop complex with two containers of coffee and a lemon Danish for each of us. While he munched his, I smoked a cigarette, and then we were back on the road. We stopped once more for coffee and a back stretch, then we drove straight through the remaining four hours to the town of Boothbay.

My initial reaction to Boothbay Harbor was a picture postcard come to life. Narrow streets lined with shops, restaurants, and ice cream parlors, tourists everywhere, sun and salt sea air; all that was missing was Norman Rockwell and a little dog.

The view of the harbor alone was worth the price of admission. Wide and filled with every type of boat imaginable, the harbor was obviously the center-ring attraction. Walt and I stood on the edge of a long dock along with hundreds of others and scanned the collection of boats. Yachts, power boats, sailboats of all sizes littered the landscape.

"That one," Walt said and pointed to a thirty-two-foot-long sailing vessel moored a hundred yards into the bay.

I didn't ask how Walt picked it out. The name in bold lettering on the forward side read *Melissa One,* Melissa being Koch's wife.

I could see activity on deck. Too far away to make out faces. I watched as a man in a dinghy was lowered by a motorized crane to the water. Once the boat was floating, the man started the engine and steered toward the dock.

"My bet is that's our ride," Walt said.

The dinghy came closer. The man piloting it wore a bright yellow pullover shirt and tan chinos. As he came closer, I could see he was a large man with a baby face.

"Does he know it's us?" Walt said.

"The only two men wearing business suits on a dock full of tourists in shorts, I think so," I said.

"It's keen observations like that which remind me why you're such a great detective," Walt said.

"Observing the obvious is a practiced skill," I said.

The dinghy arrived. The man tossed Walt a rope and stepped onto the deck. He grinned and said, "I'm Chad Handler. Which one of you is Captain Grimes?"

"That would be me," Walt said.

"Chad Handler," Chad said again, and gave Walt his right hand.

Up close, I put Chad at around forty-two, maybe forty-three years old, athletic build, sandy hair with blue eyes.

"My associate John Bekker," Walt said.

Chad didn't shake my hand. He took the rope from Walt and said, "Let's shove off. The Senator is most anxious to meet you."

"Really?" Walt said. He stepped into the dinghy, followed by me and then Chad.

"You'll stay for dinner?" Chad said. "Lobster, of course."

"Of course," Walt said.

CHAPTER 48

I know squat about sailboats. I have no idea what a thirty-two-foot-long luxury sailboat would cost, but if I had to guess, I would say it set Senator Koch back fifteen million for his floating palace. The tax alone on it would buy an average home in the suburbs.

After Walt and I boarded by the gangway ladder, Chad came up behind us and polished our fingerprints off the brass railing with a handkerchief. "The Senator is aft with Mrs. Koch," he said.

We followed Chad to the rear of the boat where Oliver Koch sat at a beautiful table with a cocktail. Melissa Koch also had a cocktail, but she drank hers from the sunken Jacuzzi centered in the deck.

"Senator, Captain Grimes and his associate," Chad said.

Koch stood up from the table. He was about six-foot-four, ramrod straight, had thick black hair that could have been dyed, and looked at us with a dark piercing stare I imagined was learned from decades of addressing Congress.

"Chad, tell the captain to take us out at seven knots," Koch said. "And then ask the chef to start dinner."

"Right away, Senator," Chad said, snapped to and went away.

"Captain Grimes, I didn't catch your associate's name," Koch said.

"Bekker," I said. "John Bekker. Retired detective. Now private."

"I see," Koch said as I handed him my business card. "Two K's. Interesting spelling."

"My roots go back to Holland," I said. "They're not very good spellers in Holland."

"I see," Koch said, dryly. "Well, come join me, gentlemen, and let's get the party started. Would you care for a drink?"

"A Coke with ice," Walt said.

"Ginger ale with ice," I said. "A twist of lemon."

"Mel, could you do the honors?" Koch said. "And make mine a gin and tonic."

The three of us took seats at the table. In my peripheral vision, I saw Melissa Koch rise up from the Jacuzzi and step out of it. She was a striking woman of fifty-three, with dark hair and a full figure. She twisted herself into a white robe before going to the bar for the drinks.

Koch drank the last sip from his tall glass and set it on a coaster. "I must admit, it came as quite a surprise when Chad told me a police captain called with new information about the old Sarah Gertz case."

"Things have a way of popping up when you least expect them," Walt said.

"Yes," Koch said. "Well, tell me what you have and how I can help with it?"

"I'll let John start, seeing as how he initiated things," Walt said.

Koch shifted his eyes to me. Behind me, I heard ice clinking in glasses and liquid being poured.

"I'm employed by a law firm to find a baby that was put up for adoption forty years ago," I said. "My—"

"Why?" Koch said.

I was immediately aware that he was a man used to interrupting and not being chaffed about doing so.

"It's unrelated," I said. "The client doesn't have long to live and he wants to leave his estate to his biological daughter after he's gone."

Melissa Koch came to the table with a tray and set the tray down. Up close she was a five-foot ten-inch beauty. "One Coke, one ginger ale, one gin and tonic."

"Thank you, sweetie," Koch said. "Please continue, Mr. Bekker."

Melissa nodded and went away. I heard footsteps as she went below deck.

"My investigation took a few twists and turns, and it turns out my client's daughter is Sarah Gertz," I said.

"That's unfortunate," Koch said. "For all involved."

"Yes, it is," I said.

"So how does her disappearance in Washington involve a police captain back east twelve years later?" Koch said. He picked up his gin and tonic and took a small sip.

"Some new—" I said.

The boat suddenly moved forward.

"We're under way is all," Koch said.

I picked up my ginger ale and took a sip, then replaced it on the tray. "Some new developments led me to contact Captain Grimes and give him the information. He felt it warranted a second look."

"I see," Koch said. "What information?"

"The FBI and Metro dusted her car and removed hair fibers and all that, but they had the car towed into evidence," I said.

"So?" Koch said.

The boat turned and picked up speed.

"So because they never drove the car, they were unaware that the seat and mirrors were adjusted for someone at least six feet two inches tall. Almost a half foot taller than Sarah Gertz," I said.

"Interesting," Koch said. "So you think someone else drove

her car home the night she disappeared?"

"Not think, know," I said. "She would not have been able to see a thing in the mirrors and would have had to sink so low in the seat she'd have no windshield visibility."

"Really interesting," Koch said. "But it doesn't tell me how I can help you."

"Now that we know she didn't drive her car home that night, it adds a new dimension to an old case," Walt said. "There is now a potential male suspect."

"Were there any prints on the steering wheel?" Koch said.

"Wiped clean, as were the doors," I said.

"How well did you know Sarah Gertz?" Walt said. "Enough to make small talk about a boyfriend or a hot date?"

"I knew her from her participation at committee meetings regarding environmental issues," Koch said. "I do remember that she was highly efficient and a good speaker in public. Two, maybe three times she addressed the full Senate and made quite an impression even on us old-timers."

"I know it's a long time ago, but did you ever see her meet anybody before or after a meeting?" Walt said. "A man, woman, anybody?"

Koch picked up his glass and took a sip. "I couldn't recall with any accuracy," he said. "Twelve years ago is a long time. Maybe at the time if the Metro police had discovered the seat thing and asked then, I might have been able to provide a better answer."

Melissa returned wearing a blue sleeveless sundress with sandals. "Chad wants to know how many lobsters to tell the chef to cook?" she said.

Koch looked at us. "Say two apiece and we'll all have a small steak on the side," he said.

"I'll tell him," Melissa said and took off again.

"This is quite a boat," Walt said.

"Yes, it is," Koch agreed. "Unfortunately I get to take her out just a few weeks during the year. Here in Boothbay and down in Florida during the holiday recess."

"Could you recall with any inaccuracy?" I said.

Koch looked at me and for the first time I saw a fleeting moment of confusion in his eyes. "Inaccuracy?" he said. "I'm not sure I understand what that means."

"Something you're not sure of and wouldn't testify to under oath," I said.

"Well, let me think about that for a moment," Koch said.

From behind me, Chad said, "Think about what, Senator?"

"It appears some new details on the old Sarah Gertz missing-persons case have come to light," Koch said. "The police now know her car was driven by a much taller person the night she disappeared. They would like to know if I remember anything about her social life that could be useful to them."

Chad slid into a chair to my left and looked at me. "Like what?" he said with a dazzling smile.

"A boyfriend or a male companion about six feet two inches tall or so seen in her company," Walt said. "Like that."

"I can't say that I have," Chad said. "Have you read the old statements from twelve years ago? Maybe something was mentioned then that might be useful."

"We did and no," I said.

"I have to admit there isn't anything I can think of that might be of help to you," Koch said. "Neither I nor members of my staff met the woman outside of a meeting situation. The only men I can remember seeing her with were fellow members of her group or my staff."

"And you can speak for your entire staff of twelve years ago?" I said. "Who they met after work, where they went and with whom?"

For the second time, Koch's guard dropped just a bit. "Why

no, I can't," he said. "But surely you don't think anyone from my staff had anything to do with her disappearance?"

"Now see here," Chad said. His face was a sudden ugly, dark mask of anger. "The Senator is about to unleash his bid for the VP nod come next election. Any hint of wrongdoing on the part of his staff, even if it's twelve years old, is a death sentence. I won't allow you to—"

"You won't allow?" Walt said.

"Relax, Chad," Koch said.

Chad sat back in his chair with a deep breath.

"I'm afraid my assistant is rather protective of me," Koch said. "To answer your question, I have no idea what most of my staff in Maine or Washington does on their own time, twelve years ago or right now. But, please understand that each member of my staff is highly vetted before hired. Even our volunteers are background checked before we allow them on board."

"Your staff isn't in question," Walt said. "Unless you think there is a reason they should be."

"No, of course not," Koch said.

"That guy," Chad said, suddenly.

"What?" Koch said.

Chad turned to face Koch. "Sure, I remember now. I didn't think anything of it at the time, who would?"

"What are you talking about?" Koch said.

Walt and I exchanged a quick, casual glance.

"That one time her car broke down and she was late for a meeting on offshore drilling," Chad said. "She said she got a ride from her friend and asked if he could wait in the House lounge. I saw him for like two seconds. I couldn't tell you what he looked like, but he was at least as tall as me and I'm six-one and a half."

"How do you know that?" Walt said.

"The split second I saw him he was standing next to her and he was a full head taller," Chad said.

"Why didn't you mention that then?" Koch said.

"It's never come up before," Chad said. "And I never gave it a thought. I mean, people get rides all the time. Who remembers?"

"It probably means nothing, but can you remember anything about this man, anything at all?" Walt said.

Chad stared at Walt for a moment, and then slowly shook his head. "It was just for that second," he said. "And a long time ago. I'm sorry."

"No need," Walt said. "It's very old dirt we're digging around in and it's probably nothing."

"Is there anything else?" Koch said. "If not, I'd like to give you a tour before dinner."

CHAPTER 49

To call the *Melissa One* grand would be an understatement. Four bedrooms, as many bathrooms, a full galley, living room with theatre, pool table, wine closet, and it was piloted by the captain from a walk-in station on the second deck.

The rich cherry wood interior glistened from coats of polish. Gleaming brass was everywhere and without a smudge or fingerprint in sight.

After the tour, we returned to the deck and the dining table portside. The boat was no longer moving, anchored about six, maybe seven miles out to sea. The water was calm. Gulls had started to gather around us as the chef served dinner. A white wine was served that the chef said complimented the lobster, but I opted for water with a slice of lemon.

Koch sat at the head of the table with Melissa opposite him. I sat to her right, Walt to her left and Chad at his place beside Koch. It was an interesting pecking order.

"It's no secret that I'm chasing the VP nod next election, so I would appreciate it if my name wasn't used in your investigation if possible," Koch said to Walt.

"Like I said, Senator, this is all preliminary and will probably go nowhere," Walt said. "I wouldn't worry about it too much."

"Captain Grimes, what my husband is trying to say in his DC speak is that in today's media frenzy age, even a grain of sand's worth of scandal can do him in and ruin his chances for the nod," Melissa said.

I shifted my eyes to Koch. He was looking at his wife with a painted smile on his lips. It was the kind of smile that, if you read it right, told you the one smiling was genuinely pissed-off mad at the person he was smiling at.

"I wouldn't let it worry you or the Senator, Mrs. Koch," Walt said. "There was very little twelve years ago and there is very little now, so media coverage won't happen unless a mysterious stranger steps forward and says, 'I did it.' "

Koch's face loosened up and he took a sip of wine. "Well, let's enjoy this fresh Maine lobster, shall we," he said cheerfully.

The sunset was shimmering off the calm waters of the Atlantic Ocean by the time dinner and dessert were consumed. A call from below on the house phone caused Koch to excuse himself. "A staff aide from DC," he said and went below.

Chad and Melissa Koch stayed on deck with Walt and I as the boat traveled at about nine or ten knots back to the harbor.

"I never get tired of the sunset at sea," Chad said.

"So what do you do now?" Melissa said to Walt.

"Go back to the office, shuffle some papers, and hope another lead pops up," Walt said. "Otherwise this old case stays old and unsolved."

Melissa looked at me. "And you, Mr. Bekker?"

"I was hired to find out what happened to a missing person," I said. "I found out."

An intercom speaker on deck crackled and Koch said, "Chad, I need you on this call for a moment."

"Duty calls," Chad said and went below.

Melissa waited until Chad was safely out of earshot, then said, "So Mr. Bekker, you found out what happened to Sarah Gertz, but you haven't found her."

"No," I said.

"You strike me as a man who never gives up," Melissa said.

"Do I?"

"Yes," Melissa said. "And I'm not so sure that's a good thing."

Walt turned his head to look at Melissa, but she was focused on the setting sun.

Nothing else was said until the boat neared its mooring point and Chad reappeared on deck.

"The Senator is still on the phone," he said. "He said to tell you to call anytime if he can be of additional help. I'll take you back to shore."

Melissa looked at me with a strange, tiny smile. "It was a pleasure meeting you, and watch your step," she said.

"My step?"

"Getting into the dinghy."

"Right."

Chad got into the dinghy first, followed by Walt and then me. We managed to watch our step. Melissa stood along the rail as Chad started the motor and we pulled away.

"Remember, Mr. Bekker, watch your step!" Melissa called out as we put some distance between us and the sailboat.

The water wasn't as calm as earlier. A wind had picked up, roughing the waters. My hair and jacket were wet with salty spray by the time we reached the dock.

Walt got out first. I was about to step onto the dock when Chad took my left arm.

"Senator Koch is a great man, an important man," Chad said. "He's a genius and the next VP and after that, who knows."

"Sure," I said. "You want to let go of my arm?"

Chapter 50

"A great man, an important man, a genius, he can kiss my ass in Macy's window," Walt said as he started his car.

"Ass-kissing in windows aside, do you believe him?" I said.

"Not a fucking word," Walt said. "That *it was so long ago* bullshit, and the way he looked at his wife when she explained what he meant at dinner, like he was outraged anyone dared question his words of immortality. I think he's a fucking ego-driven psycho with money."

"You heard his wife, that *watch your step* warning," I said.

"She wasn't talking about the gangway," Walt said. "That much I know."

"I'm not sure if the warning was about her husband or Chad," I said.

"That guy's a piece of work," Walt said. "I think he's got a little bromance going with Koch to the point he'd do anything for him."

"Believe his story about the fleeting glance?" I said.

"I think if we said the car was driven by a one-eyed female midget with a limp and a machine gun, that's what he would have said," Walt said. "I'll tell you this much, he had no fear of me, but you scared him shitless."

"Know why that is?" I said.

"I have to work within the limits of my badge," Walt said. "You don't."

"Stop for gas before it gets too late," I said. "I want to call Paul."

Ninety miles down Interstate 95 South, we pulled into a rest stop for gas, coffee, and Tums to quell the afterburn of lobster and steak.

We ate Tums first, then sipped the coffee while I placed a call to Lawrence's personal cell phone. He didn't answer. I left a message and lit a cigarette to await the return call.

It came on the second cigarette.

Lawrence was at home. I could hear a Washington Nationals baseball game in the background. I gave him the short version of our meeting, finished the cigarette, and ate two more Tums.

"It could be he really doesn't want any waves to screw up his VP bid," Lawrence said. "Or it could be he really does know something that we should but don't."

"Keep your ear to the wall," I said. "If our visit gets casually mentioned around the Bureau in the next day or so, he's hiding something and that's his way of telling us to back off."

"Oh, it will get mentioned," Lawrence said. "DC style."

"Let me know what you hear and then I'll start bugging his silver spoon ass," I said.

"Will do," Lawrence said.

We got back on the road and drove thirty miles in silence before Walt said, "I wasn't going to say anything until we got back, but you got an interview with Unicorp International."

"When?" I said.

"Two or three weeks the HR director flies up to conduct a recruitment search," Walt said. "He's already sold on you. All you got to do is sell yourself."

"What am I worth?" I said.

"About a buck ninety-seven in minerals after you're dead."

"To them alive."

"Hundred and twenty-five K plus full benefits," Walt said. "Stock options and a good ten years to build up the old 401K."

"Good thing I bought this nifty new suit," I said.

"It's not that bad a deal, Jack," Walt said.

"I didn't say it was," I said.

"Janet and the kids are worth putting a tie on five days a week," Walt said.

"I didn't say they weren't," I said.

"But you'd rather be chasing bad guys stone broke all the time?" Walt said.

"Two or three weeks, I'll be there," I said.

"A lot can happen in two or three weeks," Walt said.

I looked at Walt. "I hope so," I said.

Chapter 51

For thirty-six hours I played things close to the vest. I did a five-mile run on the beach, worked the heavy bag, took naps, and watched a ball game with Oz. Janet was free for dinner and I took her and the kids to a Mexican place near the mall. I had Tums before the meal was served and a few for dessert.

I told Janet about my upcoming job interview with Unicorp International.

"It sounds like a really good deal, Jack," Janet said.

"It is," I said. "I'll have to tell them about our honeymoon plans, but I don't think they would object knowing about it going in."

"Does this mean you won't have time to practice baseball with me anymore?" Mark said.

"I'll probably have more time," I said. "As I'll be living with you."

"Cool," Mark said.

"Yeah, cool," Janet agreed.

That was the moment Paul Lawrence chose to call me on my cell phone. I had it on vibrate, excused myself from the table, and went to the men's room.

"Paul, Jack," I said.

"What's that echo?"

"I'm in the men's room of a Mexican restaurant."

"Alone?"

"And door's locked. Go ahead."

"It seems Koch's assistant made a few calls to the Bureau to discreetly inquire as to the status of the Gertz missing-persons case," Lawrence said.

"He give a reason?"

"He said a local police captain and private investigator claimed they reopened the case based on some new evidence," Lawrence said. "He said they met with Koch over dinner and discussed the details."

"We had lobster and steak," I said.

"Yummy."

"Gave me heartburn. Still got it. What did the Bureau tell old Chad?"

"Koch's assistant?"

"His name is Chad."

"Peachy," Lawrence said. "He was told the Bureau has no plans to reactivate the case unless some new evidence comes to light."

"He buy it?"

"Doubt it, but what's his choice?" Lawrence said. "So what are you going to do?"

"Use my charm and winning personality to beguile the good senator," I said.

"Put a bug up his ass," Lawrence said.

"And anywhere else it will fit."

"Walt?"

"Hang by my side until a coconut falls from the tree."

"Update me as much as possible."

"More, even."

I hung up and returned to the table.

Janet had the look on her face. "Everything okay?"

"Better than okay," I said, thinking about *Okay*. "What should we have for dessert?"

"How about some Tums?" Janet suggested.

Chapter 52

From my favorite perch in the lawn chair, I lifted my coffee mug, took a sip, and lit a cigarette. Then I called Chad on the cell number I got from Walt. A recorded message took me to his voicemail and I left a message.

It was three minutes past eight in the morning.

Chad was probably asleep in his luxury stateroom.

I killed some time by thinking about Unicorp International. I'd been a cop for sixteen years, a drunk for twelve, sober for one, and the last time I had a job that required going to an office was never.

I could talk myself blue in the face trying to convince myself that director of security for a health insurance company would be interesting work, but I knew in my heart that it wasn't.

What it came down to was stability for my soon-to-be ready-made family. I owed that much to Janet and more to Regan. I owed them everything, so a jacket and tie and a little boredom was a small price to pay for my balance due.

The upside was a lot more steady income for very little hard work. Not a bad tradeoff for ties, meetings, and the gobs of paperwork that I was sure came with the position.

I went inside for more coffee, lit another smoke, and dialed the number for Chad again. His recorded message took me to the voicemail and I left a second callback message.

I thought about Unicorp International a bit more to kill some time, and when I placed a third call to Chad's cell phone it was almost nine-twenty. I toyed with the idea of making some breakfast, didn't, and decided a trip to town with Oz was what the doctor ordered.

I was about to go in and change when my cell phone rang. I checked the incoming number, saw it was Chad, and let it ring three more times before I answered the call.

"John Bekker Investigations," I said as I lit a fresh cigarette.

"Mr. Bekker, Chad Handler," Chad said. "I'm returning your call. I assume you have a question or some new information to share."

"A break, possibly," I said.

"Really?" Chad said in a tone of slight disbelief.

"I found a witness that was overlooked twelve years ago," I said.

"Witness?"

"She was on her way to the airport and just entering a cab when Sarah's car arrived and a man got out," I said. "She lives in Sarah's building, but was gone a month visiting her daughter in Florida and was never interviewed. She still lives there, which I found out when I got curious about remaining tenants in Sarah's building."

"What did she say?" Chad said.

His voice had a slightly anxious tone in it.

"She said she had a real good look at him as she entered the cab," I said. "She described him as about thirty, six-one or -two, blond hair and blue eyes, athletic build. Sarah wasn't in her car, but the witness assumed she'd lent it to him and he was returning it."

"Isn't that description twelve years old?" Chad said. "Wouldn't that person look much different today?"

"Not necessarily," I said. "I would bet you look pretty much the way you did ten years ago, minus a few lines around the eyes. Am I right?"

There was a short, tension-filled pause in the conversation.

"Anyway, why I'm calling you is to see if possibly the man you saw with Sarah that day fits the description of the man I just described," I said.

"Except for the height, I really couldn't say with any accuracy," Chad said. "It was a long time ago, and as I've already told you, it was a fleeting glance at best."

His voice was cold to disguise his anger. I've heard that tone before, many times before when I've struck a nerve interviewing a suspect.

"Do me a favor and think about it," I said. "Something might pop up. I'll call you in a few days, okay?"

"We'll be traveling," Chad said.

"I'm sure I'll be able to reach you," I said. "And you know how to reach me."

"Goodbye, Mr. Bekker," Chad said and my phone went dead.

As they say in old detective novels, the game was afoot.

Chad did his best to hide his annoyance, but it seeped into his voice despite his best efforts to appear cool and calm. Below the surface, Chad was seething with rage.

Because I had the audacity to disturb his sleep?

Because he saw through my ruse and knew I was talking about him?

Because I was baiting him?

Or because, like most of the beautiful privileged, he felt he was beyond questioning?

Maybe all.

I took Oz for breakfast and thought about it.

For the moment, Unicorp International was forgotten.

CHAPTER 53

Percy Meade looked at me from across his desk. I had just presented him with receipts for travel expenses and requested an additional ten thousand dollars. He scanned the receipts and reports compiled expertly by Oz, then shifted them to the corner of his desk.

"Mr. Gordon is fading fast, I'm afraid," Meade said. "He no longer has the strength to get out of bed except for a few minutes at a time."

"I'm sorry to hear that," I said.

Meade nodded. "Will you stay on after he passes?"

"It's gone beyond that at this point," I said.

"I don't understand."

"If you settled my bill and said my services were no longer required, I would continue on my own time and pay my own way," I said.

"Why?"

"I don't know," I said. "Maybe because Sarah Gertz can't speak for herself and somebody has to, and there isn't anybody else?"

Meade nodded as he opened a bottom desk drawer and removed a fat white envelope. "That's twelve thousand," he said. "I anticipated on the high side."

I picked up the envelope and tucked it into my right pants pocket as I stood up. "I'll be in touch, Mr. Meade," I said.

"You meant what you said about continuing on even if funds

are cut off?" Meade said.

"I did."

"Even if we lose Mr. Gordon before you reach a conclusion, I'll make sure you're funded well enough to carry on," Meade said.

"Why?"

"Maybe because Sarah Gertz can't speak for herself," Meade said.

Chapter 54

Boothbay Harbor was crowded to the breaking point. Every available parking space at the five municipal lots I passed on my walk from a back street to the waterfront was full.

I parked on a narrow side street fifteen minutes from downtown where curbside parking was allowed, and free. I wore casual chinos with a white collared shirt and loafers. I wore my best sunglasses, which, needless to say, were twelve bucks off the local drugstore counter.

I made the drive alone. I didn't tell Walt, Lawrence, or Janet where I was going, I just got in the Marquis and drove north until I arrived at Boothbay Harbor.

I had no real plan in place, unless winging it was considered a plan.

I lit a cigarette as I reached the edge of the dock. People were lined up by the hundreds for whale-watching tours, fishing expeditions, and so on. I stayed back to finish my smoke, then mingled my way through the crowds until I could see the *Melissa One* moored in the bay.

Some activity was taking place on deck. I was too far away to make it out and I didn't have binoculars, but I spotted the next best thing. I made my way to the bank of quarter-fed, stand-mounted binoculars and dropped in two quarters.

I swung the heavy binoculars and zoomed in on the *Melissa One*. Chad was talking to Melissa Koch. She was dressed casually in a summer pantsuit, straw hat, and sunglasses.

Together, they climbed into the dinghy. Chad started the engine and steered toward the dock. I stayed put at the binoculars under cover of the thousand tourists milling about.

The dinghy arrived. Chad got out first and gave a hand to Melissa as she stepped up to the dock. They said a few words, then Chad got back into the dinghy and headed back to the *Melissa One.*

Melissa Koch slowly made her way through the milling tourists to the street. She paused for a moment, then turned left and started walking.

I stayed about a half block behind her as she went into a women's boutique, an antique store, a bookstore, and then crossed over to the other side of the street. She hadn't purchased anything yet. She repeated the in-and-out procedure in six more shops.

She wasn't window-shopping. She wasn't shopping at all. She needed something to occupy her time and fill the wasted hours of Jacuzzi and cocktail sessions.

At the end of the block, Melissa crossed to the next street. The browsing continued for another hour or so until she stopped at an outdoor café for a cup of coffee.

I watched from across the street as a waiter brought her the coffee. She delicately picked up the cup and took a sip, held it under her nose, and stared off into space.

I crossed the street at the end of the block and came toward Melissa as she was taking another sip. Her gaze fell on me and she blinked as if startled.

"Mrs. Koch," I said. "Well, this is a surprise."

"Mr. Bekker," Melissa said. "What are you doing here?"

"Sightseeing," I said. "May I join you for a cup?"

"I . . . don't think that would be a good idea," she said with a slight hesitation.

"I won't bite," I said. "Just a cup of coffee and some friendly chit-chat."

Melissa grinned at me from under her straw hat. "I doubt you've ever made chit-chat in your life," she said. "You don't look to be the chit-chat type."

I slid out the chair opposite Melissa and waved to a waiter. "One coffee for me, please," I told him.

"You've been following me, haven't you?" Melissa said.

"Not intentionally," I said. "I spotted you and got curious what you were doing."

"Killing time, taking a walk," Melissa said. "There is only so much you can do on a boat, Mr. Bekker."

"No bodyguard or escort?"

"Dressed as I am, who would recognize me?" Melissa said. "Would you recognize the wife of the senator of your state alone in public?"

"I wouldn't even recognize the senator," I said.

The waiter set a cup of coffee in front of me. I took a small sip. It was pretty good.

"So unintentional or not, why did you follow me?" Melissa said.

"Curious about your warning," I said.

"What warning is that, Mr. Bekker?"

"Watch your step, not sure if it's a good thing if I don't give up," I said. "That."

Melissa took another sip from her cup and set it down. "I was just making chit-chat," she said.

"No, you weren't."

"It's not polite to call the wife of a senator a liar," Melissa said.

"It's also not polite to assume I'm stupid," I said.

"Is that what I'm doing?"

"Look, Mrs. Koch, we can tap dance all afternoon, but I have better things to do," I said.

I started to stand up.

"Wait," Melissa said. "Sit. Please."

I sat. "You forgot to say good boy and give me a treat."

Melissa Koch showed me a genuine smile and it was a dazzler.

"So how many women has your husband cheated on you with, and was Sarah Gertz one of them?" I said.

The smile slowly faded.

"Am I that much of a foregone conclusion?" Melissa said.

"No, but your husband is," I said. "He reeks of wolf in heat."

Melissa sipped coffee and then sighed. "Do you know what happens to men when they gain power and go to Washington?" she said. "They become little boys with giant libidos. Oliver is no exception. Oh, he's discreet, I'll give him that, and he did slow down a bit until that damn Viagra came along, but to give you a number, I couldn't guess."

"Sarah Gertz?" I said.

"I have no idea," Melissa said. "Oliver doesn't share his conquests with me."

"How does he keep a lid on things?"

"Chad runs interference, mostly," Melissa said. "Gets him women at the DC house, which is in Chad's name, by the way. Chad worships the ground Oliver walks on, as I'm sure you picked up on already."

"The warning is about Chad, isn't it?" I said.

"Chad can be quite ugly when he feels Oliver is being threatened," Melissa said.

"Violent?"

"He's a screamer for sure, but I've never seen him resort to violence."

"Scream at you?"

"Even Chad isn't that stupid," Melissa said. "He'll lower his voice and give me the look, but I draw the line at being yelled at."

"So what happened today you felt the need to get away?" I said.

"A slight tiff."

"About?"

"The campaign trail," Melissa said. "Chad is arranging a schedule of personal appearances around the country for me and I don't want to do it."

"Why not?"

"I have my reasons," Melissa said. "Now I've said enough and I have to go. Chad will be coming back for me shortly."

"I'll walk you back," I said.

"Not necessary, Mr. Bekker. I'm a big girl."

"I know, but I feel like aggravating Chad," I said.

Melissa stared at me for a moment, then showed me her smile again. "That might be fun at that," she said.

I left a ten-dollar bill to cover the two cups of coffee, then escorted Melissa to the dock, where in the distance I could see Chad getting into the dinghy. The crowd had thinned out. Most of the larger tour boats were out on excursions. Chad would have a clear line of sight to the dock and us.

From about fifty yards away, Chad spotted us. I could see an immediate change in his posture. As he steered the dinghy, his back went stiff, his body language showing his aggravation.

"Someone isn't happy," I said.

"It appears so," Melissa said.

The dinghy arrived. Chad jumped out onto the dock. His face was a hard mask of calmness that did little to disguise the fury bubbling under the skin.

"What are you doing here, Bekker?" Chad spat out.

"My friends call me John or Jack," I said. "People like you usually call me Mister Bekker or sir."

Under her straw hat, Melissa did her best to hide a grin.

"I asked you a question," Chad said.

"Which I'm under no obligation to answer," I said. "To you or anyone else."

"Mel, get in the dinghy," Chad snapped.

"Don't bark orders at me, Chad," Melissa said.

I turned to Melissa. "Thank you for the coffee and a wonderful conversation," I said. "I enjoyed both."

"What conversation?" Chad said and took Melissa by the left arm.

I put my hand on Chad's chest and shoved him backward into the water.

"Cool off, college boy," I said.

I took Melissa by the right hand and assisted her into the dinghy. "See you again, Mrs. Koch," I said.

Melissa grinned at me. "Probably not, Mr. Bekker," she said. "But then, who knows?"

CHAPTER 55

The call from Koch came less than twenty-four hours later. I was in my lawn chair having morning coffee with Oz. It was one of those perfect days at the beach. Eighty degrees without a cloud in the sky. The horizon beyond the beach was a wall of deep blue.

Oz had his notebook on his lap, a pen in hand, and reading glasses perched on his nose. "So you going to DC tomorrow morning and coming back the same day why?" he said.

"Build up my frequent flier miles," I said.

"And first class," Oz said.

"More leg room."

Oz looked at me over the rims of his reading glasses.

"And two bags of peanuts," he said.

"I'll save those for you," I said.

My cell phone rang. I scooped it up from the card table and checked the number before pressing Talk.

"Good morning, Senator," I said. "How are you?"

"Never mind the good morning crap," Koch snapped. "What do you think you're doing pushing my assistant into the water yesterday?"

"It was more like shoving," I said.

"Call it what you will, but you better have a good fucking reason."

"I didn't like the way he manhandled your wife," I said. "I'm funny that way."

"What are you . . . he did what?"

"I took a chance and drove up to see you," I said. "I met your wife on the dock and Chad went off the deep end for some reason. When he grabbed her arm, I gave him some cooling-off time."

After a short pause, Koch said, "I see."

"I'll pay for his dry cleaning if you'd like," I said.

"That won't be—what did you want to see me about?" Koch said.

"I'm going to DC to interview a witness that was overlooked twelve years ago," I said. "I know you said you couldn't remember seeing Sarah's friends or associates outside of meetings, but I have a decent description of the man seen driving her car. It might jar your memory."

"I see."

"About six foot two, athletic build, light blond or sandy hair, blue eyes, would have been about thirty at the time," I said.

"I would have to think on that," Koch said.

"Sure, no problem," I said. "I'll give you a call when I get back from DC."

"When are you leaving?"

"Tomorrow at eight on US Air," I said. "Returning at six forty-five."

"I'll think on it," Koch said. "Call me tomorrow evening."

"Bye, Senator," I said.

I set the phone on the card table and picked up my coffee.

"I don't think it's such a good idea pissing off a heavyweight senator like that, Bekker," Oz said.

"The way to force a cool-headed opponent into making mistakes is to remove the cool and make him angry," I said. "The more pissed off, the more mistakes he makes."

I scooped up my phone and dialed the cell number for Paul Lawrence. For once he answered his phone.

"Paul, John Bekker," I said.

"Well, don't you sound chipper," Lawrence said.

"Free for lunch tomorrow?" I said.

"Why, you coming here?"

"I am."

"Because?"

"To see if someone follows me."

"Wouldn't a trip to the store accomplish that?"

"I want to see to what lengths he will go."

"He being?"

"Our friend in Maine."

"Ah, code words," Lawrence said. "What time?"

"I'll be on the ground at ten and on the Mall by eleven," I said. "Let's meet at our favorite bench."

"All those benches, which is our favorite one?"

"The one with me sitting on it."

"Hey, bring a bag of—"

"Already on my list," I said.

"See you then," Lawrence said.

I tossed the cell phone on the card table and lit a fresh smoke.

"You think the Senator will make a stink?" Oz said.

"No," I said. "That would be like a guilty sign around his neck. He'll make some quiet inquiries to his powerful DC friends and let it go at that."

"For now?" Oz said.

"Yeah, for now," I agreed.

CHAPTER 56

I was playing a dangerous game of cat and mouse with a very powerful United States senator who had bigger claws than I have. I was trying to figure out how that was a good idea when the plane took off and we were suddenly airborne.

I chose first class because it boards first and I would have a bird's-eye view of the remaining two hundred and eighty passengers as they boarded the business flight to DC. Of them, I narrowed the field to an empty-handed man in a business suit who sat three rows behind first class, a large man wearing shorts and a Hawaiian shirt loud enough to cause blindness, and a skinny man in a suit with beady eyes.

The empty-handed man struck me as odd because on a business flight, business people are always loaded down with business-type junk. The Hawaiian shirt appeared too casual, like he had to work at it and the result caused the opposite effect. The beady-eyed guy made my list simply because it was my opinion beady-eyed guys were always up to no good. I had no proof of that theory, but I had no proof of a great many things that were true.

I waited until both bathrooms in first class were occupied, then I got up and strolled down the aisle to the two bathrooms at the rear of the plane. Empty-Hands had his nose buried in the complimentary airline magazine and didn't glance up as I passed him. Hawaiian Shirt had on earphones and was air-banding a drum solo, much to the discomfort of the man and woman on each side of him. Beady Eyes looked right at me as I passed him. Nothing registered, as he was just a looker, seeing what he could see, at least on the surface.

I stood in line for five minutes, then turned around and returned to my seat. I didn't get up again until the plane landed. Since I had no luggage except the box of Pat's Donuts I'd carried on, I scooted through baggage claim and outside to the cab stand.

I got in back of a very long line. As the line grew shorter, I stepped off to fake a call on my cell phone. I scanned the line and sidewalk. I didn't see Beady Eyes or Empty-Hands, but I picked up Hawaiian Shirt at the rear of the line. I got behind the four people behind Hawaiian Shirt and waited.

The line moved slowly. Even with cabs lined up around the block, the demand was too great to keep up with the ever-growing supply of new passengers. I could see Hawaiian Shirt start to fidget as he moved closer to the cab dispatcher. With me now behind him, he'd lost his advantage of following me. He'd have to rely upon his information and hope I didn't change my meeting place with Lawrence.

When he was third in line, Hawaiian Shirt suddenly spun around and announced loudly, "Anybody want to split a fare to the Mall! Going to the Mall, I'll split the fare."

I moved out of line. "Sure," I said.

A man behind me did the same. He moved up to me and we joined Hawaiian Shirt at the front. The dispatcher opened the rear door of the cab and we piled in with me on the right and Hawaiian Shirt on the left. I tried not to elbow the poor sap in the middle.

"Good idea," I said to Hawaiian Shirt.

"Saves a few bucks," he said.

Nothing else was said until we arrived at the Mall and split up the fare and tip. I took off toward the massive crowd inside the Mall grid. Hawaiian Shirt went in the opposite direction.

I lit a cigarette and hung back.

Hawaiian Shirt entered a coffee shop and reemerged wearing a dark gray, short-sleeved shirt that he must have had on underneath the brightly colored island shirt. He turned right and started walking at an even pace.

I skirted through the crowd and walked quite a way until I found an empty bench, took a seat, and fired up another cigarette. On my right side, I caught sight of Paul Lawrence as he walked with the crowd toward the bench.

When he arrived, I held out the bag as Lawrence took a seat next to me.

"Wait for it," I said.

"A tail," Lawrence said.

"A pro," I said. "Wore a shirt that wouldn't fit in on Hawaii and made sure I noticed it, then switched to a dark gray a while ago so I wouldn't be looking for it."

I smoked the cigarette to the filter, lit another, and then Lawrence said, "Gray shirt coming up on my left. About six-one or so, heavyset."

I let my peripheral vision do the work. "That's him," I said.

Gray Shirt walked past the bench without giving us a glance and continued on until I lost sight of him in the crowd.

"Koch's man?" Lawrence said.

"Or Chad's."

"Either way, the buck stops with Koch," Lawrence said. "So tell me what this is all about."

I gave Lawrence the short version of my little escapade on the dock with Chad and my conversation with Melissa Koch.

"So the good senator is a member of the all-boys club after all," Lawrence said.

"That in itself doesn't link him to Sarah Gertz," I said.

"No, but his discreet call to the Bureau, coupled with Gray

Shirt there, points the needle to G," Lawrence said.

"Of infidelity, not murder," I said. "How rare a thing is infidelity in this town?"

"About as rare as sand in the desert," Lawrence said.

"So Koch could be worried about his squeaky clean image and losing the VP nod?" I said.

"Something I'm curious about," Lawrence said. "Why do you think Melissa Koch refused to hit the campaign trail for her husband? If she's known he's cheating on her for years, it has to be something else."

"My guess is she just can't stand the guy anymore, but I plan to ask her that question a second time," I said. "In the meantime, let's go to lunch."

"Where?"

"Someplace we need to cab it so it drives Gray Shirt crazy trying to keep up with us," I said.

We walked to the edge of the Mall to the city cab stand and caught a ride to the Hill, where we had a pleasant lunch at a sidewalk café. If Gray Shirt managed to follow us, he was out of sight. We lingered over coffee and cake, then caught another cab to the airport where I left the driver a hundred dollars to cover Lawrence's trip back to his office.

"Call me when you hear something," Lawrence said. "Even if you think it's nothing."

"I don't think the Bureau will get another call from Koch," I said. "Not until I bug his wife some more."

"Have a good trip home," Lawrence said.

"Don't eat all those donuts alone," I said. "You might hurt yourself and I'd feel responsible."

I entered the terminal and wandered around for a while, then stopped at a café for a coffee. After that, I browsed in a large Hudson News stand, picked up the *Post,* and went for another coffee, where I skimmed the headlines.

I tossed the newspaper and wandered around the US Air terminal a bit more until I spotted Gray Shirt in the Hudson News stand, where he had his nose in a book. The book was upside down. His eyes were scanning faces over the top of the book. Before he picked me out, I turned and darted outside to the sidewalk.

Gray Shirt did exactly what I would have if I blew the tail and I knew where the tail would be at a certain time, namely US Air for a six-forty flight. I'd go there and wait for him to show up.

Except that I had booked a second flight home one-way on Delta that left in one hour and five minutes. I skirted into the Delta terminal, went through security to my gate, and was halfway home before Gray Shirt realized he'd been had.

Chapter 57

Keeping track of a US senator isn't that difficult if you know how the system works. When Congress is in session, their votes are recorded for public knowledge and much of their time is spent in the halls or their offices. When home on recesses, most post their schedule of activities on their websites. Town hall meetings, fundraising events, and so on. It's not difficult at all to figure out where and when they will be and for how long.

I used a computer at the library to access Koch's website, where I pulled up his schedule of events. He was the main speaker at a fundraiser for the governor in the grand ballroom of the Portland Marriott in two days. Tickets were two hundred and fifty dollars a plate. Some tickets were still available. I purchased one online with a credit card.

From the library I drove to the mall and rented a black-tie-affair tuxedo for three days at the wedding store.

When I arrived back at my trailer, Oz was seated in his favorite chair with his notebook on his lap. He peered over his reading glasses at the shopping bag with the wedding store logo on the side.

"Wedding's not for three months, isn't it?" Oz said.

"Eleven weeks if I count right," I said. "But this isn't a wedding tux. It's a black-tie-affair tux."

"For?"

"A gala event I will be attending to honor the esteemed governor of Maine for all his accomplishments," I said.

"You even know who the governor of Maine is?"

"No, but the main speaker is none other than Senator Oliver Koch," I said.

"The plot thickens," Oz said.

"It do, it do," I said. "Feel like a steak and a ball game?"

"Who don't?"

I filled the grill with new coals, squirted them with fire starter, and set them ablaze with a match. As the coals heated, I brewed a fresh pot of coffee and took it outside.

"So what are you planning to do at this event?" Oz said as I filled his mug.

"Nothing," I said as I filled my own.

"Just gonna sit there and listen to political speeches all night?" Oz said.

I took my chair and lit a smoke. "Ever see *Cool Hand Luke*?"

"Maybe?" Oz said. "Old prison chain-gang movie?"

"Paul Newman says after he wins at cards by bluffing, he says, 'Sometimes nothing is a real cool hand.' "

Oz took a sip of coffee and nodded. "Let them come to you?"

"Or at me," I said. "Either way is an admission of guilt."

"But about what?"

I got up to check the coals. They were graying just fine and would be ready for the steaks soon. I returned to my chair.

"Do you know what they got Al Capone on?" I said.

"That movie with the pretty boy said tax evasion."

"They couldn't get him on murder, so they settled for the next best thing," I said. "Anything to get him off the streets."

"Anytime you want to make sense, I'm all ears," Oz said.

"Anything to get him out of Washington," I said.

"And you gonna bring down a powerhouse senator by doing nothing?" Oz said.

"Worked for Paul Newman." I stood up from my chair. "How do you want your steak?"

Chapter 58

I spent a quiet morning that went into the afternoon with Janet and the kids at the beach. Oz came along and we grilled burgers and dogs and ears of corn. I noticed Regan was becoming quite the body surfer and the board surfers were starting to take notice of her. I rose up from my chair when one surfer-dude type decided to stop and give her some pointers.

"Jack, sit down," Janet said.

"The pimple kid is bad enough, but these surfer assholes are—"

"Jack, she's nineteen and gorgeous," Janet said. "What do you expect? Young men are going to buzz around her like bees in search of pollen."

"Yeah, well, her pollen is off limits," I said.

Mark was eating a hot dog and turned to me. "Want me to go break it up, Uncle Jack?" he said.

"Mark!" Janet cautioned.

"How?" I said.

"Go down there and be the annoying kid brother," Mark said. "Let them know she's being watched."

"Excellent idea," I said.

"No, it isn't," Janet said.

"Ten bucks in it for you," I told Mark and he took off running down to the water.

"Jack, for God's sake," Janet said.

I peered down at the beach. The surfer dude had his arms

around Regan's waist as she stood on his board with bent knees. "If God was his intention I wouldn't have a problem," I said.

"Man has a point," Oz said.

"Oh, shut up," Janet snapped. "You two are just alike."

Oz looked at me. "He don't look like no old black man to me."

Mark arrived at Regan's side and started yapping about something.

The surfer dude turned his head to look in our direction.

"Good boy, Mark," I said.

Regan stepped off the surfboard, and the dude picked it up and carried it to the waves. Regan and Mark started walking back to us.

"Really good boy," I said.

As Regan and Mark came closer, I noticed the hot pink bikini my daughter wore. I saw it earlier, of course, but it didn't register that she had the full curves of a grown woman.

"Where did that bikini come from?" I said.

"The mall, Jack," Janet said. "And to answer your unspoken question, yes, someday she will even have sex."

"I can wait for that and so can she," I said.

Regan and Mark arrived and Regan flopped into the chair to my right. "Can I get a surfboard, Dad?" she said. "I met a really nice boy who said he would give me lessons."

"In what?" I said.

"Surfing, what do you think?" Regan said.

"I think your dad is feeling a bit stressed right now, honey," Janet said.

"Why?"

Janet smirked. "He owes Mark ten dollars."

"I should have charged interest," Mark said.

Just before sunset, I tossed my overnight bag with the tux in it into the trunk of the Marquis, drove the gang home to Janet's house, then headed north to Portland, Maine.

CHAPTER 59

Portland, Maine, is a pretty little city of sixty thousand or so that sits on the oceanfront. I spent several hours the next morning walking the downtown area and waterfront section known as the Old Port.

I had lunch at a small restaurant in the bay, walked some more, and headed back to my room at the Marriott around two in the afternoon. Still worn out from last night's drive, I took a nap and awoke at four feeling like a truck hit me.

I got down on the rug and did some push-ups, sit-ups, and stretching to work the kinks from my lower back muscles. Then I ordered room service coffee. It arrived just as I finished shaving.

I filled a cup from the carafe, lit a cigarette, and looked out the window. My room was high enough to afford me a view of the city skyline and the ocean just past it.

It was a good view.

I finished the coffee and cigarette and opened the closet where I'd hung the tuxedo. I removed the plastic and hung the suit on the hook on the inside of the door to air out. I still had some time to kill before the gala event.

I polished off the pot of coffee along with three cigarettes and watched a movie on cable television. By the time the movie was finished, I was a few minutes late for the ticketed arrival time.

And by the time I slipped into the tux and made my way down to the banquet hall, I was a fashionable twenty minutes behind schedule. The doors were closed. I opened one and entered the large hall. I got the desired results. Like a Hollywood actor arriving late to the red carpet, I was noticed by half of the five hundred in attendance rather than a handful if I'd mulled in on time with the crowd.

At the front of the hall at the VIP table, Koch, his wife, and Chad turned to see who the latecomer was. As I made my way to my middle row table I could see Koch and Chad weren't pleased.

In the dim lighting, I thought I saw a fleeting smirk on Melissa Koch's lips. I took my seat and listened to some nitwit drone on for about fifteen minutes, and then there was a break for the waiters to serve dinner.

I looked over at Koch's table. He was talking to a well-dressed man to his left. It could have been the governor, but since I had no idea what the governor of Maine looked like, it was a guess. Melissa Koch did her best not to look at me.

Chad made no effort to hide his glare.

There were eleven other guests at my table. Too many witnesses for Chad to have a quiet word with me, so I obliged him by leaving the room. As I stepped out to the hall, I caught a glimpse of Chad barreling down the aisle.

There was a men's room down the hall. I went in and stood at the sink so I could see Chad when he came in behind me. I ran the cold water and tossed some on my face.

The door opened, and a very teed-off Chad came in and stood a few feet behind me. "What the fuck do you think you're doing, Bekker?" he said.

"Swearing. Yikes," I said and grabbed a paper towel.

"I asked you a question," Chad said.

"Don't stand behind me," I said. I turned around. "Or in front of me either."

"This is harassment," Chad said. "There are laws against this sort of thing."

"There are laws against buying a ticket to a fundraising event?" I said. "If so, there's four hundred and ninety-nine other guilty people in there."

Chad took a step forward. "Last time you caught me off guard," he said. "I have a brown belt in—"

I punched Chad in the gut and he folded like a greased pocket knife. "Stupidity," I said.

Chad sank to his knees and doubled over to the floor. He tried to suck in air, but his stomach and lungs were momentarily paralyzed. I took him under the ribcage and gently lifted him up.

"You're all right," I said. "Breathe in through your nose. Just don't get any snot on my tux."

I held Chad for thirty seconds or so until his breathing started to return to normal, then I let him go.

"There," I said. "Now you've gone and ruined my appetite."

Chapter 60

I waited forty-eight hours for the call that didn't come before I decided that Chad and Koch thought it best to keep the men's room episode under wraps. It was either that or Koch had the power to go behind the scenes with the Bureau and speak only to a select few in private.

My stunt was designed to let Koch know that I wasn't afraid of him and his powerful position.

His lack of communication told me he wasn't afraid of me, either, but that I already knew.

What it didn't tell me was what he would do next or how far he was willing to go in the process.

I found out the third morning after my men's room altercation. By eleven in the morning, the temperature had hit eighty-nine degrees and rising. Janet and I occupied chairs in the shade in front of my trailer. Mark was with his father, Janet's ex, for the day. Oz had gone to town to meet his younger brother for breakfast, something they had done once every few weeks since Oz got sober. Regan was down at the waves, taking lessons from Surfer Dude. I was grateful she wore a blue one-piece racing suit.

"I think she's getting the hang of it, Jack," Janet said. "She's actually quite an athletic girl."

Regan was on a board, riding a small wave to shore. She was still unsteady, but she didn't fall as the board struck sand.

"I suppose it could be worse," I said. "He could be a bungee jumper."

"Or one of those trick snowboard riders," Janet said.

"Don't put ideas in her head," I said. "Want some more coffee?"

"Yes."

I went into the trailer for fresh brew and when I returned, Regan was walking back toward us. I sat, lit a smoke, and waited for Regan to arrive.

"Jack, you really need to quit before the wedding," Janet said. "At least go back to those vapor cigarettes again."

"We'll talk about that later," I said and happily puffed and sipped.

Regan arrived and stood in front of me. "Josh lost his phone and needs to call his work," she said. "Can he use yours?"

"He has a job?" I said.

"Jack, be nice," Janet said.

"Sure," I told Regan, figuring at least I'd get to meet and speak with Surfer Dude up close and personal.

Regan turned and waved to Josh down the beach. As he started walking toward us, Regan took Oz's chair to Janet's left.

"Josh works at the surfboard shop in town," Regan said.

"I didn't know they had one," I said.

"Why would you?" Janet said.

As Josh neared us, I could see he was inches taller than me, with broad shoulders and muscular arms and legs. His chest, arms, and legs were bare, but surfers often shave their body hair like Olympic swimmers. His face was boyishly handsome, the kind young girls squeal over in movies.

When he was ten feet or so from us, I said, "Phone's on the card table. Would you like some coffee?"

"Thank you, sir, and yes, I would," Josh said as he came closer to me.

As I rose up from my chair, Josh effortlessly went into a beautifully timed spin kick with his right foot aimed at my head.

Caught in mid-stand and off balance, I had a micro-second to react.

I turned to my right like a boxer ducking a punch. The heel of Josh's foot caught me off target, but landed full force behind my left ear. I fell out of the chair to the sand. I wasn't hurt. My movement diverted much of the force, but where it landed was a boxer's worst nightmare.

A blow behind the ear with sufficient force causes the equilibrium to go out of whack. You lose balance and dizziness sets in and you stumble helplessly around the ring—or in my case, the sand.

I heard Janet and Regan scream.

I rolled, but everything was spinning rapidly and all I could see was a fleeting glance as Janet hit the card table and it broke under the force of her weight.

I saw Regan try to run and she went flying to the sand.

I heard Josh say, "What are you doing, little girl? You can't fight. Ya got nowhere to go."

His voice sounded almost gleeful as he stepped over Regan and grabbed Janet.

I saw Josh punch Janet in the face and she went down again.

I heard Regan scream, "Leave her alone!"

I got to one knee. My balance was still off, my head still spinning.

I saw Janet try to shield Regan. Josh punched her in the face again and she went flying out of my vision.

"You're all right, sweetheart," I heard Josh say. "It will all be over in a minute."

Josh's back was to me. My head was starting to clear a bit. Enough for me to jump up and grab his neck with my right arm and pull backward. I locked my left wrist over my right forearm and applied as much pressure as possible.

We went backward and down together and hit the sand hard.

Josh was no amateur. He knew exactly what to do to break a choke hold. He cracked me repeatedly in the ribs with his right elbow.

"Fuck!" Josh yelled. "Bastard motherfucker!"

I held on and took the pain.

Josh rolled left and right as he pounded my ribs. He was young and tremendously strong. I was old and tremendously strong. For a moment we neutralized each other.

"You fucking motherfucker!" Josh yelled as he rolled and pounded. "You can't win, motherfucker! I'm a pro, you fucking moron. I'll break your fucking neck, asshole."

I pulled tighter on Josh's neck. His windpipe started to implode and cut off his air supply. He made several more attempts to break my hold by pounding my ribs, but his blows were losing steam.

I felt Josh start to black out.

I rolled over onto my knees and kept my hold on his neck tight. His body folded forward. I couldn't let him go. If he recovered, he wouldn't stop. He had been paid to kill me and my family and he wouldn't stop or he'd die trying. I heard it in his voice, the joy of inflicting pain and taking life.

I mustered the strength in my legs and stood up. Josh's neck was bent forward inside my arms. I pulled backward and threw my legs behind me. Josh's neck snapped as he fell into my arms.

I let him go, rolled off him, and sucked wind for a few moments.

I fought the urge to vomit and swallowed hard.

I got to my knees.

Regan was sitting with her back against the trailer. Her eyes were wide and focused on me.

My daughter had just seen me kill a man.

I looked at Janet. She was face down on the sand and not moving.

"Regan, call nine-one-one," I said.

My daughter didn't move a muscle.

"Regan, call nine-one-one!" I shouted. "Do it now!"

Regan suddenly jumped to her feet and looked around for the cell phone. She found it in the sand and punched in the numbers.

I turned Janet over. A large welt under her right eye was quickly turning black. Her nose was pulp. Her jaw was swollen to three times its normal size. Her lips were bloody and bruised.

I lifted her in my arms and held her tight.

Regan stood over us. I expected her to collapse into regression and wind up back at the home.

She didn't.

"The ambulance is on the way," my daughter said, sounding like a composed adult.

I looked up at her. Her lips were bleeding and she had a large mouse under the left eye, but appeared otherwise unhurt.

In the distance we heard the sound of an approaching ambulance.

"Stay here, Dad," Regan said, taking charge. "I'll walk down a ways and point them in the right direction."

I choked back tears and nodded.

And watched my daughter rush down the beach to flag the approaching ambulance. The little girl was gone. A woman had taken her place.

Chapter 61

The town and beach belongs to the county sheriff's department and they, along with an ambulance, responded to the 911 call. Two EMTs and four deputies were frozen by the sight of one dead man and another man cradling an unconscious woman in his arms.

"Call Sheriff Morgan," I told a deputy. "Tell her it's John Bekker."

I sat in my lawn chair while I gave Sheriff Jane Morgan the story. Regan had gone with Janet in the ambulance, along with Oz, who had just returned from breakfast with his brother.

I've known Jane twenty years or more. I was a rookie cop the first time we bumped heads on a jurisdiction case. She was a deputy sheriff then, but I knew she would climb the county ladder when she was ready to come to blows with me after I wouldn't back down. Neither would she.

Around five foot four, with shaggy blond hair and blue eyes, Jane is as tough as any cop I've ever met, while still managing to raise four sons covering a twenty-five-year marriage. She supervises a hundred and fifty deputies as well as the county jail and courthouse.

Jane picked at her unpolished, bitten fingernails as she took my statement.

I lit two cigarettes and gave her one to go with our mugs of coffee. She inhaled, blew smoke through her nose, and said,

"What the fuck, I'm not pregnant anymore."

Seven months ago, at the age of forty-six, Jane suffered a miscarriage.

"I should have seen it coming," I said.

"Why, Jack?" Jane said. "How could anyone know in that situation?"

"I poked him," I said. "I went out of my way to aggravate him and then I let my guard down. That's the first cardinal sin in police work. I failed to expect the unexpected."

"The kid you killed?" Jane said.

"He left me no choice."

"I know that," Jane said. "What else do you know about him?"

"Not a thing," I said. "Just one of a hundred surfers on the beach. He offered to give Regan lessons a few days ago. I didn't make the connection we were being watched. The bastard waited until we were all together because he knew my guard would be down and he could get to me."

"Down or not, you took the fucker," Jane said.

"Like I said, it was him or me," I said. "I couldn't let him take me because . . ."

I raised my coffee mug and spilled some on my shirt. I set it on the sand and drew in hot smoke from the cigarette to steady my hand.

"I put it at the top of the list to ID the son of a bitch," Jane said. "Maybe we can trace him to Koch or that other bastard, what's his name?"

"Handler," I said. "First name, Chad."

Jane nodded. "Let me read back your statement," she said. "Tell me if I missed any details."

In the distance, a sedan entered the beach. I recognized it. "Walt," I said.

"I called him right after the ambulance left and you were inside for a moment," Jane said.

I nodded. My hand was steady enough for me to lift my mug and take a sip without drenching my shirt.

Walt's sedan came to an abrupt stop beside Jane's cruiser. He got out and left the door open as he walked to us.

"How bad?" he said.

"I don't know," I said. "Regan seems to be in one piece. Janet, not so good."

"The attacker?" Walt said.

I looked at my oldest, closest friend. "I broke his fucking neck."

Walt slumped into the third lawn chair. "Jesus Christ, Jack."

"I'd have done the same, some asshole puts his hands on my cubs," Jane said.

"I don't mean that," Walt said. "I'm talking about Koch. His true colors have just shown through like a fucking beacon. So what do we do about it?"

I took another sip of coffee, then tossed my spent cigarette to the sand. "Nothing," I said. "I want you to do nothing. The both of you."

"Jack, that's—" Walt said.

"I got a dead man in my jurisdiction, Jack," Jane said.

"I know it," I said. "I made him dead."

"And you want to do nothing about the asshole who—" Walt said.

"Forget the two decades as a cop, the both of you," I said. "Walt, you're my best man at the wedding, if there is one now. Jane, you and your family are at my table. That's how far we go back. I'm asking for a blind eye, at least for a little while. I need some time to work this out."

"Work what out?" Walt said. "Lawrence at the FBI will be—"

"This is Jane's backyard, Walt, not yours," I said.

We looked at Jane.

"How long?" Jane said.

I lit another cigarette, drew in smoke, and exhaled slowly. "I don't know. At least until I've had some time to sort things out."

"This guy might be right behind the president in the size of the stick he holds," Walt said. "And it seems to me the shoe is now on the other foot."

"Goddammit, Walt, are you going to do what I asked or not?" I snapped.

"Of course, you asshole," Walt snapped back.

"Jane?" I said.

"I suppose since he's a dead John Doe, I don't have to make too big a deal out of it," Jane said.

"I'm going to the hospital," I said.

"I'll drive you," Walt said.

"I'll follow in the cruiser," Jane said.

I stood up and walked toward Walt's sedan, made it about six steps and paused. Walt and Jane were right behind me.

"Walt, I—" I said.

"Don't think it," Walt said. "Let's just go."

Chapter 62

We found Regan and Oz on the sixth-floor ICU unit in the waiting room. The television was on, but neither they nor the other seven people seated in chairs paid it the slightest attention.

Oz had a large container of coffee on his lap. Their eyes turned to us when we walked in, and Regan jumped up and ran to me. I hugged her tight and pressed her face to my chest.

"Where is she?" I said.

"In an ICU room with the doctors," Oz said.

I released Regan and turned to Oz. "Why?"

"There's a nice cafeteria one floor below," Oz said. "Why don't we go there for a bit?"

We sat at a large square table against a peach-colored tiled wall. Except for Regan, who had a soft drink, we each had a container of coffee, although no one had yet taken a sip.

"I'm listening," I said to Oz.

Regan reached into her pants pocket. "I took notes from the doctor," she said.

"Want me to read it?" Oz said.

Regan shook her head. "I'll do it."

"Go ahead," I said.

"According to the doctor, Aunt Janet has a broken right eye socket, a broken nose that will need surgery, a broken right jaw bone, a dislocated left shoulder, and is under critical watch for brain swelling and leakage," Regan recited from her notes.

"Jesus Christ," Walt said.

"He said she took a kick or punch to the head like a boxer takes a knockout punch," Regan said. "He said her brain free-floated and caused her to black out or be knocked out. They said that could cause the swelling or leaking. They're not sure."

Regan set the paper down and looked at me.

"What room is she in?" I said.

"Dad, they said she can't—" Regan said.

"What room?"

"Jack, maybe we should wait until the doctor calls us?" Walt said.

"She's in good hands, Jack," Jane said. "You gotta let them do their job."

Regan stood up and held out her right hand to me. "You coming?" she said.

A doctor told us we had five minutes. He said he'd known Janet for a dozen years and worked with her on many a case. He said she was a very strong woman with a determined will and a stubborn streak, but I already knew that. Both worked to her advantage.

Regan led me into the room. She had yet to let go of my hand. I realized she wasn't holding my hand to give her strength, but the other way around.

To say Janet's face was a mess would be an understatement. I hardly recognized her, the swelling and purple bruises were so bad. Tubes and wires were everywhere. I wanted to touch her face, to let her know I was there, to say how sorry I was this happened, but that would have to wait for another time.

Right now it was all I could do to hold it together.

I broke free of Regan's hand, turned, and went to the window. Regan came and stood beside me. If there was a view, I couldn't tell you what it was, I was so out of focus.

I lost Carol because of my self-absorbed need to play cops and robbers with life and death. I couldn't lose Janet the same way. I wasn't strong enough and I knew it.

So, apparently, did my daughter.

She spoke in her soft, little-girl voice, but it was different now, filled with the quiet authority of a wise adult. "Don't even think about getting drunk," she said, so quietly I almost didn't hear her. "I won't allow it."

I turned and looked at my daughter.

"I'm not going to put a helmet on and beat my head against a wall," she said. "Not anymore. I remember everything and Mom wouldn't want that for me. She would want me to be normal and happy, and you, too. Aunt Janet has spent the last year and a half taking care of me and now I'm going to take care of her. I won't stand for it if you start drinking because you feel guilty about what happened. Do you hear me, Dad? I won't allow it."

My daughter's face told me she was all business. Where did it suddenly come from? Had this inner strength been locked away all these years? Then I realized it had always been there and it's what got her through a decade of living hell.

"I won't," I said. "I promise."

Regan nodded and patted my hand. It was a simple gesture to let me know who was in charge.

"Do you know why he did this?" she said.

"I think so."

"Do you know who sent him?"

"I think so."

Regan looked up at me and I saw something in her eyes I'd never seen before. Hatred. "Dad, when you find him, I want you to do something for me," she said.

"What's that?"

Regan turned and looked at Janet. "I want you to really fuck him up."

Chapter 63

I sat in my lawn chair for three days and nights, drank coffee, smoked cigarettes, and listened to the waves crashing on the beach. I ate little, slept even less, and waited for reports from the hospital on Janet's condition.

Walt and Jane took turns shuttling Regan and Oz to and from the hospital. It was felt best to shield Mark from the truth. He was told his mother had an accident, she would be fine, and he could visit her soon. His usually idiotic father Clayton stepped up to the plate and took care of the boy, and did his best to hide his concern for his ex-wife.

I wasn't vegetating.

I was allowing my mind to free-fall ideas. Allow roaming thoughts to flow unobstructed, and eventually something sticks to the wall and takes shape.

Around four in the afternoon on the third day, Walt drove Regan and Oz from the hospital to my trailer. I could see from the smile on Regan's lips the news was good.

"She's awake and talking," Regan said. "She asked for you."

"They operated on her eye socket, jaw, and nose this morning," Walt said. "She won't be on solid food for a while, but she can whisper, and boy is she pissed-off mad."

"Get cleaned up, Dad," Regan said. "Visiting hours are until eight."

★ ★ ★ ★ ★

Janet was still heavily sedated and asleep when I arrived. Almost her entire face was wrapped in white bandages. I sat in a chair and held her hand, and after an hour or so she opened her eyes and looked at me. She tried to move her lips, but the oxygen tube wouldn't allow her.

"Don't try to talk," I said.

Janet squeezed my hand.

I nodded.

I felt a tear well up in my eye.

Janet gently shook her head and I used my left hand to wipe the tear away.

A doctor came in then and said, "She's awake. Good. Can you give us a few minutes alone?"

I gave Janet's hand a gentle squeeze, stood up, and walked out to the hallway where Walt and Regan were standing against the wall.

"She's awake," I said. "She recognized me right off. I don't think there's any brain damage. I've had my bell rung enough to know the signs."

"Let's grab some coffee and come back after the doctor leaves?" Walt suggested.

"She's going to be all right," Walt said as he sipped coffee from a cafeteria cup. "She's one tough woman, I'll give her that."

"She saved my life," Regan said.

"Mine, too," I added. "If she hadn't gone head to head with him, I wouldn't have had those thirty seconds for my head to clear."

"That reminds me," Walt said. "Jane got a solid make on your little surfer dude. He's a pro out of Hawaii."

"Long way from home," I said.

"He's well known on the islands as an enforcer for the local drug smugglers," Walt said. "Likes to use his hands. One-time MMA and cage fighter. It's suspected he's responsible for seventeen or more pro hits."

Regan looked at me, but kept silent. I knew a thousand questions were running around in her mind, but she knew there was time for them later.

"I haven't seen a paper or looked at the news," I said.

"No need," Walt said. "Jane buried it practically underwater."

"Good," I said as I sipped coffee.

"Mr. Grimes," Regan said, "I appreciate your letting me stay at your house the past few days, but I'm going home with Dad tonight."

"I won't be going to Janet's, honey," I said.

"I know," Regan said. "I can fit on the sofa just fine, and besides, I think you need the company."

"Are you sure?" I said.

Regan nodded. "Maybe we can stop at the grocery store on the way home?" she said. "I doubt you have anything but chips and coffee."

"I'm sorry to see you go, Regan," Walt said. "I'll have to eat Elizabeth's cooking."

I looked at Regan. "You've been cooking?"

"Aunt Janet is a good teacher."

"She is that," I said. "About a lot of things."

Janet was gone when we returned to her room. The ICU nurse told us she went for an MRI to check her brain and skull for leakage.

"It's normal," the nurse said. "The doctor is just checking. She's in good hands, so I suggest you go home and come back tomorrow."

I dug out a business card and gave it to the nurse. "You probably don't call people at home with . . ." I said.

"I've known Janet fifteen years," the nurse said. "I'll call you when she gets back to the room."

"Thank you," I said.

"Let's go food shopping," Regan said. "I'll make you a nice dinner."

"You don't suppose I could stay for . . . ?" Walt said.

"Not a problem," Regan said. "I think Dad might even have three dinner plates that aren't chipped."

CHAPTER 64

I made a bonfire in the pit of stones in front of the barbeque grill. I do that a lot in winter when the nighttime temperatures drop to fifty degrees and Oz and I sit and watch the stars.

Tonight there were no visible stars. A thick overcast haze blocked out all but a sliver of a moon. The tiny sliver illuminated nearby clouds, causing them to glow white against the dark sky.

Walt sipped coffee from a mug. I smoked a cigarette to go along with my own mug.

Regan did dishes in my tiny trailer kitchen. Earlier, she'd baked mac and cheese to go along with breaded, Italian-style pork chops. I helped by grilling potatoes. Walt helped by eating. We had chocolate cake for dessert, store bought but still good.

"She's come a long way in a short time," Walt said.

"Yeah."

"Want to tell me about it?" Walt said.

"What?"

"What?" Walt said. "Whatever is going through that thick head of yours, that's what. What did you think I meant, mac and cheese recipes?"

I got up for a moment to toss a hunk of driftwood onto the bonfire, then plopped back into my lawn chair. "Just letting ideas flow," I said. "See what turns up."

"Bullshit, Jack," Walt said. "We've been friends too long for you to throw crap like that my way. I'm in this to stay, so you might as well lay it on me."

"That son of a bitch is going to confess," I said. "To attempted murder on three counts and to whatever happened to Sarah Gertz."

"Interesting," Walt said. "How?"

I tossed my spent cigarette into the bonfire. "I have no idea," I said.

"I think if you're going to bring down this prince of freaking darkness it's going to require a bit more than that," Walt said.

I was about to light another cigarette when Regan came out and snatched it from my lips. "And this you don't need," she said.

Walt grinned. "The worm has turned for you, Jack," he said.

"Never mind worms," Regan said. "Somebody has to look after this blockhead I call Dad or he'll self-destruct in no time."

I looked at Regan. In her jeans and T-shirt she appeared delicate, almost tiny. However, I was quickly learning that inside that small body beat the heart of a lioness, and why not? She'd endured more than a lifetime of hardship in just nineteen years.

She would have to endure a bit more before this one was over.

"I'm going to ask you a favor, no questions asked," I said. "Both of you."

"As a cop or a friend?" Walt said.

"I'll let you decide that," I said. "Very soon I'm going to ask you to take Regan in for a while, and Regan, I want you to go. No questions, no arguments. Agreed?"

Walt shifted his eyes over to Regan. She nodded to him.

"How long?" Walt said.

"That's a question," I said.

"Dammit, Jack, if you're asking me to assume guardianship of Regan at least tell me for how long?" Walt demanded.

"I can't because I don't know," I said.

Walt sighed and looked at Regan again. "What do you say,

sweet pea, want to give my wife some cooking lessons?"

"I don't think either of us can stop him, so yes," Regan said. "I'll go."

"Just tell me when," Walt said and stood up. "But right now I've got to go home."

Regan stood up and kissed Walt on the cheek. Then she turned to me. "Want some more coffee, Dad?"

"I would."

Regan took my mug into the trailer.

I stood up and walked Walt to his car.

"If something goes wrong and I don't . . ." I said.

"Do you need to even ask?" Walt said.

"No."

"Then shut up and enjoy that nice bonfire with your daughter, and when you figure out whatever you're figuring out, you let me know," Walt said and got into his car.

I returned to my chair. Regan came out with a fresh mug of coffee, then sat next to me. We watched the bonfire for a while, sharing a father-daughter moment without the need for words.

My squirt had grown up through no fault or doing of my own. The priests and nuns at the home punted and Janet caught and ran with it, and the end result was the very grownup nineteen-year-old by my side.

"I'll stay with Walt and Elizabeth while you go off and do what you do, but now it's my turn to ask for a favor," Regan said.

"What's that?" I said.

"I want to be there at the end when you finish this," Regan said. "Aunt Janet is the kindest, most loving person there is and I want to be there when you make him pay for what he did."

"Did the priests and nuns teach you about vengeance?" I said, trying to make light of what she just said.

My daughter looked at me. "No, Dad, you did."

Chapter 65

Three days later I finally got off my ass and sent Regan to stay with Walt and Elizabeth. Then I took a long drive north to Portland, Maine, to the lighthouse where Sarah Gertz either bought or received the globe as a gift.

Up close, the lighthouse was huge and imposing and could be seen for miles in every direction. It had a long and storied history, but I wasn't all that interested in that at the moment. I was there for the gift shop. I went in and shopped around and found a display counter with six identical snow globes on it. I snatched up all six and took them to the counter.

"Do you have any more out back?" I asked the girl behind the counter.

"We usually keep more in the storeroom," the girl said. "How many more would you like?"

"All of them," I said.

I left with eighteen snow globes that cost me thirty dollars a pop.

I got a receipt for Meade, of course.

I also had a printed copy of Koch's schedule of events for the rest of the month. Later this afternoon, he was hosting a town hall meeting in Augusta, the state capital. I checked my road-map and headed north about sixty miles.

Fifty minutes later, I arrived one hour early for the meeting. It was being hosted at a civic hall, and since Koch was the star attraction, security was tight. Six local deputy sheriffs patrolled the lot and stood watch at the doors. There was room for fifty cars, but only three spots were taken.

I parked in the rear of the lot, lit a cigarette, and waited. Slowly, the lot filled. I noticed that people walking from their cars to the hall held yellow tickets in their hands. There was little chance of crashing the meeting without a ticket.

Five minutes before start time, Koch arrived in his black sedan. Chad was behind the wheel. Koch got out and, escorted by two deputies, entered the hall through the front doors.

Chad drove the sedan back to the street and made a right turn. I started up the Marquis and followed from a safe distance. At the corner, Chad made a right turn and went down the block, then entered a municipal parking lot.

I drove around the block and on the return to the lot I passed Chad on the sidewalk. He was casually dressed in dark trousers and white shirt. Chad didn't notice me as I turned into the lot, took a ticket at the gate, and found a vacant spot a dozen rows behind Koch's sedan.

The front windows were rolled down.

I removed a snow globe from the shopping bag on the passenger seat. I carefully wiped it down with a handkerchief, then opened the glove box, and pulled out the rubber gloves I keep there for You Never Know.

Gloves on, I carried the snow globe to Koch's sedan and gingerly set it on the driver's front seat.

The drive home was very long, but oh so enjoyable.

Chapter 66

My little stunt got to Chad Handler. The following morning he called my cell phone and I let the call go to voicemail. As I sat in my chair outside the trailer, I smoked a cigarette, sipped coffee, and listened to Chad's message.

"Bekker, you son of a bitch," Chad ranted. "What the fuck you think you're doing? Stalking a US senator is a fucking felony, asshole. Lucky for you Koch doesn't want me to call the FBI, fucker. I'd have your nuts otherwise, but the Senator is a forgiving man. Stay the fuck away, motherfucker. You've been warned."

I waited a bit and called him back on his cell.

"Bekker, you got some balls of stone pulling that stunt like you did," Chad snarled.

"What stunt?" I said.

"What stunt?" Chad said. "You know what stunt, asshole."

"Chad, listen to me carefully," I said. "My girlfriend is in the hospital and I killed the man you sent to kill me and my family. You crossed the line when you involved my family. Normally, I would have killed you and been done with it, but you're a small fish and I want the whale."

"What are you talking about, what man?" Chad said. "I didn't send anybody anywhere."

"You're denying you sent a man to my trailer to kill me?" I said.

"You're crazy," Chad said. "I'm the personal assistant to a

US senator, not one of your street thugs."

"I don't believe you, Chad," I said. "And now the shoe is on the other foot. My foot."

"What the fuck does that—" Chad said just as I hung up.

I went inside for fresh coffee and when I returned, my phone was ringing again.

"Don't hang up, Bekker," Chad said.

I hung up.

Chad immediately called back.

"Do me a favor and call the FBI in Washington and ask for Special Agent Paul Lawrence," I said. "He's an old friend of mine from way back. Tell your story to him and see how much sympathy you get for Koch."

There was a long pause in the conversation.

"What, no hollow threats to make?" I finally said. "No 'fuck you motherfucker'?"

"I don't . . . okay, look, I admit I can be a hothead," Chad said. "The Senator is a great man, an important man, and in a lot of ways a genius. The country needs him. Naturally I'm upset when someone comes along and implicates him in a crime from more than a decade ago. That stunt you pulled at the fundraiser, what do you call that if not harassment?"

"You implicated him by your behavior," I said. "All I did was ask some questions. That stunt, as you called it, was to see if you spooked. You did. You contracted for my life and it very nearly cost me my girlfriend and daughter. Now it's my turn."

"I swear to God I had nothing to do with that," Chad said. "Neither did the Senator."

"I don't believe you," I said. "Now fair warning. You seriously injured the woman I love and put my daughter in danger and I can't stand for that. I won't stand for that. If I was you, I'd run. A long fucking way and pray I don't catch you."

"Bekker, I—" Chad said just as I hit Off and set the phone down.

I turned the phone off, stuck it in my pocket, and took a drive to the hospital to visit Janet, my mood just a little bit cheerier.

Chapter 67

Janet was sitting up in bed when I arrived at her room. Regan was in the chair beside the bed. They were drinking slurpies through thick straws and laughing about it like mother and daughter.

"This isn't as easy as you think when you have a broken face," Janet joked as I grabbed a second chair.

The heavy wraps had been removed from Janet's face. White gauze and tape covered her nose. A white eye patch covered the right eye. The swelling in her jaw had gone down considerably. "How do you feel?" I said.

"You know those charred burgers, fatty hot dogs, and greasy pizza you're always sneaking to Mark? What I wouldn't give to be able to eat one of those right now," Janet said.

"No problem," I said. "I'll toss one of each into a blender and make you a shake."

"Yummy," Janet said and sat up against the pillows. "Regan, can you give me and your father five minutes alone?"

Regan stood up, kissed me on the cheek, and took her slurpie with her when she stepped outside the room.

"It's amazing how strong she is after all she's been through," Janet said.

"That's because of you, not me," I said. "And I wouldn't be much without you, too, and that's the truth."

Janet sighed. "This is my fault, Jack," she said and motioned to her face.

"How do you figure that?"

"Before I asked you to talk to Gordon, I knew you would dig in like a pit bull and not let go, and I asked you to do it anyway," Janet said. "Against my better judgment. So what happened wouldn't have happened if I simply never brought it up. I wouldn't be sitting here with a broken face and Regan wouldn't have had to see you kill a man to save our lives."

"What happened, happened because Oliver Koch is a power-hungry scumbag who killed a young woman and got away with it," I said. "And you're the one who saved our lives. His surprise attack clipped me behind the ear and I was dizzy for about twenty seconds. If you hadn't taken him on the way you did, we'd all be dead."

Janet turned her face to focus on me with her left eye. "I'm not so pretty anymore, am I?" she said. "Still want to marry me?"

"More than ever."

"We'll have to postpone the wedding," Janet said. "I'll require several reconstructive procedures over six months. Then another three to six for healing."

"No, we won't postpone anything," I said. "We'll just have a private ceremony. Us, Regan, and Mark, Walt and Elizabeth, Oz. Who else do we really need?"

"A priest would be nice," Janet said and started to cry.

"You don't need a priest, you need a doctor," a man behind me said.

I turned around to look at him.

"Jack, this is Doctor Strauss, the surgeon who played Humpty Dumpty on my face," Janet said.

"No crying," Strauss said. "You'll melt your face like that wicked witch."

I gave Strauss my right hand. He shook and said, "I need to change bandages and check out my work."

"I'll go for coffee," I said.

I met Regan in the hall and we walked down a flight of stairs to the cafeteria. I grabbed a coffee and we took a table by the window.

As Regan licked her straw, I pulled out the cell phone. There were seven additional messages from Chad. I deleted them and dialed Walt's direct line.

"Just wanted to see if you're in the office," I said.

"I am and with my shoes off and feet on the desk," Walt said.

"Put your shoes on," I said. "I'm coming by and don't feel like smelling your feet."

CHAPTER 68

I took Regan with me. We stopped at the Italian deli by the hospital for three meatball subs and some bags of chips on the way to the police station.

Walt had his shoes on and his feet were flat on the floor behind his desk. "Is that what I think it is?" he said as he eyed the shopping bag Regan set on his desk top.

"If you think it's three foot-long meatball subs, three bags of garlic chips, and a two-liter bottle of Coke, then yes, that's what it is," I said. "If you thought it was a bag of bribe money, then no, I have to disappoint you."

Regan dug out a sub and gave it to Walt.

"Why do I have the feeling this foot-long bundle of joy is softening me up for something?" Walt said.

"I need a favor," I said.

"Of course you do," Walt said as he opened the white paper around the sub.

Regan dug out napkins and handed Walt a stack.

"Home address for Koch and his buddy Chad," I said. "No sense denying me, I can find them on my own. It will just take me a bit longer is all."

Walt shifted his eyes to Regan, who by now was happily biting into her sub.

"We talked about it," I said.

Regan grinned at Walt as red sauce dribbled down her chin.

She swiped at it with a napkin. "I'm good, Uncle Walt," she said.

"Call me a bit later," Walt said.

"Sure."

"I didn't have time to stop in this morning," Walt said. "How is Janet today?"

"Cussing Dad and drinking slurpies," Regan said. "She wants a hamburger."

"Cussing your father seems to be a popular hobby in this town," Walt said.

"He's that kind of guy," Regan agreed.

In the Marquis, I gave Regan a choice, head back to the hospital or the beach for the afternoon. She chose beach. On the way, we stopped to pick up Mark and Molly the cat at Clayton's condo.

When we arrived at the trailer, Oz walked over and took his customary chair next to mine. Regan and Mark tossed a Frisbee down by the water while Molly sat nearby and watched.

"Amazing how she has no fear of being here after what happened," Oz said.

"Regan said Sister Mary Martin told her that if you fall off a horse, you get right back on or you wind up afraid of it," I said.

"Know a lot about horses, the nuns do?" Oz said.

"No, just teenage girls," I said.

My cell phone rang. It was Walt.

"What do you got?" I said.

"Koch lives in a three-million-plus estate in a town called Cape Elizabeth," Walt said. "Chad has himself a place just shy of a million in the town of Falmouth. They live well, to say the least."

"Let me write down the addresses," I said, grabbing a pen and Oz's notebook off the coffee table.

Walt recited. I scribbled.

"So what's on the pea-sized brain of yours?" Walt said.

"Nothing specific," I said. "Mentally doodling."

"Doodle all you want, but don't do shit without running it by me first," Walt said.

"Top of the list, no shit-doing without telling Walt first," I said and hung up.

I checked missed calls and found three more from Chad. I deleted them and set the phone back on the coffee table.

Regan and Mark ran back to the trailer with Molly at their heels.

"We decided," Mark said. "Bonfire and hot dogs tonight."

"And who decided you'd be staying after dark?" I said.

"It was sort of mutual," Mark said. "And I could really use a break from Clayton."

"Oz, get some wood together for a fire," I said. "Me and the two mutts here are going to town for supplies."

"Don't forget chips," Oz said.

CHAPTER 69

As I drove through the town of Falmouth, Maine, Oz said, "Pretty little town, ain't it? Looks like a lot of money lives here and likes to show it off."

We left before sunrise so we would have time for a nice lunch somewhere along the ocean with a great view. I stopped just once to hit the bathroom and get gas, and we arrived in Falmouth just after twelve-thirty.

Oz was right, it was a pretty town and full of money. We drove past the high school, which more resembled a small university, and then skirted around some side streets to a narrow road that led up a steep hill.

The hill was a private driveway where, five hundred feet set back, Chad's palatial home sat isolated and surrounded by woodlands. The house was maybe four thousand square feet, blue with white trim, and had a neatly manicured lawn out front. A white fence protected the backyard.

I pulled into the long driveway and left the motor running.

"Reach around back and grab me a globe from the bag on the seat," I said.

Oz reached around for a snow globe and handed it to me.

"Be right back," I said.

I got out, walked to Chad's front door, and placed the snow globe on the Welcome doormat, then returned to the Marquis.

"I'm not sure this is legal," Oz said.

"What's illegal about leaving someone a gift," I said as I backed out of the driveway.

"Gift seems more like a threat to me," Oz said. "They can be both, you know."

"So what do you want for lunch?" I said.

"We're in Maine, ain't we?" Oz said.

"Right."

I reset the GPS for Cape Elizabeth. We hit a bit of afternoon traffic on the turnpike and crossed the bridge to South Portland, arriving at the promontory of Cape Elizabeth forty minutes later. I drove around back roads and side streets until I located the oceanfront road the Koch mansion was located on.

About a half mile down the road, situated on several acres of walled-in property, the Koch mansion overlooked the ocean. From the second floor, he must have had quite a view. From the road it was impossible to tell if anyone was at home when I slowed to a stop by the iron front gate.

"Going to leave another gift?" Oz said.

"I'm a generous guy," I said. "I just love playing Santa."

I left the Marquis, carried a snow globe to the iron gates, and reached between the bars to set it on the pavement.

I returned to the car, got behind the wheel, and we took a leisurely cruise to the end of the road where a small lighthouse and restaurant overlooked a rocky coastline.

Oz got two lobsters and a bucket of steamers. I didn't feel like driving with my insides churning so I opted for a bucket of chicken with fries.

Not ten minutes after lunch, Oz spent twenty minutes in the bathroom. I wandered down to the rocky coast and took a seat on a bench. I fired up a smoke and enjoyed the salty sea breeze on my face.

When Oz returned, his usually coffee-colored complexion

seemed almost gray. He plopped on the bench beside me and rubbed his beard.

"Gonna be one long-ass ride home," Oz said.

Chapter 70

It was late when I dropped Oz off at his trailer. Our trip was stalled several times for bathroom breaks along the way. Oz stumbled from the Marquis to his front door, unlocked it, and went inside. I resisted the urge to grin.

I drove the Marquis to my trailer, went in to brew some coffee and then took my chair and lit a cigarette.

I turned my cell phone on and checked messages. There were eleven missed calls from Chad. I deleted them and dialed his number.

After four rings, I was directed to Chad's voicemail box.

I hung up, waited a minute, and called back.

This time Chad answered after two rings.

"Bekker, I've been calling you," Chad said. "The Senator is very upset with your little gift that you left him. Me, too."

"I'm just getting warmed up," I said.

"What's that mean?"

"Means I'm going to fuck with you and fuck with you and then fuck with you some more until you break down and give me what I want," I said.

"There are laws against stalking a US senator," Chad said.

"Fuck the laws," I said. "You messed with my cubs and besides that, Koch is a murderer and I intend to prove it and take you down along with him."

"You're insane."

"No, just pissed."

"I already told you we had nothing to do with what happened."

"And I already told you I don't believe you," I said. "Koch is a womanizer. Even his wife knows it. When I'm done the whole country will know it."

"That doesn't make him a murderer," Chad said.

"Maybe I can't prove it, but I sure as hell can ruin his career and yours right along with it," I said. "And the FBI will find who sent the hit man, you can believe that. Paul Lawrence is a bulldog once he gets a sniff."

"You leave me no choice but to contact Justice and have them order you to stop," Chad said.

"I don't give a fuck what Justice says," I said. "This is a personal vendetta on my part and by the time I'm through you're going to see some apocalyptic shit go down. Koch couldn't get the nod for VP of the local kennel club by the time I'm through with him. I was you, I'd start brushing up the old résumé."

"Bekker, listen to me," Chad said. "I understand that you're angry. I'd be angry, too, but the Senator had nothing to do with the Gertz girl's disappearance or the man who tried to kill you. I give you my word."

"Wow, the word of a career politician who makes his living selling gift-wrapped bullshit," I said.

"What if . . . what if we met?" Chad said. "The three of us."

"Sure," I said. "Nothing I'd love more than to call that scumbag a liar and murderer to his face."

"At least just listen to the man?" Chad said. "What can that hurt?"

"When?"

"Say tomorrow?"

"Say where?"

"Someplace isolated," Chad said. "We can't have this go public."

"Don't worry about that," I said. "I won't go public until I have proof enough for the FBI to make an arrest."

"Do you agree to meet or not?"

"Sure."

"There's a tide breaker at the Portland Breakwater Lighthouse," Chad said. "It runs about a half mile out. We'll meet at the wall, say eleven tomorrow night. There are some benches. We can sit and talk. Just the three of us in private."

"I'll be there," I said and hung up.

I glanced at my watch, then dialed Jane Morgan's cell phone. She answered on the second ring. "Morgan."

"Jane, John Bekker," I said. "You busy?"

"My old man's making a play for my left boob, otherwise no," Jane said.

"Feel like playing—"

"Hold on," Jane said. I heard her set the phone set down and say in the background, "I swear to Christ I'll cut it off and feed it to the goldfish if you don't leave me the fuck alone."

I heard the phone being lifted.

"Least he could do is put a goddamn raincoat on it, the sonofabitch," Jane said. "So what can I do for you?"

"I need backup," I said.

"How many?"

"Just you."

"For?"

"A private meeting with Senator Koch and his assistant," I said. "At night, in the middle of nowhere. We'd have to leave around noon."

"Want I should bring an M-16 or a standard sniper rifle with a silencer?" Jane said.

"Surprise me."

"Sniper rifle is oh so pretty," Jane said.

"Works for me," I said. "See you around noon. I'll give you the details on the drive."

"You buy—get the fuck off me, asshole—you buy lunch, and I ain't cheap," Jane said.

"Like lobster?" I said.

"Goddamn giant roaches," Jane said. "Find a steakhouse. I like mine bloody, like my senators."

Chapter 71

We arrived two hours early and I took a walk along the breakwater to the lighthouse on the point a half mile away. Consisting of thousands of massive, cut granite boulders stacked in the bay, the breaker rose about fifteen feet out of the water and cut the bay in half to reduce the high tide and calm the surrounding waters.

When I started walking a few couples holding hands were strolling about, but by the time I reached the lighthouse, I was alone. Some fog was rolling in and the salty mist was cool on my face.

I pulled the tiny flashlight from my pocket and checked around the lighthouse for hidden weapons. I didn't see any.

As I walked back to the small park that surrounded the tide breaker, the fog grew denser and soaked my hair.

At the end of the rocks, I found a bench facing the narrow road in, sat, and lit a cigarette. I waited until the second cigarette to retrieve the thermos of coffee from the car and fill the cap.

I didn't look at my watch until the headlights of an approaching car came into view on the narrow road. The fog was really thick now and the car was nearly invisible behind the headlights.

The headlights suddenly went dark. The car rolled along and came to a slow stop beside mine. It was Koch's sedan. The windows were too dark to see who was behind the wheel.

The driver's door opened and Chad slowly emerged. He walked through the fog toward me and stopped six feet in front of the bench.

"Where's Koch?" I said.

"In the car," Chad said. "He wants me to make sure you're not wearing a wire."

I set my thermos cup aside, stood up, raised my shirt, and then sat back down.

Chad took two steps backward, reached into the small of his back, and produced a Glock 9mm pistol. He aimed it directly at my chest. "Oliver Koch is an important man," he said, sounding a bit crazed. "The next vice president and in eight years the front-runner for the big seat. I can't allow you to ruin his greatness, not a worm like you. Now get on your feet."

"I don't think so," I said, and retrieved my cup.

"What?"

I took a sip.

"You didn't ask me if I was wearing an earpiece," I said. "Which I am, and right now a high-powered sniper rifle has dead aim on your back. Jane, show him."

Two silenced shots rang off the sidewalk beside Chad's right foot.

"Now put two in his heart," I said.

"Wait!" Chad said and dropped the Glock at his feet.

"Make that one in the heart," I said. "One in the head."

Chad dropped to his knees. "Goddammit, Bekker, wait!"

"For?"

"The goddamn thing isn't even loaded," Chad said. "I was just going to scare you, that's all."

"I don't think so," I said. "I think you were going to walk me out to the lighthouse, hit me on the back of the head, and toss me into the ocean a half mile off shore. It's a fifty-fifty shot I'd wash in or drift out, but either way I'm out of your hair and it looks like just another accident off the slippery rocks in the fog."

"No!" Chad cried. "I swear it."

"Jane, if he twitches, put one in the back of his head," I said.

I stood up from the bench and retrieved the Glock. I removed the magazine. It was empty.

"See," Chad said.

I dug out the Browning .45 pistol from the small of my back, racked the slide, and aimed it loosely at Chad. "This one is loaded," I said. "Go sit your stupid ass on the bench."

Chad got to his feet, walked to the bench, sat, and looked at me.

"Jane, come on out," I said.

From thirty feet into the shadows, Jane slowly appeared. Dressed in black jeans and a black T-shirt that was stretched to the limits to contain her very large breasts, she walked into the light with the Remington 7mm rifle cradled in her arms. The deadly rifle appeared even more imposing with the eight-inch silencer attached to the muzzle.

"Chad, this is Jane," I said. "She is nobody to mess with when she's in a bad mood and right now her mood couldn't get any worse."

Jane stopped just short of the bench and looked at Chad. "Dickless piece of shit," she said, and smacked Chad in the jaw with the butt of the heavy rifle.

Chad slumped over to his right. His face hit the seat of the bench.

"You remind me a lot of my husband," Jane said. "He's a dickless piece of shit, too, but I do love him so."

I lit a cigarette as Chad slowly sat up. The side of his face was already swelling up and blood dripped from his lower lip.

"What do you think, Jane, give him what he was going to give me?" I said as I tucked the Browning down my pants.

"Walk this idiot out to the lighthouse and toss his useless ass into the ocean?" Jane said. "I love it."

"You're joking," Chad said.

I grabbed his shirt, yanked him to his feet, and threw him over the bench. "Am I?" I said.

"Nothing sexier than a man throwing another man over a park bench," Jane said.

I walked around the bench, grabbed Chad by the shirt, and yanked him to his feet. "Time to walk the plank, Captain Morgan," I said.

"Don't fight over me, boys," Jane said. "There is enough of me to go around."

"For God's sake, this is cold-blooded murder," Chad said.

"God has very little to do with it," I said. "And my blood is pretty hot right now. Move."

Jane poked Chad in the belly with the Remington. "Let's just shoot him," she said.

"I really don't feel like carrying his ass to the lighthouse," I said. "All that blood."

"Good point," Jane said.

"You people are insane," Chad said.

"We're also the ones with the guns," Jane said. "Walk."

I shoved Chad toward the tide breaker.

"Stop," Chad said. "Just stop."

I shoved Chad again. "I need a reason to stop or so help me God, I'm going to kill you in cold blood and go for a burger afterward."

"Two in the brain works best," Jane said. "Like a double tap."

"Yeah." I pulled the Browning and whacked Chad in the gut with it. He fell to his knees. I stuck the heavy .45 against his head.

"You win!" Chad cried. "You win, Bekker."

I shoved the Browning down my pants, grabbed Chad, and shoved him onto the bench. "What do I win?" I said.

"I'm not willing to die for him," Chad said. "What do you want?"

"What do you got?" I said.

Chad sighed. "Can I smoke?"

"I could go for one," Jane said.

"Let's all smoke," I said.

I lit three and passed two around. Chad inhaled deeply and exhaled slowly.

"Here's what I know," he said. "Oliver Koch goes through women like they were M&M's. About thirteen years ago, Sarah Gertz caught his eye and he asked me to introduce her to him after a meeting in private. Stupid son of a bitch knocked her up and she didn't want to have an abortion. He, and by he I mean me, offered her one million dollars to have an abortion, but she refused."

I blew a smoke ring and glanced at Jane. She was blowing smoke through her nose like a pissed-off dragon in heat.

"And?" I said.

"And nothing," Chad said. "That's it. That's all I know."

"Now, Chad—" I said.

"I swear it," Chad said. "Soon after I made her that offer, she disappeared. Vanished. No contact with Koch, nothing."

"Did she love him?" I said.

"Adored him," Chad said. "Worshipped at his feet. She told me if she couldn't have him, she would keep his baby. Something like that. I forget her exact words."

Jane and I exchanged glances.

"She told you she wanted the baby and not the million?" I said.

"In no uncertain terms," Chad said.

"So he couldn't bribe her to get an abortion, panicked that the scandal would ruin his future career, and he killed her," I said.

"No way," Chad said. "Not Oliver."

"Why not?"

"He's not violent," Chad said. "I've been with him twenty years or more and I've never even heard him raise his voice. He's a first-class hound, I'll give you that, but he's no killer."

"That doesn't mean he didn't hire it out to someone who is violent to do his dirty work for him," I said. "Someone, say, like you?"

"No way," Chad said. "I didn't even put bullets in my gun."

"Someone contracted the flying Hawaiian to kill me and my family," I said.

"Koch wouldn't risk his VP nod on something so stupid," Chad said. "And neither would I."

"You just did, asshole," Jane said.

"I admit what I did was very stupid," Chad said. "But you drove me to it, Bekker. And I'm going to say this one last time and be done with it. Neither Koch nor I had anything to do with that—what did you call him?—flying Hawaiian hit man and what happened to your family."

I sat on the bench next to Chad. I lit two fresh cigarettes and gave him one.

"Aw, hell," Jane said and sat next to me.

I gave her my smoke and lit another.

"So what now?" Chad said.

"I'm going after Koch and you're going to help me," I said.

"I can't do that," Chad said.

"You can and you will because if you don't, I'll have a certain FBI friend of mine investigate you for soliciting prostitution for the Senator, withholding evidence in the Gertz investigation, and attempted murder," I said. "And, oh yeah, Jane just happens to be a county sheriff and trust me, you don't want to spend one minute in her custody. You're not tough enough. Come to think of it, neither am I."

Chad looked at me, then past me at Jane.

Jane blew smoke through her nose and showed him her best smile.

"You said Koch is a great man," I said. "Is he great enough for you to do twenty years for?"

Chad sat back on the bench and sighed. "What do you want me to do?"

"Nothing," I said. "Say nothing, do nothing, interfere with nothing, and if asked, you know nothing."

"Nothing's not all that hard to do, Chad old boy," Jane said.

Chad nodded his head. "I can do that," he said.

"Now that we have that settled, let's go for some coffee and ice cream," Jane said. "This fog is ruining my hair."

Chapter 72

"Do you really think Senator Koch is capable of murdering that young woman and sending a hit man after you?" Chad said.

"Chad, honey, you're a cute man and all, but you really do live in a bubble, don't you?" Jane said. "People are capable of all kinds of vile, hateful things, especially if they have a great deal to lose when their dirty little kept secrets threaten to become public knowledge."

"I know that, but I also know the Senator and it's hard for me to believe he could do what you said," Chad said as he ate some chocolate ice cream from a dish.

We'd found an all-night restaurant not far from the lighthouse and occupied a window table. In the distance, I could see the lighthouse beacon as it rotated its powerful beam three hundred and sixty degrees.

"They all say that," Jane said. "He was such a good neighbor, always so quiet and polite. Right up to the time he raped and murdered that two-year-old little girl."

"Maybe so, but being a womanizer doesn't make you a murderer," Chad said. "Isn't it possible someone else is behind this?"

"Like who?" Jane said.

"Whoever really did kill the Gertz woman," Chad said.

"My guess is, whoever did kill her is who sent the Hawaiian after me," I said. "And my other guess is, it is Oliver Koch."

"I've got people checking Hawaii for contacts and leads,"

Jane said. "It's just a matter of time before a trail from Hawaii to Koch is established."

"And that trail is going to lead right into Koch's office door," I said. "With a federal warrant."

"And take you down in the process," Jane said.

"Unless you do exactly as I say," I said.

Chad spooned some ice cream into his mouth and followed that up with a sip of coffee. "And that is what?" he said. "Exactly."

"You go about your business as if tonight never happened," I said. "You conduct your regular duties as normal, keep your mouth zipped, and maybe this will all go away on your end. You keep me advised of his schedule and changes in his schedule, meetings, phone calls, and if and when he steps out on his wife again. That's my deal. Take it or leave it."

"Leave it and you take a ride with me to the county jail," Jane said. "I broke a nail tonight because of you and manicures ain't cheap. Also, my hair's a mess, so it won't be a fun ride to the clink."

"I suppose a man has to look out for his own skin," Chad said.

"You suppose right, cutie pie," Jane said.

"But while I'm looking out for my own skin and helping you tear down a true giant in the political field, I want some assurances," Chad said.

"Such as?" I said.

"My name doesn't come up," Chad said. "Ever. Not in an official document, in court, anywhere, and especially in the media. I still have to live and work in DC circles after this and all I have is my reputation. That's my end of the deal."

I looked at Jane. She nodded.

"We can do that provided you don't try to cross us," I said. "I smell something I don't like and you're done. Agreed?"

"Like I said, a man has to look out for his own skin," Chad said. "And I like living in mine."

Jane looked at me. "He's not as dumb as he looks," she said.

Chapter 73

"Think he'll keep his word?" Jane said from the passenger seat of the Marquis.

"Yes."

I reached for my cigarettes on the dashboard and passed the pack to Jane. She removed one, gave it to me, and removed another.

"Because?" she said.

"To start with, he's a complete imbecile," I said. "He's also a coward and a worm and I believe him when he said he has to look out for his own skin. We put visions of sugarplums and prison in his head and he's scared right down to his hundred-dollars-a-pair socks. If it comes down to it, which it has, he'll choose sugarplums over a jail cell."

"There's no loyalty in the world anymore, Bekker," Jane said. "He works for the man twenty years and sells him out to save his own ass. Saddening."

"Any truth to what you said about your contacts in Hawaii?" I said.

"Not a word," Jane said. "The island paradise is a hotbed for drugs, gangsters, and other such assorted creeps. You'd have to really know the islands to make that kind of connection. You really mean all that bullshit you said?"

"Which part?" I said. "I said a lot of bullshit."

"Keeping imbecile's name out of it?" Jane said.

"If possible," I said. "It may not be, but if he's in the dark as he says I see no reason to prosecute provided he keeps his word."

"And Koch?"

"Whatever it takes," I said. "You in?"

Jane blew smoke out her nose and looked at me. "Just try to keep me out."

CHAPTER 74

Regan held my hand as we walked along the beach.

"Aunt Janet comes home in three days," she said. "I'll be moving back in, okay?"

"I don't see why not," I said. "As long as I'm staying there to help you guys out."

"Is that what you call it now?" Regan said.

"What?"

"Watching out for us."

"Well, I'll be doing some of that, too," I admitted. "And when I'm not there, Oz will be. Agreed?"

"Agreed. And Mark, I think he's had enough of Clayton."

"Don't forget Molly," I said.

"Molly goes where Mark goes."

"Sure," I said. "So where's your little boyfriend these days?"

"Dumped."

"You dumped him?"

"He dumped me."

"He dumped you?"

"For a girl with zits who works at the pizza place at the mall," Regan said. "She has giant . . . you know."

"Like moths to a flame," I said. "There will be plenty of others."

"Not a priority," Regan said. "I want to go to school."

"College?"

"I have my high school diploma," Regan said. "I think I'd

like to try college."

"You're certainly smart enough to study whatever you put your mind to," I said. "Any ideas what you want to study?"

"You won't laugh?"

"I don't know. Are you going to tell a joke?"

We stopped and Regan picked up a shell and skipped it across the water. I did the same. Her skip was better than mine.

"There's a lot of bad people, Dad," Regan said. "I'd like to try law school and help put some of them where they belong."

"Become a lawyer?" I said.

Regan nodded. "A prosecutor. What do you think?"

"How long have you been thinking about this?" I said.

Regan turned and looked up at me. "Since I was five years old."

"Revenge against other evil people won't bring your mother back," I said.

"I know."

I picked up another shell and skipped it on the water. It disappeared in the waves after several skips.

"But if I can prevent some young girl from spending her life in a home wearing a helmet, I think I want to try," Regan said.

"It just so happens that a very old friend of mine from the old days is a prosecutor," I said. "Would you like to talk to her?"

"I would."

"I'll give her a call and see what I can do," I said.

"Thanks, Dad," Regan said. "Any idea what college would cost?"

"I'm guessing around forty thousand a year for seven or eight years," I said.

"That much, huh?"

"A really bad man did a very nice thing," I said. "And now is probably a good time to tell you about it."

"I don't understand," Regan said. "What man?"

We continued our walk. I told Regan about Eddie Crist, the East Coast mob boss I believed responsible for her mother's death. While I was busy drinking for a decade, Crist set up a trust fund for Regan and then one day sent for me via a kidnapping. He cleaned me up and then, as a deathbed request, he asked me to find the man who murdered Carol even if it turned out to be his only son. I found the man, and Crist died somewhat at peace with the life he chose, and who knows, maybe redeemed himself with the man upstairs.

That trust fund was still in effect, and would provide Regan with ample funds for college and long afterward.

When I finished the story, Regan sat down in the sand and started to cry softly to herself. I sat beside her and placed my arm around her shoulders.

"Is this what you would call ironic?" Regan said.

"Same thing with what happened to Janet," I said.

"What do you mean?"

"You didn't say ten words in a whole day," I said. "I knew last year this bright young girl was locked away inside you and it took Janet needing you to bring her out. Now I can't shut you up and you want to go to college. I don't believe it's true that everything happens for a reason. I think some things just happen and they cause other things to just happen. Sometimes those things are good."

"Like me?" Regan smiled.

"Yeah, like you. So you want to walk or you want to cry?"

Regan stood up. "I can do both."

Chapter 75

While fresh ears of corn roasted on the grill, I called Paul Lawrence in Washington.

"Can you use your almighty power with the Bureau to do a financial check on Koch?" I said. "His actual worth in cash, assets, and homes."

"What are you looking for?" Lawrence said.

"Something I can stick in and break off," I said.

"A lot of these wealthy elite use their wives to hide assets," Lawrence said. "Put the vacation home and boat in the wife's name to reduce the taxes and such."

"So check Melissa Koch while you're at it," I said.

"Jack, you're not going to bring down Oliver Koch with a paper tiger," Lawrence said. "And neither is the Bureau. This one shot has to count. If you miss, hell hath no fury like a powerful senator scorned."

"If you could—Hold on," I said and went to flip the ears of corn. "If you could do a rush job on this it would be great."

"It would be great if I'd been born Fabio, too, but I'm stuck with what I got," Lawrence said.

"Is that your way of telling me to be patient?" I said.

"Rome and all that cliché shit," Lawrence said. "Maybe tomorrow night."

After I got off the phone with Lawrence, Oz came by with two giant steaks he'd picked up in town on my nickel and tossed them onto the grill. The immediate sizzle set our mouths to watering.

We sat to wait.

I lit a smoke.

"I put all your notes in the book," Oz said. "I noticed something and—oh, your handwriting needs a lot of work, by the way. Your *i*'s look like *j*'s. Anyway, I noticed something and thought I'd ask, figuring you already thought about it."

I got up to flip steaks and corn, sat back down.

"The girl, what if she turned down the million in exchange for an abortion because the baby was worth a lot more alive?" Oz said.

"A million a year until the kid turns twenty-one?" I said. "Yeah, it has crossed my mind once or twice."

"Be a strong motive to get rid of her, wouldn't it?"

"It would."

"But?"

"I think it's like the imbecile said. She was gaga over his lord and master of the Senate seat," I said. "I think she wanted the baby and Koch, and for him to leave his wife and the whole fairytale ending little girls are brainwashed into believing."

"Which would ruin his future plans for the big seat down the road," Oz said. "And create an even greater need for the girl to disappear."

"It do fit nicely," I said.

"It do, it do," Oz said. "Except there isn't a shred of evidence to prove all this bullshit, is there?"

"Melissa Koch's tale of her husband's infidelity," I said. "Chad's confession he pimps women for the Senator. A snow globe from Maine inscribed *With Love, Okay.* No hard evidence of the girl's death or disappearance and not a single witness. Not exactly an episode on your favorite cop show."

"But despite all that you're moving forward," Oz said.

"Right after we eat our steaks," I said.

"Do I get to witness this major event?"

"I expect you to keep notes," I said. "It's full steam ahead."

"Best sharpen my pencil," Oz said.

We ate our steaks and watched the sun sink below the horizon. It was a warm night, too warm for a bonfire, so I clicked on the outside floodlight. Down at the pitch black beach, invisible waves crashed loudly as they broke against the sand.

I lit a smoke and hit redial for Paul Lawrence's personal cell number. My call was forwarded to his message box.

"Paul, Bekker," I said. "One quick thing. Call me back right away if possible."

I hung up and sat back in my chair.

"You call that full steam?" Oz said. "More like dripping water."

"Best I can do on a full stomach," I said.

I went into the trailer for dishes of chocolate ice cream and mugs of coffee. When two of the three scoops in my bowl were gone, Lawrence called back.

"Three hours is your idea of patience?" Lawrence said.

"A small request," I said.

"What?"

"Can you have it leaked that the new interest in the Gertz disappearance has led to a new discovery?" I said. "A single hair fiber found in her car that forensics is testing for DNA."

"Leaked?"

"Quietly to Koch or his people," I said. "I want to see if we get any sort of reaction out of the Senator."

"Leaked how?"

"That's your area," I said. "My area is the more in-your-face kind."

"Leaking false information is a crime," Lawrence said.

"So is murder," I said. "And who do you arrest if the leak

and evidence doesn't exist?"

"Well, I have some informants I could use, but they cost," Lawrence said.

"I'll reimburse you plus expenses," I said. "And I'll throw in a box from Pat's."

"You're a bastard, Jack," Lawrence said. "You know that?"

"Bastard is my middle name," I said.

"If you get a reaction, I know before anyone," Lawrence said.

"Sure."

I hung up and finished my ice cream.

"Of course, we could all wind up in prison if this blows up in your face," Oz said.

"Three squares a day and free clothes is a sweet deal," I said. "Want some more ice cream?"

"They serve ice cream in prison?" Oz said.

"On Christmas," I said.

Oz handed me his empty bowl. "Fill it up," he said.

CHAPTER 76

Chad called me late in the afternoon after I returned from a six-mile run and was beating on the heavy bag outside my trailer.

"Mr. Bekker, I don't know if this is important or not, but the Senator has canceled his schedule for the rest of the week," Chad said.

"He say why?" I said as I took my chair.

"No, but it came after he took some private calls from Washington," Chad said.

"How private?"

"He excused me from his office in the middle of an event planner."

"Any idea who he was talking to?"

"No, but the conversation started out friendly and then his face sort of dropped, and that's when he asked me to leave his office," Chad said.

"Does that happen a lot?" I said.

"Him excusing me?" Chad said. "Not in twenty years. Not even when he's talking to some babe I've prearranged."

"What was his schedule like?" I said.

"A fundraiser in Bangor, a speech for a friend in New Jersey, a meeting with some EPA group over funding, a luncheon with the governor of New Hampshire, a charity event on his boat," Chad said.

"What's he going to do in place of?" I said.

"I don't know."

"Find out."

"And then?"

"You tell me."

Chad sighed. "Should I be worried?"

"Only about me and what happens to you if you cross me up," I said. "Play Koch as normal and see if you can find out who was on the other end of that call. Maybe he doodled on a pad or took notes. Any more schedule changes and you let me know right away."

"I feel dirty, Bekker," Chad said. "I didn't think I would, but I do."

"If it will make you feel clean, think about what happens if I press charges against you for attempted murder, then think about how dirty prison is," I said and hung up.

I returned to the heavy bag for another thirty minutes, did some push-ups and pull-ups, and then went inside for fresh coffee. I took a mug to my chair, lit a smoke, and called Paul Lawrence.

"Got the donuts this morning," Lawrence said. "I assume you aren't calling to make sure they arrived safely."

"Did your snitch leak the bogus hair DNA story?" I said.

"Cost me a thousand dollars plus dinner and expenses," Lawrence said.

"It's covered," I said. "And Koch had a very distinct reaction when he received the news. He tossed his assistant from the room and then canceled all his appointments for the week."

"Interesting," Lawrence said.

"Ain't it, though," I said.

"Of course, he could be sweating out the fact that the hair could prove he had an affair with the girl," Lawrence said. "Which is still a far cry from murder, Jack."

"Remember that asshole congressman who had an affair with a murdered girl?" I said. "He had nothing to do with her murder, but the affair ruined his career. What's he doing now, anybody know?"

"Make Koch pay either way," Lawrence said. "Works for me."

"I'll call you when I know more," I said.

I sat and thought things through, mulling over facts and lack of, and I reached the conclusion a ruined career wasn't good enough.

Not this time.

Attempted murder on three counts, Janet in the hospital, and my daughter witnessing her father kill a man adds up to a lot more than a ruined career.

The bastard no longer had to answer just for Sarah Gertz. Not anymore.

If I had to flush the son of a bitch out and kill him with my bare hands, he was going to pay for his crimes.

I lit a smoke and sat back in my chair.

He put hands upon Janet and my daughter with intent to kill.

That was a no-no of the highest order in my mind.

Unforgivable.

And now my mind was in a completely different place.

A place usually reserved for men like Eddie Crist.

And once you go there, you don't come back.

CHAPTER 77

Janet came home with very little fanfare. She got out of the Marquis and walked into her house under her own steam. The first thing she did was fill a tall glass with ice and eight ounces of white wine and take it to the backyard.

I grabbed a ginger ale from the fridge and followed her through the sliding kitchen doors. We took chairs on the lawn in the shade and sipped our drinks. I lit a cigarette and for once Janet didn't object.

A large white bandage covered the bridge of her nose. Her jaw was still swollen a bit, but barely noticeable. Her right eye was still bruised and blackened, but healing nicely. A second surgery for her nose was scheduled for thirty days down the road if the skin was healed enough.

"Next time I ask you to do something for me, feel free to say no, and loudly," Janet said as she took a sip of wine.

"Even if it's that little spot you like me to rub with my—" I said.

"Oh, shut up," Janet said. "If you make me laugh my face will split open."

"Walt will be bringing Regan and Mark home in a bit," I said. "We have time enough to fool around."

Janet turned her head to glare at me.

"Or not," I said. "Either is fine."

Janet gulped wine and then lowered the glass to the lawn. "I wasn't afraid at the time," she said softly. "All I saw was that man attacking Regan and I just reacted. I didn't think. I just—is that how it is with you? All those years, all those bad guys?"

"Sometimes," I said. "Most of the time, no. As a cop you're trained to react to certain situations, but most times reacting without thinking is a mistake."

Janet touched the bandage on her nose with a finger. "I'll say."

"The silver lining, if you could call it that, is that Regan has grown a dozen years in so many days," I said.

Janet nodded, and then the floodgates opened and she had a really good cry. It was the delayed reaction victims feel after the danger has passed and the idea that they may have been killed really sets in and takes root.

They have counseling for rape victims and victims of violent crimes set up for just such occasions, but I knew time and distance were the only real cures. Put enough time and distance between event and the memory, and the memory will eventually be replaced by life, because life does go on, with or without you, and *with* is a strong magnet.

Regan proved that every day.

She chose life. Janet would do the same.

I've been blessed with strong women.

I heard a car arrive out front.

Like a switch had been flipped, Janet composed herself. Regan and Mark raced around the side of the house, and she stood up to embrace their hugs. Even Molly the cat got in on the act and pawed Janet's ankles.

Walt appeared on the fringe of the lawn. I stood up and walked over to meet him.

"You got that look in your eye," Walt said.

"What look?" I said.

"That take no prisoners look I first saw twenty years ago when we started out as partners," Walt said.

"Where I'm going could cost you your pension," I said. "If we don't wind up in prison. Are you in or out?"

Walt looked past me at Janet as she smiled at Regan and Mark.

"What's that you always used to say when you were about to do something really stupid?" Walt said.

"Three squares a day and free clothes is a sweet deal?" I said.

Walt looked at me. "Yeah, that," he said.

Chapter 78

Oliver Koch was hosting a town hall meeting in Bangor, Maine, three days after Janet came home. Chad called me with the info, but claimed he couldn't find out about the mysterious caller from the other day. With Oz staying over, I made the drive north the night before and stayed at a nearby Comfort Inn. I grabbed a pizza for a late dinner and ate in my room with the television on low volume for company.

I was going to that ugly place now and there wasn't room for outsiders. If you aren't lucky enough to be born without compunction, committing evil is hard work. It takes a certain mindset to do something you know is morally wrong and yet do it anyway.

Even hardened criminals have a code of honor. Put a child molester in any prison yard in America and murderers, drug dealers, and thieves will take him out almost overnight.

To go past that code of honor meant wandering into the danger zone where serial killers and rapists dwell.

It's an ugly place.

In my career, I've put away maybe a dozen or so who live on that side of the tracks. They're capable of almost anything and oftentimes things we can't even imagine, or maybe don't want to.

Eddie Crist the mob boss lived in that place most of his life. Toward the end, when he felt his conscience twinge, he managed a bit of salvation by his actions toward Regan.

I'll forever be grateful for that.

My cell phone rang. I checked the incoming number and answered the call.

"You knew, didn't you?" Lawrence said.

"Knew what?"

"That I'd find out Koch has two homes in the islands," Lawrence said. "One on Maui and another on the Big Island."

"Remember Hawaiian Shirt from Washington who tailed me on the plane?" I said. "And then the hit man from Hawaii. It's no coincidence."

"Koch has connections on the islands," Lawrence said.

"Halfway around the world where he thinks they can't be traced," I said. "Anything on his financial records yet?"

"Loaded doesn't cover it," Lawrence said. "Puts a lot of shit in his wife's name to hide assets and avoid certain taxes. Both homes in Hawaii are in her name. The stupid sailboat and some other stuff."

"What about a prenup or other documents that prevent Melissa Koch from divorcing him?" I said.

"Airtight prenup gives her half a million for life," Lawrence said.

"Not bad, but not exactly the lifestyle she's used to," I said.

"No. So what's going through that thick skull of yours?"

"Still shaking the tree," I said.

"Don't let a coconut hit you on the head," Lawrence said.

I hung up and called Chad. His voicemail picked up and I left a message for him to call me right away.

Then I took a nap while I waited for him to call me back.

My phone rang forty-five minutes later. I checked the number as I lit a cigarette. It was Chad returning my call.

Except that it wasn't.

"Chad?" I said.

"This is Homicide Investigator Michael Lange of the Maine

State Police. To whom am I speaking, please?" a strange voice said.

"My name is John Bekker," I said.

"Are you a friend of Chad Handler, Mr. Bekker?" Lange said.

"No, I'm not," I said.

"But you called his cell phone?"

"Yes, I did," I said. "About an hour ago."

"May I ask why?" Lange said.

"May I ask why you're asking why?" I said.

"Three hours ago Mr. Handler was found dead in his home in Falmouth," Lange said. "Is that a good enough reason for you?"

"Natural causes?" I said.

"Suicide. He left a note. Said the strain of it all was too much for him to bear. He asked for forgiveness," Lange said. "Do you know anything about that?"

"I think we should meet," I said.

"I think that would be a good idea," Lange said. "Where are you?"

"Comfort Inn, not far from the Bangor Airport."

"I'll be there in an hour," Lange said. "And Mr. Bekker, as soon as I hang up I'm having the Bangor PD take a ride to your room to make sure you stay put."

"Ask them to pick me up a coffee," I said and hung up.

Chapter 79

Michael Lange more resembled a marine corps drill instructor than a state police officer, right down to his white-walls crew cut. About six feet tall, ramrod straight, Lange wore a lightweight summer suit that did little to hide his imposing physique.

I waited for Lange in the motel lobby, where I could see the police cruiser parked in the lot. Lange arrived in an unmarked car, spoke a few words to the officer in the cruiser, and then I went out to greet him.

We immediately went to the coffee shop across the street from the motel, to get out of the heat. We both ordered coffee.

I placed my ID on the table for Lange to review. He read my license, checked my photo, and passed it back to me.

"I'm retired from Special Crimes, Homicide, and Vice," I said. "I've been hired to find a missing person and the trail led me to Washington. The woman in question had an affair with Senator Koch about twelve years ago, right before she vanished. Chad Handler was acting as an informant for me concerning the Senator's schedule and activities."

Lange stared at me for a moment. "You're shitting me," he said. "Senator Koch is the crown fucking jewel of this whole goddamn useless state."

I pulled out my pen and pocket notebook. I scribbled for a moment, tore out the page, and passed it to Lange. "Captain Walter Grimes, FBI Special Agent Paul Lawrence, call them and ask to verify what I'm telling you."

Lange looked at the paper, folded it, and tucked it into a pocket. "You think the Senator had something to do with the girl's disappearance?" he said.

"I think he killed her, or had her killed," I said.

Lange stared at me with his stone-chiseled face.

"The woman was pregnant and refused to have an abortion even after Koch wanted to pay her a million to have one," I said.

"Do you have any idea what the fuck you're saying?" Lange said.

"I do."

"Oliver Koch is a shoe-in for the next VP nod, hands down."

"That doesn't make him innocent or incapable of murder."

"Can you prove any of this?"

"I can prove he had the affair and that Chad covered it up," I said. "I can't prove murder at this point. I can't prove he hired a professional hit man to kill me and my family. My future wife will need six months of reconstructive surgery and my daughter escaped injury only because I killed the bastard with my bare hands. With additional cooperation from Chad, I might have linked Koch to murder one. I still might, but it will take a bit longer now with him out of the picture."

"Hold on," Lange said as he dug out his cell phone and my slip of paper.

I drank my coffee while Lange punched in the private numbers for Paul Lawrence's cell phone. While Lange identified himself to Paul, I took our empty cups to the counter for refills. By the time I returned, Lange was off the phone.

I set the cups down and reclaimed my seat.

"Shit," Lange said.

"Sounds like Paul," I said.

"No, what he said was he would appreciate it if we cooperated with and didn't impede *your* investigation," Lange said. "And he would especially appreciate it if it was kept very quiet and off the record. Code words for stay out of your way."

"Sounds like Paul," I said.

"I've been a cop twenty-eight years and just when you think nothing can surprise you anymore, something comes along and knocks your socks off," Lange said.

"How did Handler kill himself?" I said.

"Wood support beam runs across his living room ceiling," Lange said. "Tied a noose and jumped off a chair. That's how he was found by the sheriff's department."

"What made them go to his home?" I said.

"He didn't report for work at the Senator's office," Lange said. "After several phone calls and text messages, the Senator called the sheriff's department and asked if they could check on him. Handler was dead several hours by that time and there was nothing they could do."

"Where's the body?" I said.

"Morgue in Portland."

"Have photos?"

"In my laptop."

"Let's go back to my room," I said. "I'd like to take a look."

I watched the digital photos on Lange's laptop. They weren't pretty. The deputy took initial photographs, then the state police lab followed up with a dozen or so more.

Chad hung himself from a support beam that appeared to run the length of his lavish home. He was fully dressed as if about to leave for work. White shirt, red tie, black trousers, no jacket.

I lit a cigarette and took a sip from the container of coffee I'd picked up on the way out of the restaurant. "So he got dressed for work, changed his mind, and decided to hang himself?" I said.

"It does appear so," Lange said. "Nothing disturbed in the house except for the overturned chair. Nothing missing that was determined. No fingerprints anywhere other than his own. No sign of forced entry at the doors or windows. No marks anywhere on his body except for his neck. Unless otherwise directed by the forensics lab, this one stays a suicide."

"Can you enlarge the rope around his neck?" I said.

Lange used his mouse pad to enlarge the rope. "Any photos of just the rope?" I said.

Lange skipped through several photos and displayed several of just the rope hanging from the beam and several more on an evidence table.

"That's not a noose," I said. "What kind of knot is that?"

"That is called a fisherman's knot," Lange said. "A small loop around a large loop, overlapped five times and tucked into the small loop and pulled tight. One of the best knots for securing a hook to a fishing line."

"Chad spent a lot of time on Koch's boat, so he probably knew how to tie that knot from fishing," I said.

"Probably."

"Can you print me a hard copy of the rope?" I said. "And one close up of the knot?"

Lange looked at me.

"For my files," I said.

"Anything else?"

"Take a ride with me to see the Senator in the morning?" I said.

"He's issuing a statement to the press in the morning," Lange said. "I doubt he'll want to see anyone after that."

"Convince him," I said.

"Eight-thirty okay?" Lange said.

"Make it eight," I said. "I'll treat you to breakfast."

Chapter 80

"Suicide, my bony ass," Paul Lawrence said when I called him after Lange took off.

"Know what a fisherman's knot is?" I said.

"The last time I held a fishing rod, I was eight years old and it was one of those pocket deals my dad kept in the glove box," Lawrence said.

"Catch anything?"

"A cold from standing in a freezing stream."

"I do some surf casting with Oz at the beach," I said. "It's a knot made with a small loop around a larger loop with five wraps and a tuck. The more it's pulled on, the tighter the knot is. That's what Chad Handler tied to hang himself. A fisherman's knot instead of a noose."

"He probably had no idea how to tie a noose," Lawrence said. "It isn't easy if you've never been shown how. He spent a lot of time on Koch's sailboat and probably picked up that fisherman's knot thing from fishing with the Senator."

"Yeah."

"That state cop cooperating with you?"

"We're going to see Koch in the morning, right after he gives a statement to the media," I said.

"What's your gut tell you, suicide or something else?" Lawrence said.

"Something else, but don't ask me what," I said.

"Think you'll pick up something from your visit with him in

the morning?"

"I'll find out and let you know," I said.

After hanging up with Lawrence, I sat back against my pillow and lit a cigarette. It was too late to call Janet or Regan. It was too late to call Walt and run things by him.

It was too late to do anything but think and sleep.

First, I thought. Decades ago, when Walt and I first became detectives, a wise older detective took us under his wing. One of the first things he taught me was about coincidence in an investigation. If a witness disappears just before he or she takes the stand, or evidence suddenly goes missing, or the murder weapon happens to pop up at just the right time, it isn't coincidence, it's planned.

A woman goes missing after she announces to her powerful, married lover she's keeping the baby. The assistant to the same powerful man takes his own life after agreeing to help with the investigation. In between the two, a hit man from Hawaii shows up with a contract on me after I get a bit too nosey about the Senator's habits, and it just so happens, the Senator owns several homes on the islands.

"When the facts lie, go with your gut," the old detective told me. "Because figures can lie and liars can figure."

After a while I quit thinking and went to sleep.

Sometimes that helps, too.

CHAPTER 81

Michael Lange wore his uniform the following morning when he arrived at my motel exactly at eight a.m. His rank was lieutenant, but I wasn't sure if that carried over to plain clothes.

I didn't ask, but the uniform was probably to impress and intimidate Koch. That might have worked on a local politician, but he was Washington power and used to uniforms of every type.

Seeing them, and having power over them.

I didn't point that out to Lange. No sense making an enemy of someone who could be useful down the road. We had a pleasant breakfast at the same diner where we'd had coffee the night before and were on the road before nine.

The drive to Cape Elizabeth took nearly three hours. The gates to Koch's estate were open and manned by two state police officers. They seemed startled to see Lange behind the wheel of a cruiser, then they snapped to attention.

"We miss the press conference?" Lange said.

"It started about fifteen minutes ago on the back lawn," a trooper said. "We have two men posted there for added protection."

"Against what?" Lange said.

The trooper stared at him. "I . . . I don't know, sir," he said.

"Don't announce us," Lange said.

"Yes, sir."

Lange feathered the gas, and we drove past the two troopers

to the long driveway and the front of the Koch mansion. Up close, I estimated the room count at twenty and the value of house and property at six to seven million.

We left the cruiser and walked along a stone path to the backyard where Koch stood at a podium in front of a dozen or more members of the media.

"I'm sorry I can't take questions at this time," Koch said. "I just don't have enough information to provide adequate answers. All I can tell you is what I said in my opening statement, that Chad was a dear and trusted friend and I can't begin to express the sorrow I feel at this untimely loss."

"Senator, will the state police be handling his suicide as a matter of routine, or will they take it a bit more?" a reporter said.

"A bit more?" Koch said. "Are you referring to possible foul play in Chad's death?"

"Just asking, Senator," the reporter said. "I'm sure they will look at all points of interest in a high-profile death such as this."

"You'll have to ask the state police that question," Koch said.

"Do you have a name? Who do we contact?" the reporter said.

Easy as you please, Lange strolled to the podium and stood beside Koch. "That would be me," Lange said. "Lieutenant Michael Lange, Maine State Police."

Koch was a smooth, experienced operator and Lange's interruption didn't faze him in the least. He stepped to Lange's side and let Lange take center stage.

Immediately, reporters started firing questions at Lange as recorders and cameras rolled. Lange fielded the questions by raising his hands to quiet the reporters.

"Good morning," he said. "I won't take questions, but I have a short statement that should answer some of them for you. At this time, the death of Chad Handler is being treated as a suicide until evidence dictates otherwise. We are searching for the motive behind this untimely suicide, but all indications are that Mr. Handler acted alone in taking his own life. When I have more details, they will be released to the media. Thank you."

Lange stepped back. Koch stepped back up and gave a short thank-you statement, and the reporters started to file out. When the last of them was gone, Koch turned and noticed me for the first time.

"What the hell is he doing here?" Koch said to Lange.

"We came together, Senator," Lange said. "And we'd like a few moments of your time alone."

Koch's home office had an entrance from the backyard garden. It was built to mirror his office in the Senate, only not at the taxpayers' expense, as he put it when we entered.

Koch immediately sat behind his large and imposing desk. Lange and I stood.

"Lieutenant, this man has been a pain in my ass," Koch said. "He's been harassing me for weeks about a missing person from twelve years ago. He seems to think I had something to do with her disappearance even though the FBI and Metro Police cleared me and my entire staff at the time she disappeared."

Lange looked at me. "Is that right? Are you harassing the Senator?"

"No," I said. "I'm plain-out fucking with him and enjoying every fucking second of it, and I don't plan to stop for any reason."

"Now see here," Koch said.

"And I'll tell you something else, Senator," I said. "You killed Sarah Gertz after you knocked her up and we both know it. You sent a man to kill me and my family and we both know that, too. I believe you had Chad Handler killed and made to look like suicide because you discovered he was helping me gain evidence against you. And I'm not going to stop or go away until I have the evidence to put your miserable fucking ass in prison for life or you get the death penalty. Either is fine with me."

Koch stared at me until he slowly rose up from his chair. His face tinged red as his anger mounted. "Leave my house this instant," he said. "And be prepared to hear from my attorney concerning a lawsuit."

"Fuck you," I said. "And fuck your attorney. Your ass belongs to me and we both know it."

Koch started to come around his desk. His eyes were wide with fury.

"Stop right there or get dumped on your regal, senatorial ass," I said.

Koch froze in place. Slowly his eyes returned to normal as common sense won out over anger. "Lieutenant, you're a witness to his threats. My attorney will contact you for a statement, and you can be sure I will contact the governor and let him know you allowed this to happen in my own home. Now the both of you leave at once."

"Make sure your attorney spells my name right," I said. "Two *k*'s."

"Get out this instant," Koch said.

We left.

On the way out the garden doors, Lange paused and turned around to look at Koch.

"I'm sure glad I didn't vote for you last election," he said.

Chapter 82

"You're out of your mind," Lange said as he drove the cruiser toward the highway. "Do you how much punch Senator Koch has? He's the fucking King of England around here."

"I don't care if he's the fucking Prince of Tides," I said.

I lit a cigarette inside the cruiser. Lange didn't remark on my violation of the statewide smoking laws. He did, however, push the button to lower the window.

"A man lays hands on your wife and daughter with intent to kill, what would you do about it?" I said.

Lange looked at me.

"Exactly fucking right," I said.

Lange drove in silence for a bit. I chain-smoked in silence for a bit. Lange broke the silence first. "So what now?"

"I press on," I said. "You don't have to do a thing. It doesn't involve you or the state police."

"What if he gets his lawyer to file a complaint?" Lange said. "If I'm subpoenaed I'll have to state what I heard."

"He won't get a subpoena," I said.

"No?"

I pulled out my cell phone and called Paul Lawrence. I filled him in on the new updates and the brief but fiery encounter with Koch. "Can you give him a quiet jingle and request that he doesn't move forward on his threatened restraining order and lawsuit?" I said.

"Since when does a little lawsuit bother you, Jack?" Lawrence said.

"It doesn't," I said. "I just want the Senator to know he doesn't have as much power as he thinks he does. Once he understands that, I'm going to rattle his cage until he falls out and into my lap."

"It will have to be an unofficial call," Lawrence said.

"I don't care if you make it with two tin cans and string, just so long as Koch gets the message," I said.

"Okay, Jack," Lawrence said. "I just hope you know what you're doing."

I said goodbye to Lawrence and tucked the phone away. As I lit a fresh smoke, Lange glanced at me.

"What?" I said.

"You're serious?"

"As a heart attack."

"When this goes down, I'd like to be there," Lange said.

I blew a smoke ring and watched it sail out the open window. "Welcome aboard," I said.

Chapter 83

I sat in the waiting room of the surgeon who would be doing the operations on Janet's nose and jaw. She went in at ten in the morning and didn't resurface until eleven forty-five. I found out later they were picking out new noses for Janet and while the surgeon was at it, he could tighten up the old jawline and remove those crow's feet around the eyes.

I whittled away the time by mulling thoughts around in my head to see if something jumped out at me. Chad Handler's suicide still made no sense. He was young enough and wealthy enough to survive a scandal if it came down to it, and any chance his name would be released when the time came would have been a by-product at best.

After three days, Chad's suicide was old news and forgotten by the media. Even Koch had moved on, announcing on his website he was rescheduling town hall meetings for the coming weeks.

Paul Lawrence made the call to Koch on the QT. I didn't ask for details, but Lawrence told me the Senator wasn't a happy fellow.

Neither was I.

Progress had stalled.

Without Chad Handler as my liaison, I'd lost my in to Koch's daily activities. The reality that Koch could ride out this mess right to the White House VP seat seemed more and more probable with each passing day.

It was turning out I was just a fly on the horse's back, a pesky annoyance to swat with its tail.

The surgeon opened a door and poked his head out. "Can you come in for a moment?" he said.

I followed him to the office where Janet sat at a desk with picture books and a computer. She looked at me.

"What do you think?" she said.

I looked at the computer screen. The image of Janet with her new nose and eye and chin tuck made her look thirty-five or younger.

"I always wanted a child bride," I said.

"Surgery is set for five weeks," the surgeon said. "Give the scar tissue more healing time before I operate."

"Make her any younger and they'll think I'm robbing the cradle," I said.

"Well, we could do a little work on you, if you'd like?" the surgeon said.

Janet laughed, stood up, and thanked the doctor.

I drove to my trailer, where I fired up the grill and we ate lunch at the card table. The afternoon was bright, the tide was low, and for once the beach was empty of surfers. Gulls gathered on the fringe, squawking and fighting for scraps of food they anticipated would be tossed their way.

"I'm not a vain woman, Jack," Janet said as we sat in our chairs and sipped after-lunch coffee. "You know that. Vanity has never been a fault of mine."

"I know."

"I always thought I would age gracefully and accept things as they came."

"I know."

"I'm thinking of having my boobs enlarged as long as I'm having the nose job," Janet said.

"That's nice."

"Jack, where are you right now?" Janet said. "I could recite chicken soup recipes and you'd say, 'I know.' "

"Sorry," I said. "Something is bugging me and I don't know what."

"Could it be that you didn't ride in on a white horse to smite the bad guy and save the day?" Janet said.

"It's not—who says smite?"

"I do, and if that's not it, what is it then?"

I grabbed my smokes and lit one.

"That bad, huh?" Janet said. "When you reach for your crutch, I know it's serious."

"I had him and he slipped away," I said. "Chad Handler was murdered to protect Oliver Koch's dirty little secrets. I could beat my chest and make threats all day long, but the bottom line is Koch beat me. In seven or eight months, when they kick off the campaign crap for the next election, he waltzes away with the VP nod for his crimes."

Janet took a sip of coffee, carefully avoiding the small white bandage covering the bridge of her nose. "Are you angry because he beat you or because he got away with murdering a young woman and nearly us in the process, Jack?" she said as she set the cup down.

"Both," I said. "But something else, too."

"What?"

"When Carol was murdered and Regan suffered, I wanted to kill Eddie Crist," I said. "Not arrest and trial, but murder with my bare hands. That day he brought me to his home and sobered me up, it was all I could do not to strangle that old man in his wheelchair. I feel that way now. I don't care anymore about the Gertz woman and the law, or Robert Gordon. I just want to kill Oliver Koch in cold blood for what he did to you and Regan, and I know that is a very dark place for my mind to be, but there it is."

Janet turned her head and looked at me. "And that's what's bugging you?" she said. "That you want to kill a man for revenge for hurting people you love?"

"I'm supposed to know better," I said. "Hotshot cop, super detective and all that crap, but when you come right down to it, I'm no better than Eddie Crist."

Janet stood up and walked into the trailer.

I crushed out the butt of my cigarette in the tiny tin pie plate on the card table. I grabbed my pack of smokes and lit another.

I heard Janet reemerge from the trailer. A quilted blanket flew past my head. I turned around and looked at Janet. She was wearing nothing but her birthday suit, and as birthday suits go, hers was hard to beat.

"There isn't a soul on the beach and Oz is at my house," Janet said. "So I'm going to lie down on this blanket and if you're so inclined to remove your clothes and lie down with me, I would very much appreciate it."

"Your shoulder?" I said.

"As long as you don't put your two hundred and twenty-five pounds on it my shoulder will be fine," Janet said.

She spread out the blanket and then took a seat. With her right hand she patted the spot next to her. "Be a good boy and I'll give you a treat."

Afterward, we went inside for a nap. Janet fell right off to sleep. I lingered in between sleep and consciousness in that place where dreams lack, but your mind goes blank.

My eyes suddenly snapped open.

I sat up in bed and carefully unwrapped Janet's legs from mine. I stood and tossed on shorts and a T-shirt, went outside, and took my chair.

I lit a cigarette.

It suddenly occurred to me.
Vanity.
One of the seven deadlies.

CHAPTER 84

"We're out of our fucking minds, all of us," Walt said.

"It does appear that way, don't it?" Jane said.

We were in a van courtesy of Paul Lawrence. The van was loaded with the latest in surveillance and electronic equipment. The van was parked across the street from the town hall meeting where Oliver Koch was giving bullet points of some tax plan or another to a crowd of about three hundred.

In that crowd of about three hundred were twenty reporters in a front row.

Of those twenty reporters, one was a CIA freelance operative, a femme fatale of the highest caliber. A drop-dead gorgeous strawberry blonde with deep green eyes, she was used mostly for spy work in foreign countries when some high-ranking official needed to be seduced.

And then killed.

Paul Lawrence introduced her to me as Susie. I doubted that was her real name, but it was possible Lawrence didn't know it either. We met at my trailer the morning Lawrence and Susie flew in from Washington.

"I assume you want him seduced, and not killed?" Susie said.

"For Christ's sake, Susie, he's a US senator," Lawrence said.

"And?" Susie said.

"I don't want him killed," I said. "I want him seduced and I'd like you to wear a wire while you do it. We can wire you up right before—"

"I have my own equipment," Susie said. "Not the crap stuff the government uses."

"Okay, good," I said. "How much for a few hours' work?"

"What do you want done?" Susie said.

"We want him seduced," Lawrence said.

"Yes, you said that," Susie said. "Do you want him fucked, tied up, and begging like a dog in heat or just naked with photos and film? What?"

Lawrence looked at me. "What, naked and photos?"

I nodded.

"Since this is a favor to Paul, I'll give you my bargain-basement rates," Susie said. "Fifteen grand covers it all."

"Come on, Susie, that's—" Lawrence said.

"Cash?" I said.

"Of course cash," Susie said. "I don't even have a real Social Security number."

"We leave tomorrow," I told Susie. "I'll pay you in advance before we hit the road."

So now Lawrence, Walt, and Jane kept me company in the van while we listened to Koch drone on to the crowd about tax plans, job growth, and some other assorted political promises that those in attendance had heard a thousand times before.

It was obvious Koch was measuring the crowd for their reaction to his bid for VP. He seemed pleased by the general reaction and ended with a Q&A period that lasted about thirty minutes.

As the meeting ended, we could hear reporters rush Koch and barrage him with questions. That was the first time we heard Susie speak on tape.

"Senator, Senator, a moment of your time?" Susie said.

There was a short pause, then Koch said, "Why, certainly. And you are?"

"Susie."

"Well, aren't you just so cute," Koch said. "Susie."

I could almost feel Koch's leer. After that, it was up and running.

Susie peppered Koch with a few questions concerning his VP bid, then guided him toward some personal questions, and finally hooked him when she asked for a private interview.

Maybe they could go for coffee?

The interview lasted fifteen minutes before they were on the way to Susie's motel room just off the highway. She had him naked and ready in no time. He asked if he should stay the night since his wife was at their vacation home in Hawaii.

Susie said that wouldn't be a good idea and then said we could come in now.

Paul Lawrence opened the door and we filed in one by one. Me, Walt, and then Jane. I politely closed the door behind us.

Naked as a jaybird, Oliver Koch gave us a hard stare. "What is the meaning of this?" he barked.

"You tell us, Senator," Lawrence said as he flashed his identification. "You're the one naked on camera."

Jane squinted at Koch's naked body. "I sure hope that's a grower, because it's not much of a shower," she said.

Chapter 85

In the interrogation room at the nearby state police barracks, Oliver Koch glared at us from across the table. He wasn't handcuffed to the table, as he wasn't under arrest. He had a container of coffee in his right hand and he took small sips from it as Lawrence fiddled with a recorder.

"Is that necessary?" Koch said of the recorder.

"You tell me, Senator," Lawrence said. "As of thirty minutes ago, I've officially reopened the Sarah Gertz missing-persons investigation and you're the number-one person of interest on my list."

"This is preposterous," Koch said.

"Is it?" Lawrence said. "You're the one naked on camera with a CIA freelance operative."

"That's entrapment," Koch said. "And you have no legal warrant or cause."

"I doubt anybody in the media cares," Lawrence said. "This time tomorrow your political career is ruined and your wife will be asking for half in divorce court. Your choice is talk to me or don't. Choose *don't* and you make YouTube's top one hundred by tomorrow morning."

Koch glared hard at me. "Why are they in the room?"

"Captain Grimes is here because the Gertz woman is from his district and the girl's father is implicated in a crime, as you already know," Lawrence said. "Sheriff Morgan is here because the hit man you contracted acted inside her jurisdiction. Bekker is here because this is his show and he hates your fucking guts. Any more questions, Senator?"

Koch sipped some coffee. "Should I have my lawyer here?"

"Do you want him here?" Lawrence said.

"Am I under arrest?"

"Not for solicitation," Lawrence said. "You didn't pay for Susie's services. You just fell for her charms, but in that you're not alone. What's it going to be, one million hits on YouTube or talk to me?"

Koch nodded. "What do you want to know?"

"What you know concerning Sarah Gertz," Lawrence said.

"I leave here with the only copy of that tape and your written word that what happened tonight doesn't leave this room," Koch said. "Those are my terms in exchange for my co-operation."

"No good, Senator," Lawrence said. "What you have to say may be useless to me, in which case I will proceed with a full-scale investigation into the girl's disappearance."

"You're bluffing," Koch said.

"Test me," Lawrence said.

Koch stared at Lawrence for a moment. Then he sighed and took another sip of his coffee. "I've always had a weakness for women," he said. "And they've had a weakness for me."

Jane rolled her eyes and stifled the groan in her throat.

Koch looked at Jane. "I make no mistake that my wealth and power serves as an attraction," he said. "And I make no bones about it that I've used my wealth and power to seduce them. Now, what do you want to know about the Gertz woman I haven't said twelve years ago to the Metro Police and FBI?"

"Did you kill her?" Lawrence said.

"No, I did not," Koch said. "I met her at an EPA committee meeting and we sort of hit it off right away. One thing led to another and she became pregnant. After that—"

"Women just don't become pregnant," Jane said. "You knocked her up."

"Yes, I did," Koch said. "Though unintentionally, I assure you."

"And after that?" Lawrence said.

"She came to me and said she wanted to keep the baby," Koch said. "In the face of political ruination, I offered her one million dollars to have an abortion. She wouldn't. Shortly after that she disappeared."

"And you had nothing to do with that?" Lawrence said.

"No."

"And the contract killer who came after Bekker and his family, what do you know about that?" Lawrence said.

"Not a thing and if you have some evidence that says contrary, I'd like to see it," Koch said. "Because maybe you can ruin my political future and maybe my wife will divorce me and a sympathetic court will award her more than our prenup, but do you think I can't rebound from those financial setbacks and scandals? Bill Clinton ring a bell? Reagan divorced before Nancy ring a bell? So charge me with something or get out of my way."

"You're forgetting one thing, asshole," I said. "I have a snow globe that reads *With Love, Okay,* code for Oliver Koch. They promised not to go public with your little motel room junket this evening, but I made no such promise not to bring my story to the media and present the snow globe as evidence. A little fuck you from me to you with love, JB."

Koch looked at Lawrence. "Are you going to allow this man to threaten me as if I were some junkyard dog?"

"What threat?" Lawrence said. "Anybody hear a threat?"

"Nope," Walt said.

"I heard a mouse fart," Jane said. "Lucky I'm downwind."

I stood up from the table. "Next time you see me it will be when I put the cuffs on you," I said.

"Hold on," Koch said. "Just hold on."

I looked at Koch.

"I've long held the suspicion that Chad Handler had something to do with her disappearance," Koch said. "He . . . that note, what did it say. Oh, yes. The strain was too much for him to bear, something to that effect. I think the pressure you put on him made him finally crack and take his own life."

"Why would he kill for you, Senator?" I said.

"To protect me from harm," Koch said. "The man was like one of my own children. His devotion was steadfast. I wish to God he was alive for you to question, but as he isn't, I can't help you beyond that. Maybe if you checked more carefully into his activities, you might gain some insight. Ruin me if you must, but that's all I have to say."

Lawrence turned around to look at me.

I nodded slightly.

"Okay, Senator," Lawrence said. "This is how it's going to go. We'll hold off on your little close encounter tonight while we investigate Handler's background and activities, but make no mistake about it, we will look at you every which way possible and if we find something, anything, it's game off."

"You won't," Koch said.

"Sound pretty sure about that," Lawrence said.

"You won't find anything because I'm innocent of the girl's disappearance," Koch said. "And if you go public with that tape, I will have a team of lawyers waiting to send each of you to the poorhouse, starting with you, Bekker. Keep me advised how the investigation goes, will you?"

I turned and walked out of the room.

CHAPTER 86

I sipped coffee, then slid the cup away from me in disgust. We were in a booth at a late-night diner not far from the state police barracks.

"Son of a bitch is telling the truth," I said.

"How are you so sure?" Jane said.

"Jack's right, he is telling the truth," Lawrence said. "And it's by his reflex actions and verbal communication. Liars and the guilty can't hide their stress and guilt for very long when confronted. They will do something or say something that gives away their guilt and eventually traps them in their own lies."

"Koch gave us none of that," Walt said.

"So this Handler could be the guilty one?" Jane said.

"Could be," Lawrence said. "And I now have cause to check every nook and cranny of his life and suicide to find out."

"I hate to be the one to say it, Jack, but we may be at square one," Walt said. "Less, even."

I grabbed my cup and took a sip.

"On the other hand, we might get lucky with Handler," Lawrence said. "It is possible from his visits to Koch's Hawaii locations that he made some connections with the seedy type. Maybe he was into drugs or little boys? Who knows until we start really digging, and he was the right height to fit the girl's car seat the way it was set."

"And he did know the girl from meetings and knew she was pregnant," Walt said.

"Sometimes you got to let things go and cut your losses, Jack," Lawrence said. "This might turn out to be one of those times."

I took another sip from my cup.

"Or we could get lucky and find something that links Handler to the Gertz girl," Lawrence said.

"And that email from a long-lost cousin in England telling you an uncle in India died and left you a million dollars just might be true," I said.

I stood up and tossed a twenty on the table. "It's a long ride home."

Chapter 87

I sat in the chair opposite Percy Meade's desk and watched him count out twenty thousand dollars in owed expense money. I had yet to submit a bill for hours, but I was in no hurry.

I briefed Meade prior to giving him my expense report.

"So that's it, then," he said as he put the final hundred-dollar bill on the stack on his desk. "I don't see how you could possibly do anymore, and don't forget it was a very long shot at best."

I nodded. "How is Gordon these days?"

"Responding to treatment better than expected," Meade said. "It was felt he wouldn't last two weeks, but they give as much as three months now. Who really knows?"

"Can he have visitors?" I said.

"If he wants," Meade said. "Do you want to give him your report in person?"

"I think so, yes."

"Want me to call him and arrange a visit?"

"No," I said. "I think I'll take my chances at stopping by unannounced. You'll get my final bill in the mail."

"Very well," Meade said.

We shook hands and I left his office.

I drove to the post office to pick up two weeks' worth of mail, tossed it on the back seat, and steered the Marquis to Robert Gordon's house.

A live-in nurse from the hospital answered the door. It took some explaining, but I finally convinced her that Gordon would want to see me. I waited in the living room while she went to a back bedroom. She returned a few minutes later and said, "Mr. Gordon will see you, but please make it quick. He hasn't the strength for a long conversation."

Gordon was propped up on pillows in a king-size bed. His weight was down to around a hundred and twenty pounds. As with Eddie Crist, cancer was literally eating him alive.

The nurse left us alone.

Gordon stared at me with eyes that told me death was close at hand.

"I didn't want to make my report to Meade," I said. "I wanted you to hear it directly from me."

Gordon nodded. "Go ahead," he said in a soft, raspy voice. "I have nothing to fear anymore."

"It took some doing, but I located the family that bought your daughter," I said. "Nice family in Queens, New York. They raised her right. She went to college for political science and moved to Washington to work for environmental groups. About twelve years ago, she was knocked up by a horny senator in one of her groups. Soon after that, she disappeared and hasn't been heard from since. I believe, but can't prove, that she was murdered to protect the senator's future in politics. If I were you, I'd figure out whom to leave my millions to, because she's gone and won't be heard from again."

Gordon stared at me.

"So now I'll tell you what I really came here to say," I said. "If you hadn't sold your daughter she would probably be alive here today, sitting by your side to comfort you as you die in peace. But she's probably dead and it's your fault and if you think that you being a doctor makes up for that, you're wrong. Have a nice death, Mr. Gordon."

I left him there on his deathbed.

I could feel his eyes on the back of my head as I walked out of the room.

He could live another three months or die the next sixty seconds; it made no difference to God where he was going.

Or to me, either.

CHAPTER 88

Janet and I watched Regan and Mark body surf on the incoming waves of high tide. We brought our chairs from the trailer to the beach, and as the tide rose, water covered our ankles.

Janet wore a blue cover-up over her one-piece suit, a straw hat, and owl sunglasses. Except for the small white bandage over the bridge of her nose, she looked pretty much normal. Surgery was less than a month away, our wedding less than two months, give or take.

It was time to take stock of my life. I had a beautiful woman, a pending new job, my daughter had advanced more than I could have hoped for, and I had a few bucks in the bank with a fat paycheck on the way.

Life goes on and moves on, and it was time I joined that move.

Unlike in your favorite cop show on television, many times the bad guys win.

This time I lost.

The bad guys came out on top.

It was time to cut my losses and move on with my life and the life I would soon share with my newly formed family.

Still . . .

Exhausted from riding the waves, Regan and Mark came and flopped by our chairs. "I'm hungry, Mom," Mark said.

"Me, too," Regan said.

Janet looked at me.

"I'll go fire up the coals," I said.

As soon as I vacated my chair, Mark made a beeline for it. Regan tackled him at the legs, and then took a seat.

"No fair," Mark said. "I can't hit girls."

"Get used to it, little brother," Regan said.

I turned and looked at Janet. It was the first time we'd heard Regan refer to Mark as her little brother. Janet gave me a tiny nod and smile that told me she approved.

I walked back to my trailer. Molly was asleep on the card table, her body curled in a ball on top of the stack of unopened mail I'd picked up from the post office. I let Molly be and filled the grill with fresh coals, splashed on some starter fluid, tossed on a match, and went inside for some fresh coffee.

Armed with mug and cigarette, I claimed my chair to wait for the coals to heat. I was upwind and too far away for Janet to whiff the cigarette smoke, so I happily puffed away. Molly sat up, yawned, and vacated the stack of mail.

I grabbed the stack and started whittling it down. A few bills, a credit card statement, junk mail, and a large, flat envelope from Michael Lange. I tore it open and removed several eight-by-eleven photographs of the knotted rope Chad Handler used to hang himself with.

The rope was standard hardware store supply and could have come from anywhere. I studied the knot. I studied the rope. I saw nothing that jumped out at me or clicked.

I tucked the photos into the envelope, set it on the card table, and went to check the progress of the coals.

About an hour later, as we sat around and stuffed our faces with hot dogs and burgers, Janet peered down the beach at an approaching car.

"It looks like your mirror image is about to arrive," Janet said.

I got up and tossed a couple of dogs and burgers on the still-hot grill, then returned to my chair. A few minutes later, Walt parked his car next to the Marquis and got out.

"I hope a few of those are for me," he said.

"Just about ready," I said. "Grab a seat."

Walt took Oz's chair next to Janet.

"What brings you by in the middle of the afternoon?" I said.

"Paul Lawrence asked me to find out why you don't answer your calls," Walt said.

"My phone is turned off," I said.

Janet looked at me.

"I needed a few days of quiet," I said.

"Want I should tell him that?" Walt said.

I shook my head. "I'll tell him later."

Walt nodded.

Regan stood up and grabbed a large paper plate. "Hungry, Uncle Walt?"

"Starving."

The afternoon wore on. Jokes were told, laughter echoed on the empty beach, spirits were high, and Sarah Gertz was forgotten, if only for the moment.

As the sun slowly began to set, I packed Janet, the kids, and Molly into the Marquis and followed Walt's sedan off the beach.

When I returned to the trailer a while later, Oz had a bonfire going and was in his usual chair.

"Spent the afternoon with my brother," Oz said. "Had dinner with him and his wife, and I love my brother, but the man's wallet is glued to his back pocket."

"That reminds me," I said and unlocked the trailer door, went inside, and returned with a white envelope for Oz. "It should take some of the sting out of the dinner bill."

"What's this?" Oz said.

"Three grand for services rendered," I said.

Oz peeked inside the envelope. "Case closed?" he said.

"It will be in a minute," I said.

I turned on my cell phone and called Paul Lawrence.

"Had my phone off, Paul," I said. "I was on overload."

"I understand," Lawrence said. "Interested in how the Handler thing is shaping up?"

"Why not?"

"Everything we've found in his home leads us to believe he worshipped at the altar of Oliver Koch," Lawrence said. "Even found a supply of the same rope in his basement and it matches the rope and knot used to secure the small dinghy from Koch's yacht. Place is littered with fingerprints and hair samples, but he entertained a lot in the name of Koch, so it was expected. I'm afraid there's not much more we can do at this time, Jack, unless something new and damning comes across my desk."

"I know," I said. "It was worth the shot, and if Handler is guilty, he's paying for it now."

"That's it, then."

"Yeah."

I set my phone on the card table and lit a fresh cigarette.

"Even Koufax lost once in a while," Oz said.

"Koufax isn't dead and can speak for himself," I said. "Sarah Gertz is and she can't."

"I guess I'll go put this away," Oz said and stood up with the white envelope in his right hand.

I nodded and watched Oz slowly walk toward his trailer. After he entered and lights came on, I sat and looked at the stars. Too bad they couldn't talk; they were witness to everything since day one.

I was about to call it a night and get some sleep when something struck me.

Something Janet said earlier when Walt arrived.

"It looks like your mirror image is about to arrive," she'd said.

So what?

I lit another smoke, sipped lukewarm coffee, and thought about *so what.*

A cylinder fired.

Then another.

Pretty soon my brain was racing like a new Porsche.

Mirror image.

"Son of a bitch!" I said and jumped out of my seat, raced to the trailer, and clicked on the outside floodlight.

I raced back to my chair, grabbed Lange's envelope, and pulled out the photos. I stared at them long and hard. Then I went inside for a moment to look for some rope. I found a six-foot piece under the sink and returned to my chair.

I sat and tied a fisherman's knot.

I held it up side-by-side with the photo.

The knot in the rope Chad Handler used to hang himself was tied left-handed.

A mirror image of mine.

That's what was eating away at me all this time. The thing I couldn't put my finger on was right in front of my nose.

I closed my eyes and blocked out the sound of waves crashing at the beach, and nighttime gulls squawking over bits of food. I went backward to the first day I met Chad Handler in Boothbay Harbor. Walt and I waited on the long dock as he approached us in the small dinghy.

He tossed and secured the rope with his right hand. He steered back to the sailboat the same way, right-handed.

He pushed me with his right hand.

He aimed his gun at me with his right hand.

I opened my eyes and set fire to a cigarette.

It was a safe bet Chad Handler was a righty and didn't tie a left-handed knot.

I tried to tie a fisherman's knot with my left hand. It was awkward at best and the knot was next to useless.

I looked at the photos again. The knot was perfect. It wasn't likely Handler was ambidextrous. Most people use one hand or the other, and very few good enough with both to be classified in that category.

I inhaled on the cigarette, closed my eyes, and let the smoke slowly drift out my nose. On the sailboat, she'd sipped her drink with her left hand. At dinner, she ate with her left hand. In town, she held her coffee cup and carried her purse left-handed.

My eyes snapped open.

And the wheels spun round and round.

Chapter 89

After nineteen hours and one very long layover in Los Angeles, my plane touched down on the Big Island of Hawaii at 4:15 in the morning. I had a carry-on bag in the overhead compartment and no checked luggage, so I scooted past baggage claim and went directly to the car rental counter.

I requested a car with a GPS, and once I was behind the wheel, I fed it the address for the Koch estate. The drive took forty-five minutes and guided me along a winding road into the mountains where it skirted cliffs and the beach below.

The scenery illuminated by my headlights was gorgeous, but I wasn't there to sightsee and send postcards home. The massive gates to the Koch estate were open. I pulled in and drove to the roundabout where a BMW and a Lincoln were parked.

I got out, stood for a moment, and looked at the estate. The mansion was massive, but I expected no less. Floodlights illuminated the immediate area. The fence surrounding the house was disguised with flowers of every type, and I followed them around back where an hourglass-shaped swimming pool dominated the backyard.

The sun wasn't up yet, but soon. It was the time of the morning where it was still mostly dark, but just light enough to see faint images and outlines. A man sat in a recliner beside the pool. He was sipping coffee.

I removed my shoes, walked on the balls of my feet across the grass, and came up behind him. My right hand went into my pocket for the ChapStick I always carry with me.

I came up behind his chair and pressed the ChapStick on the top of his head.

He froze.

"One twitch and your brains will be on your lap," I said. "Do you believe me? Say yes or no."

"Yes," he said without moving.

"Are you the man who tailed me on the plane to Washington?"

"Yes."

"Never wear a Hawaiian shirt on a plane if you want to blend in."

"Sure."

"Do you work for her?"

"No."

"Are you her lover?"

"When she's in Hawaii."

"Do you want to live past this morning?"

"Yes."

"Ever been to Falmouth, Maine?"

"Yes."

"Tell me where she is."

"Walking," he said. "She likes to walk at dawn."

"Where?"

"Path at the edge of the gate," he said. "Overlooks the beach. Goes on for a mile and a half. She takes a morning walk there every day, sometimes at night, too."

"How tall are you?"

"What?"

"Your height, what is it?"

"What?"

I pressed down harder with the ChapStick. "*What* ain't no country I ever heard of, motherfucker," I said in my best Sam Jackson voice. "Do they speak English in *what*?"

"Six two and a bit," he stammered.

"The right height to drive Sarah Gertz's car."

"I drove it, but I didn't kill her," he said. "She hired local here on the Island. I swear it. All I did was drive the car."

"Do you want to get out of here?"

"Hell, yes."

"Which car is yours?"

"Lincoln."

"Get up slow and turn around."

He rose up from the recliner and slowly turned around. Just as his jaw came into my view, I punched him square on it with my full weight behind the blow. He crashed over the chair and spilled to the grass.

I stood over his unconscious body, removed his belt, and used it to tie his hands behind his back. By the pool was a stack of white robes. I grabbed one, removed the terrycloth belt, and used it to tie his legs together.

I retrieved my shoes and then walked to the edge of the yard where a gate led to the path. I opened the door and started walking along the path. It was well worn, with wildflowers and brush growing on the left side. On my right about six feet away, the hundred-foot-high cliffs overlooked the ocean and beach below.

It wasn't quite light enough yet to see the beach.

Soon.

I lit a cigarette as I walked. This high up, the breeze off the ocean was cool and filled with the scent of salt. I walked about a half mile when I saw Melissa Koch power-walking toward me.

She held weights in each hand.

She saw me and didn't break stride until the gap between us narrowed to twenty feet or so. Then she slowed to a stop.

I kept walking and stopped in front of her, blocking her path.

We looked at each other.

Her eyes were defiant.

"I should have had Herb just shoot you and be done with it," Melissa said.

"Why?"

"Because my idiot husband can't keep his dick in his pants," she said. "Because I've invested too much time and trouble in his career to let him piss the White House away on some stupid bitch with a schoolgirl crush on him. Stupid girl goes and gets herself knocked up and I'm supposed to suffer because of it. I think not."

"So you made her disappear?" I said.

"Yes."

"Where?"

"I don't know."

"Herb make the arrangements for the hit man that came to my house?"

"Yes," Melissa said. "Herb will do just about anything for me, you see. He loves me, the dope."

"Your husband know any of this?"

"My husband is a fool, as you might have gathered by now," Melissa said. "If it weren't for me, he'd still be a councilman in Portland, advising on the lobster catch and blueberry crop."

"With millions."

"That he inherited and which I multiplied many times over," Melissa said.

"And Handler?"

"He's nothing." Melissa showed me a tiny grin. "Although he proved very useful there at the end, didn't he?"

"Herb kill him?"

"He hoisted his unconscious body, but as I'd guess you figured out, I tied the knot," Melissa said. "Now, as you have no proof of any of this and never will, I will ask you this once to leave my property. After that, I will call nine-one-one and tell them I have an intruder."

She accented her point by holding both weights in her right hand and pulling a tiny cell phone from her waistband with her left.

"Sun's coming up," I said.

"So it is," Melissa said.

"The White House that important you'd kill for it?"

"Yes, and it's been done before in history," Melissa said. "Now get out of my way before I call the police."

I stepped aside.

She looked me in the eye. "Speak one word of this and my attorneys will take away all that you have and all that you ever will have, including that girlfriend of yours and your pretty little daughter. Understood?"

"Yes."

The grin reappeared. "Good day, Mr. Bekker."

I took a deep breath and filled my lungs with salt sea air.

The breeze was cool on my face.

Off on the horizon just a tiny sliver of sunlight brightened the dark sky.

The first light of a new day gave the promise of hope.

I had regained my soul not yet a year ago and I wasn't prepared to lose it again. Third chances are few and far between. I closed my eyes for a brief moment. My inner voice told me what the right thing to do was.

I ignored it.

My eyes opened.

The look in Melissa Koch's eyes told me I was already dismissed and forgotten.

I took a step to my right to allow her to pass.

As Melissa Koch stepped around me, her left foot made contact with my left ankle. She stumbled forward, lost her balance and tumbled to her left. I turned to catch her, but her forward momentum carried her to the soft dirt at the edge of the cliff where she landed with a thud.

I spun around quickly.

"Are you all right?" I said.

"Yes, you buffoon, I am all right and no thanks to you," she said.

"Let me give you a hand." I started to walk down to the edge.

"I don't need your help," she said.

I stopped about six or seven feet from her.

Slowly, Melissa Koch stood up. The soft, rain-soaked dirt of the cliff started to give way under her weight. She looked at me with fear in her eyes.

"Jump!" I yelled.

She placed her weight on her left foot as if to jump. The dirt at her feet crumbled. She slipped backward and fell again.

I started toward her and the dirt beneath my feet slid forward, almost taking me along with it. Melissa Koch slipped farther toward the collapsing cliffside.

"For God's sake help me!" she screamed as gravity took her partway over the edge.

Another step forward and I would join her. I removed my belt and got down on my belly. "Grab my belt and hold on," I said.

Just her upper body was visible now, gravity working its magic.

I stretched out and tossed the belt toward her hands. It fell about two feet short.

"Reach forward and grab it," I said.

She stared at the belt, paralyzed by fear. "I . . . can't."

"Yes you can. Grab the goddamn belt."

The dirt was crumbling more quickly now. She sank under her own weight.

"Now! Do it now!" I shouted.

I saw her right hand reach for the belt. The soft dirt at the edge of the cliff gave way completely. There was a split second of eye contact between us and then she was gone.

Slowly I stood up and stepped backward to the hiking path. The sky was light now, that first light of the new day warm on my face.

It seemed forever ago that I'd stood on Koch's yacht where Melissa Koch gave me her warning. *Watch your step,* she said.

That was good advice.

She should have followed it.

ABOUT THE AUTHOR

Al Lamanda is the author of the mystery/thriller novels *Dunston Falls, Walking Homeless, Running Homeless, Sunset and Sunrise.* He has also written several screenplays. A native of New York City, he is presently working on his latest novel.